Christmas in Mistletoe

by Clare Lydon

custard
books

First Edition November 2020
Published by Custard Books
Copyright © 2020 Clare Lydon
ISBN: 978-1-912019-50-2

Cover Design: Rachel Lawston
Editor: Cheyenne Blue
Typesetting: Adrian McLaughlin

Find out more at: www.clarelydon.co.uk
Follow me on Twitter: @clarelydon
Follow me on Instagram: @clarefic

Also by Clare Lydon

Other Novels
A Taste Of Love
Before You Say I Do
Nothing To Lose: A Lesbian Romance
Once Upon A Princess
One Golden Summer
The Long Weekend
Twice In A Lifetime
You're My Kind

London Romance Series
London Calling (Book One)
This London Love (Book Two)
A Girl Called London (Book Three)
The London Of Us (Book Four)
London, Actually (Book Five)
Made In London (Book Six)
Hot London Nights (Book Seven)

All I Want Series
All I Want For Christmas (Book One)
All I Want For Valentine's (Book Two)
All I Want For Spring (Book Three)
All I Want For Summer (Book Four)
All I Want For Autumn (Book Five)
All I Want Forever (Book Six)

Acknowledgements

If you don't know, I love Christmas. Everything about it. The lights. The food & drink. The music. The movies. But most of all, I love the luscious, tingly anticipation that precedes it. It's delicious. So when I realised I hadn't written a Christmas novel for five years, I was somewhat aghast. What had I been doing with my time? I decided to put that right with Christmas In Mistletoe. I hope my mission to put Christmas front and centre has succeeded. I've long wanted to write a book including the music industry too, having worked in it for years. I hope this gives you a taste of that world.

Thanks to Linda Em for being the inspiration behind Ruby after her amazing gig in a Soho jazz bar. You never know where inspiration will strike! Also, huge props to Trevor at Wrentham Christmas Tree Farm for giving up his time to talk me through his job – you were invaluable. Thanks to Angela for her first read and helpful comments. Also to my fantastic advanced reading team for their eagle eyes. You're all ace.

As usual, thanks to my cohort of talented professionals who make sure my books look and read the best they can. To Rachel Lawson for the spiffy cover. To Cheyenne Blue for the masterful editing. And to Adrian McLaughlin for his typesetting prowess.

Thanks also to my wife for reading this in one go on a Sunday. You're the best.

Last but definitely not least, thanks to you for buying this book and supporting this independent author. I hope this story leaves you wanting a mulled wine and a mince pie, as well as giving you all the Christmas feels!

Wherever you're reading this, have a wonderful Christmas and an abundant New Year. See you then for more lesfic goodness!

If you fancy getting in touch, you can do so using one of the methods below. I'm most active on Instagram.

Twitter: @ClareLydon
Facebook: www.facebook.com/clare.lydon
Instagram: @clarefic
Find out more at: www.clarelydon.co.uk
Contact: mail@clarelydon.co.uk

Thank you so much for reading!

For Victoria.
Never Vicky.

Chapter One

The hairs on the back of Fran Bell's neck stood up, one by one, as if preparing to applaud. She tilted her gaze at the singer in front of her, squinting against the glare of the bright stage lights. Fran didn't look away. She couldn't.

Ruby O'Connell had Fran under her spell.

Fran hadn't checked her phone once during the whole performance. Hadn't had one other thought but Ruby, with her long, willowy body, confident stare, and voice like painted gold. Fran had been to a lifetime of gigs, but only a handful had made her react like this. Ruby O'Connell's voice told a thousand bold stories. Fran wanted to hear more.

Damian, Fran's colleague, nudged her. "What do you think?" he mouthed, his blue contact lenses glowing in the dark.

She leaned in to shout in his ear. "I think she's a bloody slam-dunk."

Damian nodded his agreement.

Ten minutes later, and the whole crowd in Holborn's New Moon Jazz Club surged to their feet. Whistles sounded from the back, along with stamping of feet. A shout of "more!" from the man to Fran's right. He was just voicing what everyone was thinking.

Ruby bowed, thanked the crowd for coming, then walked off-stage. She pulled the leather strap of her acoustic guitar over her head and put the instrument down, then gave her bass player a hug.

Fran followed Ruby's movements, just in case she was leaving. When Ruby headed towards the loo, Fran turned to Damian. "She was fucking incredible. It's a travesty she's not headlining tonight."

"Totally agree." Damian pulled in his chair, his 5 o'clock shadow pronounced. He was one of the hairiest men Fran knew. "What a voice. It oozed class. Spoke to my soul."

Fran raised an eyebrow. She hadn't taken Damian for a poet, but he constantly surprised her. "I hope she listens to what I have to say. I'd love to work with her. She's a little different to Fast Forward."

Damian snorted. "Understatement of the year. But Fast Forward will be fine. I have faith. You need to get some, too." Damian turned and got his phone out. He checked it, then raised his head, giving Fran a stiff grin.

Now they'd seen Ruby, he wanted to leave. As his boss, Fran wasn't sure how long she should toy with him. Maybe another few minutes.

"Nine thirty. The final act's on in ten minutes. It's going to be at least another hour before we're done."

Fran twisted her wine glass on the round wooden table, and watched how the dim amber hue spilling from a small lamp turned her Merlot a warmer shade. She loved these venues: dark, intimate and with more than a hint of debauched times gone by. It was a far cry from London's sticky, grimy clubs. Plus, you got a seat. Fran totally got what her dad meant now when he refused to go to any gig without a seat. There was no danger of getting a pint of Stella flung at you here. As if to illustrate her point, the people beside her made room on their table for another glass of wine and a charcuterie board to share. Eating at gigs. Only in jazz clubs.

Damian's face was a stricken picture. "Really? Another hour?"

She was being unkind. But she was sort of enjoying it. Fran nudged him with her elbow. Being unkind to Damian was like toying with a puppy. "I'm only kidding." She inclined her head towards the exit. "Go. Do whatever it is young people do on a Wednesday in town."

Damian returned her look. "The same thing you do?"

Fran used to think that. But lately, as she'd just tipped over to 36, she'd begun to think otherwise. Now, at times, the lure of a cuppa was far greater than the lure of another glass of wine. Her dad would laugh at her for thinking so. But as her music industry job involved so much going out, staying in was a treat for Fran. Sofa, tea, movie. Bliss.

Damian, though, being 29, was already up and away, grabbing his jacket and legging it before Fran changed her mind. She followed his retreating form, but then her attention was snagged by the returning Ruby O'Connell.

Fran raised her chin and got up, tracking Ruby with military precision. She brushed down her navy jeans and pulled on the cuffs of her black shirt.

Ruby accepted a flurry of congratulatory handshakes.

Fran waited for the crowd to die down, and for Ruby to return to the rest of her band. Once Ruby had given her friends her first relaxed smile, Fran swooped. She'd done this enough times; she knew the drill.

She cleared her throat to get Ruby's attention. It worked.

Ruby turned, her reddish-brown hair not as vibrant away from the bright lights of the stage. However, the intensity of Ruby's emerald stare locked Fran in place. Her eyes had looked incredible from a distance, but up close, they were even more alluring. How old was she? Her smoky voice and old-soul vocals made her seem older. When she sang, Ruby could be any age. Up close, though, she was probably no more than 30, max.

Fran extended a hand.

Ruby took it.

Her handshake was firm, her stare true. This obviously wasn't the first time this had happened to Ruby.

"Fran Bell, Dronk Records." She turned up the wattage on her smile. "You were incredible. You have an absolutely amazing voice."

"Thank you." Ruby scanned Fran's face.

As Fran stared right back, her gaydar pinged, but she ignored it. Ruby's sexual preference had nothing to do with tonight or what she was here for.

"I wondered if you'd like to come in for a meeting. We'd love to work with you, have you put out a new album with us. Gigs, album, touring. The whole package. We're currently lining up our Christmas gig schedule, and I could see some venues where you'd be perfect. I know Christmas is seven months away, but it comes around quicker than you think."

Ruby gave her a weird look. "Happens every year, apparently." She paused. "You're offering me the chance to gig and make an album?"

Fran nodded. "I am."

Ruby swept her cool gaze around the room, before settling it back on Fran.

Fran kept her smile in place. She couldn't read Ruby.

"As you can see, I already do that. You're here at one of my gigs. I have an album out, too. People come to see me, they buy my music. It's already happening." As if to prove her point, Ruby broke off to sign an album for four fans, chatting with them and taking selfies.

Fran gave Ruby's band a tight smile. She felt more like a spare part than she had in a long time.

Eventually, Ruby turned back to Fran, giving her a '*see-my-point?*' smile.

Fran picked up the baton. "I totally get that you're an independent artist, one with a great platform. But what I'm offering is the chance to do so much more. Build on that. Really get your name out there. You're on iTunes now, right? All the streaming services?"

Ruby nodded. "Of course."

"We could make sure your streams go up exponentially. Give you the exposure you richly deserve. We have press contacts, venue contacts, we could put you in touch with terrific songwriters to work with, too." Fran paused. "I bet you don't make a full-time living with your music yet. That you do other jobs on the side, just to make ends meet?"

Ruby tilted her head, her striking green eyes clouding over.

Fran didn't want to see that.

"I do a little more than make ends meet. Yes, I do some voice coaching on the side, but I've built my music career and platform organically, and I'm still very much in the game seven years down the track." Ruby drew back her shoulders. "Which is why I don't need you to swoop in and save me with promises that may or may not come true." She waved an arm around the venue. "I'm not a star, but I don't want to be. Enough people know me and come to see me. I do just fine." She put a finger to her chest. "I'm my own boss, and I like it that way."

Fran gulped, no idea what to say.

A hint of contrition crossed Ruby's face. "Sorry, you just pressed a button. I've been down this road before with a former label and I don't intend to do it again. It's not personal."

Fran stood up straight, a blush crawling up her cheeks. It certainly felt personal. She knew Ruby had been with a label in her early years, but had no idea why the relationship had broken down. She'd certainly never had this sort of reaction before. A record label seeking out an artist after a show was normally a thing to be pleased about.

Ruby O'Connell was not most artists.

"How about just an hour of your time? Just to outline what I can offer. You may have been burned before, but I promise you, I'm a fan. I came here tonight to see you play live. I know you're special and I want the rest of the world to know it, too. I've helped a lot of artists before including The Grab Band, Trisha Star and Delilah, so I know what I'm doing. I'm sure you're well aware of how incredibly Delilah's career is going in particular." Delilah had blown up Fran's life, too. But that was on a need-to-know basis.

Tonight was about Ruby O'Connell.

Nobody else.

Ruby assessed Fran, as if running a lie detector down her body, seeking the truth. "You did a great job with Delilah, I'll give you that. But we're hardly the same market. She's pop. I'm not."

She wasn't going to budge, was she?

"I appreciate everyone who comes to see one of my shows. But my stance hasn't changed. I'm an independent artist doing my own thing." Ruby smiled to soften the blow. "But I'm glad you enjoyed the show. It's always what I want to hear."

Fran ground her teeth. "You were sensational. Is there anything I can do to change your mind? I can make you as famous as Delilah. Maybe even more so."

Ruby shook her head. "Not everybody wants that, though. But, thank you. It's nice to be asked."

Chapter 2

Four months later.

"Why are there pumpkins everywhere?" Ruby sat at the farmhouse kitchen table. "We're a Christmas tree farm, not a pumpkin patch." Fat orange squashes lined the wide kitchen counter, while others sat in straw-lined baskets on the floor.

Her mum leaned against the butler sink and patted the closest one. "We're selling pumpkins, like last year. Your brother ran out of room in the greenhouses, so he brought some up here to keep warm. It got frosty overnight. He takes them back to their friends in the morning." She grinned like that was completely normal.

"Frosty in September?"

Her mum's eyes widened. "This is Suffolk, remember? It's not all hot and crammed in like London."

"Scott's done a great job with the pumpkin harvest." Sat opposite, her dad rubbed his hands together. "He's grown double what he did last year and I still think we'll sell out at Halloween."

Her mum pulled out a chair and sat next to her dad.

"Plus, it brings people here and gets them thinking about buying a Christmas tree from us come December."

The kitchen smelled amazing, with sausage rolls and scones baking in the AGA cooker, and a tray of home-made ginger-and-vanilla biscuits already cooling on the kitchen table. Ruby's stomach rumbled as she looked at them. She needed a cuppa to go with them.

"Not just a tree, though." Her dad gave her a wink, pointing a finger in Ruby's direction. "Are you ready for our nailed-on money-making extra?"

Her parents had tried a multitude of ideas before, and even though none had made them their fortune, they were never fazed. Mistletoe advent calendars, gourmet marshmallows and home-made soaps, to name a few. She remembered the year they'd made multi-coloured fudge, and Ruby hadn't been able to get the stain off her hands for weeks. She readied her face so she was prepared for this year's golden ticket.

Her dad drummed his fingers on the table. "This year, we're also offering home-made Christmas crackers!"

He tilted his bald head and fixed Ruby with the same green stare as her own. Ruby had inherited her height and her eyes from her dad. From her mum, she'd got a singing voice, a love of bananas, and her distinctive shade of red-brown hair.

"What do you think, Rubytubes? Home-made crackers? Or are we crackers?"

Ruby snorted. "You have to be crackers to run a Christmas tree farm." However, this idea wasn't too bad. "So long as you make the jokes bad and the presents unique, you might have a winner. Everyone needs trees and crackers, right? You just need to get people here and give them a festive experience they won't forget."

Ruby pushed her chair back, and the noise on the stone floor made them all wince. "Sorry!" She walked to the counter and filled the kettle, then flicked it on. "Have you got enough time to do the crackers, though?" She put a hand on her hip and turned to her parents, logistics turning in her brain. "It's only six weeks until the farm goes into overdrive."

Dad nodded. "We reckon so, don't we, Mary?"

Her mum nodded, nabbing a biscuit from the wire rack. She finished crunching before she answered. "We do. We talked about it with Scott and Victoria, and they're both up for helping. As is Eric, too."

The whole family roped in. Ruby could just imagine how much they'd love that. Should she offer to help? She wrestled with her conscience, but she couldn't spare the time. She had too much work on. Plus, she was still coming back to help out in December.

"And before you offer to pitch in, don't even think about it."

Ruby frowned as she got the mugs and made the tea. Had her dad developed mind-reading abilities? She put the tea on the table.

Her mum stood and put an arm around her. "In fact, we were going to tell you not to worry about coming back for the festive period this year. Your career's important, and you've put your life on hold every December for long enough. Things are getting back on an even keel, especially now the pumpkins are pitching in with the trees. This year, we want you to put yourself first."

Ruby bit her lip. She'd love to have December all to

herself. To do some festive gigs. Fit in more private clients. But not quite yet. Her family still needed her, and she still wanted to be with them, too.

"Your mum's right," her dad added, glancing her way. "Mistletoe Christmas Tree Farm is our responsibility, and when we need family help, we'll ask Scott and Victoria. You have a life elsewhere and we want you to enjoy that."

Ruby rested her head on her mum's shoulder and sighed. "I know that. But I like coming back for the whole of December. It wouldn't feel right if I didn't. I love working at the farm." She wasn't lying. But it did put a strain on her every year.

"We're not saying don't come home. But we can hire extra help if you need to be elsewhere." Her mum kissed the top of Ruby's head and squeezed her waist. "Just think about it, okay? You could simply come home for Christmas like normal people."

Ruby laughed, straightening up. "We've never been normal people. But I'll think about it. I'm still coming back this December, but maybe next year might be different? Let's see what happens." It would mean she could really focus on her career and push things forward. Which was all kinds of scary.

Her dad nodded. "We just want you to have the best run at making it as a singer. The years slip by so quickly. We don't want to stop you fulfilling your dreams."

Ruby shook her head, her heart warmed through. Her parents' support and belief in her singing talent had never wavered. Even when Ruby had often felt like throwing in the towel herself. She leaned down and kissed her dad's bald head. "I know that, and I appreciate it."

Her dad grinned up at her. "Don't go getting all sappy, I have enough of that from your mother."

Ruby and her mum guffawed. They both knew her dad was the sappiest of them all.

They all sat and sipped their tea. Ruby grabbed a biscuit, too. When she tasted it, she closed her eyes. Her mum's baking was always divine.

Chipper, their golden Labrador, stuck his head up from under the table. His sixth sense that food was on offer was notorious. He put his soft head between Ruby's legs and she ruffled him under his ears, just the way he liked it.

"I love you Chipper, but you're not getting a crumb of this biscuit," Ruby told him.

"Besides making home-made crackers—"

"Call them artisan," Ruby interrupted.

Mum frowned. "Arty-what-now?"

Chipper barked as Ruby stopped petting him. She began again.

He dribbled on her thigh as a thank you.

"Artisan. It's the new way of saying home-made. Sounds posher. You can charge more."

Ruby had Mum's attention now. Mum grabbed her phone and made a note. "Good job you live in London and know these things, isn't it, Paul?"

Dad nodded. "We'd have no idea, that's for sure. Although maybe Michael and Dale might."

"Anyway," Mum interrupted. She gave Dad a stern look. "Besides artisan crackers, the other big news in the village is that the new owners of Hollybush Cottage have finally moved in. They're called Michael and Dale."

Hollybush Cottage was next door to her parents' farm. Sort of on it if you were going to be picky. When Mistletoe Christmas Tree Farm had been going through a lean patch around ten years ago, Mum had the bright idea of portioning off a section of the land and renovating one of the outbuildings into a three-bedroom home.

"Are they nice?"

Mum nodded. "Very." She leaned in closer. "*And gay.*" She whispered those two words as if Michael and Dale might hear if she spoke any louder.

Ruby smiled. Cool as her parents were, sometimes she forgot they still lived in sleepy Suffolk. Although having a lesbian daughter put them ahead of most. "It's about time our little hamlet of Mistletoe had a bit of male gay in the mix, isn't it? Sue and Penny will be pleased the spotlight's off them."

Chipper huffed at her.

Ruby ruffled his fur. "I know, you're a gay male, I'm not leaving you out."

Dad snorted. "I dunno. Sue and Penny revel in the spotlight. Their noses might be put out of joint now they've got competition."

"Anyway, Michael and Dale are lovely; I met them the other day." Mum brushed the front of her pale pink jumper. "Their daughter's visiting from London, so I told them to come over for a glass of wine. I thought it'd be nice, as you're here from London, too. Make her feel more at home."

Ruby's stomach dropped. She'd been looking forward to the opening night of *Strictly Come Dancing* and a glass of wine in front of the fire, not making small talk with strangers. Then she frowned. Did her mum have an ulterior motive?

"Are you trying to set me up again? Apart from anything else, just because Michael and Dale are gay, it doesn't mean their daughter is, too."

"I know that!"

Mum sounded hurt. But Ruby would bet money that had been her logic.

"I just thought you're both from London. They lived in Surrey before, so coming to Mistletoe is a bit of a change."

"I'll say." Mistletoe wasn't so much a Suffolk village, it was more a hamlet. It had a church, a Christmas tree farm, a shop, and a part-time bar. If you wanted a proper pub, you had to walk 20 minutes to the next village, Snowy Bottom.

Ruby checked her watch. "What time are they due? I have a couple of calls to make." Even though she was home for the weekend, she still had work to do.

"After seven. Drinks and nibbles. Just to welcome them."

Ruby glanced around the kitchen, with its peeling units and trusty AGA. 'Lived-in' was what some would call it. 'Weathered' was another term that could be applied. If this festive season was a success, maybe they could get a new kitchen. That was her mum's dream.

"Why don't we take the newbies to The Bar?" Ruby said. "That way, they can meet the whole village."

Mum wiggled her nose. "They're coming here first, but maybe afterwards if they want to. So long as it's not too late."

"Is Scott showing his face?" Ruby hadn't seen her little brother since she arrived this morning.

"He might. We finished planting the younger trees this week, but he still had some photoshoot trees to ship today." Dad pushed his metal-rimmed glasses up his face.

Ruby's face dropped. "Has Nettie gone?"

Her mum shook her head. "Tuesday. You should go and say goodbye before she leaves." Nettie was a statuesque 12-year-old Nordmann fir who was destined to be a photoshoot model this year.

"I'll go give her a pat tomorrow." What was it her parents had said about being unhinged? However, when you tended to a tree for a decade, you got attached. Nettie was a firm family favourite.

"I say let's take the newbies to The Bar," her dad agreed. "Then they can meet Victoria, Eric, and Scott, too. The entire O'Connell family."

They had no idea what they were in for.

Chapter 3

Fran still couldn't quite believe her parents had bought this cottage.

Although, in another way, she totally got it. It was *them* to a tee. Quaint. Full of charm. Shiny. It should be. Her parents had spent a huge chunk of money having it done up, after the previous owner had lived there for eight years with an array of dogs and an allergy to opening a window.

"Dog and chips, that's what it smelled like," Dad had told her over the phone. She'd never have known. Now, it smelled like fresh paint and promise. Plus, with Pop's favourite lemongrass and basil candles already burning, it smelled like home.

That Hollybush Cottage was lovely wasn't in doubt. It even had a holly bush in the garden.

Of course it did.

Fran's issue was that it was in the middle of nowhere, in a village called Mistletoe. Better yet, the cottage was situated on the edge of Mistletoe Christmas Tree Farm. It was like her parents had moved into a Hallmark Christmas movie. One that smelled divine, and was super gay.

In the real-life version, which Fran was reluctantly starring in, she and her parents were going around to their neighbours' house for welcome drinks tonight. Fran had endured a tough week. Delilah was number one, and Fran was still bruised from their split. Recovered, but bruised. She'd come to Mistletoe to check out her parents' new house, but also to hide away for a bit where nobody knew her. To take a moment to breathe. Drinks with the neighbours wasn't on her agenda.

However, she couldn't say no to her parents. This was their new life, and Fran wanted to support it. They'd supported her in everything she did, after all. Even when she'd ditched her art degree for a career in the music business.

"What are the neighbours like?" Fran was pretty sure she had an idea, but she wanted to hear it from Pop's mouth.

"They seem lovely." But Fran could hear the amusement in Pop's voice as she followed him up the stairs.

"Uh-oh," she said.

"No, they really are!" A gasp of laughter escaped Pop's lips as they arrived on the landing. "You know, they're just a bit… country with it."

"Which is absolutely fine," Dad added from behind, a scold in his voice. He pointed through the rustic pine door off the landing to her left. "This is your room."

"You're a bit country now, can I add?" Fran gave them both an amused look. She walked into her new bedroom, and took a breath. The views over the fields of Christmas trees and beyond were spectacular. The late afternoon sun cast an orange haze over the sea of green. In the back garden, she spied her parents' newly installed art studio. "Wow, I can see what you mean when you said it was a room with a view."

Dad put his arm around her. "We are a bit country now, too. I guess that's why we moved here. To embrace this life, with these views. Plus, Paul and Mary who own the farm have been very welcoming. Mary even brought us a casserole. Like we're in a real community."

"You had that in Surrey."

But even as she said it, Fran knew it wasn't true. They hadn't had that. The people in their Surrey village had kept themselves to themselves. Perhaps Mistletoe was going to be what her parents had hankered after for years. A thriving community who looked out for each other.

Dad took Pop's hand in his. "We didn't. But we might get it here."

* * *

Two hours later, Fran, Michael and Dale trudged out their front door, down the garden path, and then along the perimeter of the farm until they reached the main entrance. A massive wooden sign welcomed them to Mistletoe Christmas Tree Farm, although one of the three small bulbs illuminating it had blown. The painted Christmas trees on the sign could do with some touching up, too.

"Do people actually make a living growing Christmas trees in the UK?" Fran blew on her hands as she asked. Out of London, the temperature had dropped at least ten degrees, even though the forecast told her otherwise. "Also, why have we never come to a Christmas tree farm before?"

"Because we always had a fake one?" Pop replied.

"Let's not share that fact right away, okay everyone?" Dad added.

They all nodded, then started along the main path to the farmhouse.

Barking from the other side of the door greeted their knock. It opened to reveal an excitable golden Labrador, held tight by a woman in jeans and a dusky pink jumper, her short ruddy-brown hair sticking up at all angles. A bald man with metal-framed glasses appeared at her side. The woman's face broke into a welcoming smile when her glance settled on Fran's parents and then on her.

"You made it! Come in, welcome! You must be Francesca. I'm Mary. This is our overgrown puppy, Chipper, and that's my husband Paul. It's lovely to meet you!"

Paul gave them a wave, then grabbed the dog and disappeared, before returning in seconds.

Her hands now free, Mary wasted no time in hugging Fran.

Fran hesitantly returned it. There really was no other option.

Paul, who towered over Mary, did the same, before leading everyone through to their farmhouse kitchen.

"Excuse the pumpkins!" Mary added.

In stark contrast to Fran's parents' newly refurbed pad, this kitchen had seen better days. However, even though the floor was scuffed and the cupboards worn, the smell lingering in the air was divine. The table was laden with sausage rolls, cheese, crackers, chutneys and a tray of scones. There were also wine glasses in an array of shapes and sizes, as if they'd once had six sets, but now just had one glass left from each. The fridge was covered in a montage of flyers, leaflets and lists, and the mantle that adorned the room's centrepiece fireplace was laden with family photos. Dad and Pop had mentioned one daughter who lived in London, but there were clearly more children. None of them were in this room, though.

As if reading her mind, Mary walked past, patting Fran's arm. "Let me just give Ruby a shout."

Fran braced herself. She hoped she and Ruby had something to talk about. It was going to be a toe-curling evening, otherwise. Or perhaps one where she could just fill her mouth with pastry items so she didn't have to talk.

Fran was just doing exactly that — a still-hot sausage roll, so good she was worried she might have groaned in pleasure when she bit into it — when Mary reappeared.

"Found her!" Mary stepped back to reveal her daughter. Tall as a tree. Mud-red hair. Intense green eyes. A stare that Fran had been on the receiving end of before.

Fran blinked then sucked in a breath. Big mistake. A piece of sausage roll lodged in her throat and she doubled over, coughing violently. She sucked in a huge breath. That only made it worse.

In seconds, Dad was behind her, whacking her back with his shovel-like hand. Why did people insist on doing that?

Fran shook her head frantically, but was too busy choking to tell him to stop. Her insides wheezed as she fought to catch her breath, panic blaring in her brain.

Dad switched to two hands around her middle. He gripped, then pressed hard.

A huge gust of breath rushed up Fran, and the offending bit of sausage roll flew out of her mouth at speed. It landed on the toe of Ruby's right slipper, which was styled in the shape of a snowman.

Fran should have been more embarrassed, but she was

too focused on getting her breath back. She coughed some more, tears streaming down her face. She could just imagine the bemused faces all around the kitchen. She put the palms of her hands on her thighs, then took a few more steadying breaths. She accepted a tissue from Mary, a consoling hand on her back from Pop, then straightened.

It was only then she was doused in embarrassment. What a way to make an impression on her parents' new neighbours.

One of whom was the only singer to ever turn her down.

"I'm so sorry, that sausage roll went down the wrong way," Fran said.

"Don't be silly!" Mary thrust a glass of red wine into her hand. "Have a drink, that'll make you feel better."

But all Fran could see was the regurgitated sausage roll, still sitting pretty on Ruby's slipper. Where was Chipper when she needed him? Fran glanced at Ruby's face, then back to the slipper. She had to deal with it.

She put her wine on the table, then lunged forward, tissue in hand, and scooped up the sausage roll. It would have been a successful mission too, if her head hadn't met the farmhouse table on the way back up. The crack as her skull hit solid wood reverberated in the air. Fran staggered left, clutching her head.

Arms held her upright as pain ricocheted around her brain. She winced, closing her eyes, waiting for it to pass. Could this night get much worse? She *really* hoped this was the low point.

"Oh my goodness, are you okay?" That was Mary again, her voice rising as she spoke.

Eventually, Fran opened her eyes, her vision watery. When

she glanced Ruby's way, she was sure she could see the hint of a smirk under her blank features. Fran didn't blame her. She'd provided a wealth of entertainment already.

"I'm fine. I just need to stand still and not move or eat anything for a little while." Her head throbbed as she eased her dad's hands from her. "I'm not normally this clumsy."

"Don't worry about it. Ruby was a terribly clumsy child. Always in the hospital, weren't you?"

Ruby frowned. "It was once, Dad."

"Had an argument with the living room fireplace, and the fireplace won," Paul added.

Mary put an arm around Ruby, then angled her towards Fran. "Anyway, this is our daughter, Ruby. She lives in London, too. Ruby, this is Francesca."

"Just Fran." She was still holding her head.

Mary nodded. "Just Fran it is."

"Hi, again." Ruby didn't quite meet Fran's gaze. She clearly wasn't sure how to play this, either. "Are you stalking me?"

Fran smiled despite herself. "I'm not a very good stalker, am I? I haven't seen you in four months."

There was a silence, broken eventually by Fran's dad. "You two know each other?"

"Sort of." Fran leaned over and grabbed her wine. She took a swig. "Ruby's a folk singer. A really good one. I went along to one of her gigs and tried to sign her, but she turned me down." Fran met Ruby's gaze. "Maybe this is a sign you should say yes."

Ruby gave her a measured smile. "I don't believe in signs." She paused. "But this is freaky. What are the chances of you being my new neighbour?"

"What are the chances?" Paul touched his wine glass to Fran's with some force.

Fran made a face. If Paul smashed her wine glass, that would be her evening complete. Luckily, it held.

"However you two know each other, you have good taste in music, Fran. And you," he pointed his glass at Ruby, "never told us you'd been approached again. You should think about it. It might work out this time."

"And give up control of my life. We've been through this, Dad."

"We have. But sometimes, a little help can be good. Especially if it gets you into places you wouldn't get to otherwise."

Fran winced. She focused on a time when her head wouldn't be throbbing.

When she wouldn't be in this kitchen with Ruby.

Who still didn't want to sign with her.

"Enough, Paul. We have guests. I think it's lovely you two know each other. You can be friends even if you don't sign to Fran's label, can't you?"

Ruby eyed Fran. She gave a shrug.

Fran gave her one back.

It was like they were six years old, both being scolded by their parents.

"Anyway, have another sausage roll," Mary told Fran, breaking the tension. "You looked like you were enjoying the first one until you spat it onto Ruby's slipper."

* * *

The road from the farm to the bar had minimal street

lights. At 8pm on a Saturday, it was also deserted. Fran took in a fresh lungful of country air; the faint whiff of manure lingered in her nose. She could see no animals nearby, but maybe that was just what the country smelled like? She had no idea. She'd grown up on the not-so-mean streets of Surrey.

Was walking on a road like this safe? She'd never do it in London. Then again, London had wider pavements and tons of cars. They'd been walking for five minutes and hadn't encountered one. Their parents were up ahead, chatting merrily, their phone torches guiding them. Ruby was walking beside her. They hadn't spoken a word in the past couple of minutes. If Fran had been hoping that meeting Ruby in her natural habitat might break down her barriers, it appeared to be doing the opposite.

"Sorry again about your slipper." Was that a good opening gambit? Fran couldn't think of anything else.

"No problem," Ruby said. "I don't normally have that effect on women, but there's a first time for everything."

Fran smiled. A little warmer. "I was just surprised it was you. When my dads told me I was meeting someone, I could almost tell they wanted to say, 'she lives in London, you might know her!' I never expected it was going to be true."

"At least that's something we can agree on." A few more moments of silence.

"How long have you lived here?"

"I live in London."

Fran suppressed an eye roll. "I mean your family. They seem quite settled."

Ruby nodded. "They are. We moved here when I was nine. So, 20 years. At first the farm paid its way, but as time's gone on and people don't come to farms to get their Christmas trees, things are always hanging in the balance. But somehow, my parents make it work. Doing up and selling Hollybush Cottage kept them in business for a good while. They inspired me to go my own way, too."

Fran stuffed her hands further into her pockets. The chill wasn't just coming from the air. "I admire that. I'm not out to change that. You made your feelings very clear when we met before." She glanced at Ruby. There was maybe six inches difference between them, but Ruby seemed a few feet taller tonight. "Do you earn enough doing it on your own, though? I'm genuinely curious."

Ruby took a moment before she answered. "I do. I have a core group of fans, I gig, and I'm a voice coach. I get by. My parents told me to audition for a reality TV show, but I never think they're about singing. I don't want to be judged on my looks or who I am. I want it to be about my songs, my art."

Fran nodded. "I get that. But if you were judged on your looks, it wouldn't deter from your music. You've got a great voice, great songs, and a great look. You're the full package. I know you don't want to sign with me, but you will get other offers."

"I've had other offers. I've turned them all down." Ruby's tone held a warning. "I signed with a label a few years ago. It didn't work. They blew very hot, and then very cold when I didn't want to do exactly what they wanted. It wasn't a great experience, to say the least. I like having full control of my life, now."

Fran was getting that. "But isn't it a whole lot of work? Wouldn't you like some help?"

"I cope just fine."

"I won't say another word about it." Fran clicked her tongue against the roof of her mouth and they walked in silence to the end of the road. Mistletoe Stores was on the corner of Mistletoe's one and only junction. Propped up on the bench outside was a chalkboard, with 'This way to The Bar' written on it.

Ruby pointed. "My sister and her husband run Mistletoe Stores and its attached bar. They named them both. I think I got the creative gene."

Fran smiled. "I think you're right."

Chapter 4

"Ruby O'Connell! Look at you! Did you get taller in London? Are they feeding you some kind of weird magic beans that make you shoot up?"

Audrey Parrot said this to Ruby every time she came home and they met, invariably in The Bar. Audrey was one of the many locals who'd known Ruby since she arrived in the village in knee-high socks, with ribbons in her hair. Ruby had altered drastically in that time, but Audrey hadn't changed much at all. Her grey hair had always been welded to her head, and she had far too many opinions about everything under the sun. Including Ruby.

"Just the usual, Audrey. Tofurkey and vegan bacon, you know what London's like." Even though Ruby ate meat, she always replied with what wound Audrey up the most: veganism. She wasn't sure why Audrey was so offended by those who shunned meat and dairy, but she was.

Audrey leaned forward and patted Ruby's flat stomach. "You should be eating steak, and lots of it."

"I do eat steak, Audrey."

But Audrey wasn't listening. "It makes you good and strong and it'll fatten you up. If you just eat plants, how are you going to stay healthy? Look at that girl who won *Strictly*

27

Come Dancing who announced she was vegan. Nothing but skin and bone." Audrey wagged a finger in Ruby's face. "Shall I come to visit you and bring some steak-and-ale pies?"

It was tempting. Audrey's pies were the stuff of legend. However, telling Audrey her address would be a catastrophic error, because she'd definitely use it.

"Who's this you've got with you? A new friend?" Audrey might as well have put the word 'friend' in air quotes, such was her stress on the word.

Fran wasn't a friend. She'd simply landed in Ruby's lap tonight. It wasn't how Ruby had expected her Saturday night to go, but then again, Mistletoe always held twists.

Mum came to Ruby's rescue. "This is Fran, Michael and Dale's daughter. She's visiting from London. Would you believe she works in music and knew Ruby already?" Mum pushed Michael and Dale towards Audrey. "This is Audrey, the village oracle."

"Village gossip, more like," said Sue. She was the village yoga and Pilates teacher, as well as the local artist. If you looked close enough, there was always a splash of paint on Sue. Tonight was no exception; Ruby spotted flecks of yellow on Sue's elbow. Her wife Penny looked at her adoringly. Sue and Penny were what Ruby aspired to be.

"I was being polite the first time we introduce her to the newbies," Ruby's mum replied. "Audrey will know what's happening in your life before you do. You might be surprised at first, but the sooner you accept that, the better."

Michael and Dale laughed like that was a joke.

Ruby smiled; they'd learn. She moved past Audrey and towards the bar, where her brother-in-law Eric was pouring a pint of cider. Her sister Victoria sat on a bar stool. Ruby gave her a hug, before blowing a kiss to Eric. She had a lot of time for both of them, and after opening the village shop and bar, they seemed to have found their calling. Victoria claimed she'd always wanted to be like *EastEnders* landlady Sharon Mitchell as a young girl, and now her dreams had come true.

"Busy in here tonight," Ruby said.

"There was something on at the church today, so everyone's having a debrief." Eric ran a hand up the back of his closely cropped hair. This time last month, he'd had the biggest afro Ruby had ever seen. He'd shaved it for charity, but now kept complaining his head was cold.

Ruby swept her gaze around the bar. It was compact and bijou, with room for two bar stools and nine tables, along with four keg taps and two wooden pumps. Seven of the nine tables were filled, with all the usual suspects present. Each table had a bowl of peanuts and Twiglets, but Eric had resisted adding tinsel to the optics as yet. Victoria thought you needed to wait until at least November for that. For Ruby, tinsel was an appropriate decoration all year round.

Michael, Dale, and Fran rocked up alongside her, and Ruby made the introductions. The newcomers ordered their drinks, then stood back, looking awkward. Ruby avoided Fran's gaze, hoping they'd move soon.

Thankfully, Ruby's parents moved the two empty tables together, then ushered the trio to sit. Now the bar was full to capacity, and their double-table was in the middle. Michael, Dale and Fran were the star attraction, whether they liked it or not. Her mum guided Ruby to the seat next to Fran, before sitting, too.

"How did the church thing go, Audrey?" Mum leaned back on her low stool and almost fell into Audrey's lap.

"We voted for a midnight mass, and it went through. Good thing, too, the number of hours we all put in at that place. Penny and I were there for two hours this morning, getting it spick and span for the meeting."

"We're the god dusting squad, aren't we, Audrey?" Penny gave the group a wry smile.

"We certainly are, so it's a good job the vicar listened to us. Now there won't be a service on Christmas Day in the village. I've already told Victoria and Eric they need to stay open until 11.30pm on Christmas Eve, then we can walk over to the church after."

Victoria pulled up a stool. "That's against our license, Audrey. We need special dispensation for extended hours."

"Who's going to shop you? I defy them. They'd have a whole bar after them, and we can be mean when we want to be." Audrey raised her voice. "Can't we, everyone?"

Cheers from every table. That was the thing with The Bar. The tables were all within touching distance, so the whole place could be involved in the same conversation with ease.

"You tell them, Audrey!" That was Norman, who lived opposite the farm and owned the local funeral directors. He claimed to be partly deaf, but had incredibly good hearing when he wanted to.

Mum sipped her drink and smiled at Fran and her parents.

They looked a little stunned.

"You have to come along to the midnight mass on Christmas Eve," Mum said. "There's no better way to see Christmas in."

Michael frowned. "We're not really church-goers."

Dad laughed. "You don't need to be a church-goer. I'll be there and I've no religion. But who doesn't love a sing-song? It's all about wetting the baby's head. The baby being Jesus. We do that in here first, then we sing. It's tradition. The church went against tradition last year when they banned the midnight mass. They said we were too rowdy."

"Us! Too rowdy!" Audrey bumped shoulders with Mum. "I told them at the meeting today, I'd give them rowdy if we weren't reinstated. That Christmas Day mass last year was terrible. Too early and we were all hungover. Get us at our best when we're in full flow, that's what I say!"

"And Ruby can sing us a song like she did when she was a teenager!" Sue added, nodding in Ruby's direction.

Embarrassment blazed up Ruby's spine. It was true she'd been a singing prodigy when she was growing up, and she'd often led the singing at midnight mass. But it wasn't for her anymore. Whichever way she looked at it, she couldn't support a church which didn't support her.

"My church singing days are over." Ruby made sure her tone was firm. Any weakness on this and before she knew it, she'd be on the altar with a microphone in hand.

"What about you, Dale and Michael? Any vocal talent? Gay men are normally theatrical, and we welcome fresh talent in the village."

Ruby winced. Audrey was never going to win any prizes for her tact, was she? Imagine if they were vegan, too. Audrey might combust.

Both Michael and Dale shook their heads with some vigour.

"Not really our scene," Michael replied. "I can't hold a note, and Dale's more a sing-in-the-shower kinda guy."

There was an uncomfortable moment where Ruby was sure Audrey was picturing that. "What about your daughter? Didn't you say she was something in music?"

Panic flared in Fran's bright blue eyes as she shook her head. She ran a flustered hand through her dirty-blond hair. "Oh no, I'm very much behind-the-scenes, not on the mic." She guzzled her wine. "Besides, I don't think I'm going to be here for Christmas. It's a very busy time of year, and I've told my boss I'm working the whole time, so I plan to stay in London. Christmas is just another roast dinner, after all."

Every muscle in Ruby's body tightened, and she closed her eyes. Had Fran really just said that, to this crowd?

Mum was first to crack. "Just another roast dinner?" Mum's frown was deep. "It's certainly not just another dinner in Mistletoe. Not coming home for Christmas is almost a criminal offence."

Ruby glanced at Fran. "She's not wrong. When you move here, it's kinda written into the contract." Did Fran not like Christmas? Ruby could not compute. It wasn't a sentence any of the village would utter.

Fran didn't meet Ruby's eye. "The final quarter of the year is the busiest time for sales. I don't make the rules for the record industry. I just follow them."

"Maybe you need to re-jig your priorities." Ruby gave Fran a pointed stare. Music execs were all the same: money, money, money. Fran probably didn't even listen to Christmas music.

"Maybe you should open yourself up to new possibilities that might further your career," Fran countered.

Beside Ruby, her mum sat up a little straighter.

Ruby's vision flared red. "My priority at Christmas is to come home and help my family business." She wasn't going to be wound up by Fran. She glared at her.

"Even if I could give you some fantastic exposure in the weeks leading up to Christmas?"

"Even then." Fran really didn't take no for an answer, did she?

The whole bar took a collective intake of breath.

Victoria clutched her half of lager and lime.

"Twiglet?" Michael held up the bowl between them, signalling a time-out.

Ruby shook her head.

Fran did the same.

Honestly, who worked through Christmas? Ruby hoped Fran stayed in London, if only so Ruby could have Mistletoe all to herself. Her home town was Ruby's refuge, the place where everyone knew her from old. When she was here, she wasn't a struggling musician. She was just Ruby.

She certainly didn't need to be pestered by the likes of Fran Bell.

Chapter 5

Fran hadn't been kidding when she said she was busy in the run-up to Christmas: it was now a little over six weeks to the big day. One of her many gigs was this independent artist showcase that Damian had dragged her to in Hackney. He wanted to approach the headliner, Tom Darby, and he wanted Fran's opinion.

The smell of weed hit her nostrils as she walked through the front bar. Damian stopped to say hi to a couple of friends. This was his manor, after all. Fran lived a bit further out in Stratford, where the Olympics had been held. Hackney Wick was more her local hangout, or Greenwich if she was being fancy. Damian, however, was in his element.

When an artist had a label behind them, a showcase — where the artist performed a handful of songs for press and invited fans — was normally held in a private members club or swanky Soho bar, with free drinks a prerequisite. Fran was intrigued to see how it worked without a label. The location was different, for a start: a pub in Hackney.

"Did you listen to the link I sent you for this artist tonight?" Damian's eyes lit up when he spoke about music. It was one of the reasons Fran had taken him on. That, and the fact he made her laugh with his random facts in the interview.

If she was going to work closely with someone, the ability to make her laugh was high on Fran's list of wants.

She nodded. "I did. He sounds immense." The music was a crossover of country and folk, and Fran had loved the artist's depth on his vocal, as well as the fiddles. She was a sucker for a fiddle. Fran was keen to see if his voice was the same live.

They walked through to the back bar, where a healthy crowd was already gathered. The stage was on the far side of the room, with a drum kit and three mics set up. A double-bass loitered to the rear, and a bushy-bearded man was testing the guitars.

"You know who this bloke tonight would sound great with?"

Fran shook her head.

"Ruby O'Connell. Imagine his timbred voice with her smoky vocals. The folk world would go mad for it. It'd be like The Pogues and Kirsty MacColl, but with Tom and Ruby, both of the leads can sing like angels."

"Careful, people love those artists." But Fran had to agree. Ruby and Tom Darby would be a dream ticket.

"So do I." Damian leaned into her ear so she could hear him above the music, which had just been turned up. "But I have it on good authority they know each other, so it could happen."

Fran gulped, then let her gaze wander the room. Ruby O'Connell might be here? That was just what she needed. Although, if they were destined to be neighbours of sorts, perhaps she could try to talk to her. Smooth things out. Fran's parents would be pleased, at least.

Damian leaned in once more. "Your dads really moved to a village where Ruby O'Connell's parents are their neighbours?"

Fran winced at the memory. "Uh-huh. And I had a coughing fit in their kitchen, and spat her mum's delicious sausage roll onto Ruby's slippers."

"I can't believe the super-cool Ruby wears slippers." He paused. "Tell me at least they were ruby slippers, like in the Wizard of Oz."

Fran shook her head. "I hate to be the bearer of bad tidings. They were snowmen. Or snowwomen, I didn't stop to look too hard." Fran grabbed two Heinekens from the ice buckets set up on the bar. It was that or wine. Wine was dangerous on an empty stomach, so beer it was. She opened two bottles and gave one to Damian.

"Maybe you can wear her down to sign with us over Christmas drinks."

"That is doubtful. I wouldn't be able to get a word in edgeways in the only bar in the village. It's the epitome of a local bar for local people."

"The village is really called Mistletoe?"

"It totally is."

Damian tilted his head. "Do they have mistletoe hanging over the village sign when you drive in? Do you have to pull over and snog the nearest person under it to be allowed in?"

"Maybe when we get closer to December, who knows? Right now, the sign is just a regular sign with a drawing of mistletoe on it."

Damian stroked his stubble. "Do you know the origin of the word mistletoe?"

Fran shook her head. Here he went again with his random facts. "I don't. Do you?"

He nodded. "It's an English-German word, derived from the old English term for twig, along with the old German term for dung. It basically means shit on a twig." Damian gave her a wide grin.

"You're kidding."

But the shake of his head told Fran he wasn't.

"That's brilliant. I wonder if the village knows. You think I could endear myself to the locals and maybe get it on the town marketing? I'm sure they'd love it." Fran wafted a hand in the air above her, like she was reading a movie poster. "Come to this village in the middle of nowhere and buy a Christmas tree from Shit On A Twig Farm."

"I think it needs work," Damian deadpanned. He looked around the bar. "Good turn-out here, though." He held up his bottle of Heineken. "Good beer choice, too. Maybe indie is where the music business is going."

"I hope not, or we're out of a job," Fran replied. "Talking of jobs, how did the interview with Fast Forward go today? No problems? They smiled in all the right places? Tenny's anxiety didn't get the better of her?"

Their all-female, indie-pop band of the moment had been interviewed by a big Sunday paper this week. The band had been primed and media-coached, but their lead singer Tenny was still a bag of nerves. Fran hoped it had paid off.

Damian's nod was confident. "They did good. They were nervous as hell going in, but nobody's out to trip them up." He paused. "If you discount the Twitter trolls who most definitely are."

"Really?" It was a hazard of the industry, particularly for young women. The rise of the keyboard warrior meant that everything was fair game to comment on, at any time of the day or night. It was exhausting for everyone involved, but most damaging for the artists on the sharp end.

Damian sighed. "Yes, but I'm trying to ignore them and focus on the positives. Plus, their latest single broke the top 10 this week, so their trajectory is on target. When their Christmas single lands and they hit their big London gigs, we'll really see what they're made of. If they can get over their stage jitters."

All Dronk Records' other artists were pure musicians, signed on the strength of their song writing and performance. Fast Forward, on the other hand, was the label's attempt to break into the indie girl band scene with a manufactured band, albeit five women who could play all their instruments. Despite their early success, the band were still getting used to the glare. They looked the part, but they didn't quite believe it yet.

Fran grimaced. "They've certainly embraced their pre-gig nerves. We need to coach them. Or give them Valium, one of the two."

Damian spluttered. "We're trying to steer them off the drink and drugs road for as long as we can."

"Rock and roll ain't what it used to be."

* * *

Half an hour later, they were immersed in the set from Tom Darby. His songs were big, wrapping their arms around you. He had an easy stage presence, and Fran was transfixed.

"Thanks so much for coming out tonight. This gig is for all the people who've helped me along the way, and let me sleep on their sofa so I could gig around London without bankrupting myself. Especially my good friend and now flatmate, Ruby O'Connell. She's also written a new song which is an absolute killer, and I've persuaded her to debut it tonight. So please, go mad and give it up for the brilliant Ruby O'Connell!"

Fran twisted her head just in time to see a tall figure moving through the crowd.

Ruby.

Fran's insides swooped. Oh shit, Damian had been right. She really was here.

The crowd clapped and whistled, as Ruby got up on stage, giving them a confident wave.

Damian nudged her with his elbow. "I called it."

This was the Ruby that Fran remembered. Professional Ruby. Far from the one who'd scowled at her most of the night in Mistletoe. Shit on a Twig town. They were the same people, but somehow, Fran couldn't make the connection to the smiley, happy singer before her.

Was Fran the same? Confident and cool at work, snappy at her parents? Maybe. Perhaps it affected everyone when they returned to their childhood home: they reverted to what used to be.

But right now, in front of Fran, Ruby was totally in the moment. If there was anyone more born to sing and perform than her, Fran hadn't seen it in a while. Even Tom Darby was put in the shade, and Fran had been impressed by him.

When Ruby sang, time stopped, as did everyone in the

crowd. When Ruby drew a breath, the audience leaned in, desperate to get closer.

Ruby's new song, 'Pieces Of You', was immense, with a sweeping chorus that roused the whole room. Violins twanged and the double bass boomed.

She hadn't had fiddles at the jazz club. Fran swayed to their sound.

Tom Darby provided soft backing vocals, but it was Ruby who opened her mouth and created stardust, her voice mesmerising the room. She was incredible.

It was a crime she didn't want to be signed. How could Fran persuade her? Not with the cold sell. That hadn't worked the first time, or in Mistletoe. Fran had to come up with another way. Because if she could promote this single, they could have a worldwide hit on their hands. They could bring cool folk music to the masses.

"Fuck me, that was better than my dreams." If Damian's mouth could have hung open, it would. He put a hand on Fran's arm as Ruby got down from the stage, the crowd now cheering with gusto. "But it's not Ruby I'm here to see. I'm going to talk to Tom. Wish me luck."

"Good luck." However, Fran's glance wasn't on Damian. It was totally on Ruby as their gazes met. A frisson ran through Fran: a whole crowd of people, but Ruby had spotted her.

A question crossed Ruby's face, before she frowned, then walked towards Fran.

Fran pulled herself upright and wriggled her hips. She just had to try to be friendly. Get Ruby on-side. That was the first thing to get done. Part one of the charm offensive: flattery. It helped that it was genuine.

"Bravo." Fran gave Ruby a broad smile. "That was insane. That song has smash-hit written all over it."

Ruby nodded, her neck pink from exertion. She was wearing a low-cut brown and cream top with a silk scarf, and tweed trousers with big boots. It would have looked ridiculous on Fran. On Ruby, it was perfect. She was every inch the star.

Fran's scalp prickled as warmth oozed through her. She gritted her teeth. She wanted to sign Ruby, not shag her. However, the way her whole body had just heated up when Ruby got close, it apparently had other ideas.

"I didn't expect to see you here. Now I really do think you might be stalking me."

Fran held up both palms. "In my defence, you weren't on the bill tonight. We came to see Tom, but you were an added bonus. My colleague Damian was just saying earlier what a great match you two would make. Then, up you popped, and now he thinks he can predict the future. Between you and me, I might never hear the end of it now."

"Sounds like he has good taste."

There was an awkward pause as Ruby stared at her, and Fran grappled for something else to say. Dammit, she schmoozed for a living. Why did she find it so difficult to speak to Ruby O'Connell? The one person she really needed to impress and gain the trust of. She couldn't even spit out two sentences without her brain flatlining.

"How are your dads settling into the village?"

Ruby could do small talk.

Fran could conquer it, too.

"They're doing well. They're just settling into their lives, and their art studio. They're going to give Sue a run for her money."

"Sue will love having someone to talk art with."

"I spoke to them last night. Pop – that's Dale by the way, Michael is Dad. Anyway, Pop was talking about designing some gay greetings cards because he can never find good ones. So I'm expecting a 'Happy Christmas To Our Lesbian Daughter From Your Two Gay Dads' this year. Although I think that might be a bit niche, but isn't niche and indie where it's all at these days?"

Shit, she'd just come out in the most awkward, clumsy way, hadn't she?

However, Ruby's face relaxed as she took in Fran's words. "You're gay, too? I hadn't picked you up on my radar." She gave Fran her warmest smile yet. "If they make one that says 'Happy Christmas To Our Lesbian Daughter From Your Farming Family', let me know. Perhaps they could really embrace niche. I mean, it works for me."

Hang on, had Ruby just come out, too? Fran wasn't that surprised, but the confirmation of what she'd suspected sent a wave of triumph from her brain to her heart. She always loved it when cool, attractive, talented people were part of her crowd. It made Fran feel all those things by association.

"I wouldn't say you're niche," Fran told her. "In fact, I'd say having one of the most pure and natural folk voices in the country was anything *but* niche. You deserve to go mainstream."

Ruby laughed. "Are you trying to butter me up again, then slip a contract into my drink when I'm not looking?"

Fran laughed right back. "I promise, no signing talk tonight, okay? My compliments are just that."

"I'll believe you this once."

"Good." Fran let her shoulders drop. She breathed out. Could she almost relax in the presence of Ruby O'Connell? It would be a first.

"Have you been back to Mistletoe since we were there last?"

Ruby shook her head. "I've had a lot on. But I'm going back in two weeks. It'll be December 1st by then, and that's when things really hot up there. Then, I'll be back for the season."

Fran's parents had asked if she was coming to see them for a weekend before Christmas, particularly as she wasn't going to be there for the big day.

"I was planning on going back around then, too." Fran paused. "Where do you live?"

"West Ham," Ruby replied.

"Pretty close to me. I'm in Stratford. I could give you a lift home. Unless you were planning on driving?"

Ruby shook her head. "Tom and I share a van, but he needs it. I was going to get the train."

Fran splayed her hands. "The offer's there. I promise, I won't bring a contract, either."

She had Ruby's interest. A lift home was like a golden ticket in London. But would it be enough to tempt her?

"I don't know. I don't want to put you out." Ruby put a hand to her perfectly oval lips.

Fran followed it with interest.

"Although, I do have a lot of presents to bring back."

Fran shrugged. "There you go, then. No schlepping them on the tube and train. It's really no bother."

Ruby took a deep breath, sizing Fran up. "I didn't think we were going to be friends after our first two meetings."

"Just being a good neighbour. You can buy me a coffee on the way if it makes you feel better."

Why was she trying to persuade Ruby? Fran normally loved the solitude when she drove. Just her and her Spotify playlist, and the ability to belt out her favourites at the top of her voice. She wouldn't be able to do that with Ruby O'Connell in the car.

"You're on. I'll buy you a coffee *and* a sandwich. Perhaps even a bag of crisps."

"A meal deal."

"Now we're talking." Ruby pulled out her phone. "Should we exchange numbers?"

Ruby plugged in the number Fran recited. "This is not just another step in your stalking plan, is it?"

Fran gave her a butter-wouldn't-melt smile. "You fell right into my evil trap."

Chapter 6

"Good thing you don't have as many gifts as me, or we might be struggling for space." Ruby glanced at Fran's backseat, then turned around, giving Fran what she hoped was an apologetic look. Spits of rain were visible on the windscreen. Or was it snow?

"I go a bit overboard at Christmas. It's a family trait. Plus, when I knew I had a lift, all bets were off. I like to get everyone I love in the village a gift. Most of them are just fancy biscuits in posh tins, but they're exotic as they're from London. Audrey, for instance, would kill me if I didn't come back with some for her."

Fran laughed. "She was one of the more interesting characters I met at The Bar."

"Audrey doesn't hold back, but she means well. She played cards with me when I was a kid. You don't forget things like that." Ruby did up her seatbelt with a click. "By the way, I was expecting you to have a bit more of a fancy car than this."

"Creative industries don't pay well." Fran gave Ruby a *you-know-that's-true* look. "This is my dad's old car, actually." She patted the dashboard softly, as if it had to be handled with care. "My trusty Honda might be old, but she's never given me a moment of pain." Fran started the car and pulled out onto the road.

Ruby glanced at Fran's hands gripping the wheel. Her nails were polished, and short. Her hands looked strong, too. Capable. They'd only met a few times, but already Ruby knew that about Fran. Also, that she was persistent.

"In fact," Fran continued, flicking her indicator and turning right. "My parents are getting it serviced for me this weekend. I keep missing the dates they've booked in, and they insisted I didn't miss this one. It's been over two years since I had it done, which is way overdue. Is it shameful to admit that at the age of 36, I still don't pay for my car to be serviced?"

Ruby laughed. "Canny is more the word I'd choose. If I could get my parents to give me a car and pay for its upkeep, I would, too. Sadly, I don't think that's going to happen any time soon." Ruby made herself comfortable. "Has it got a name?"

Fran shook her head. "It doesn't. I just call it Car."

"Very creative. Perhaps you and my sister have something in common. You called your car, Car, and she called her bar, The Bar. Very literal."

Fran glanced her way. "Do you and your sister get on?"

Ruby nodded. "Now we do, but it was touch and go in our younger years."

"Then there's hope for us yet."

Getting out of London on a Friday evening was just as sticky as Ruby had imagined. The M11 was way too popular, and a light snowfall had just begun.

Fran flicked on her lights along with her windscreen wipers. At least she didn't need constant chat. The radio had been the soundtrack to their journey so far, which was fine with Ruby.

They were currently in a jam, with no sign of it easing. Ruby sucked on the inside of her cheek. When she glanced at Fran, she was doing the same.

"Here's the next smash hit from Delilah, called 'Losing You'," said the DJ.

Fran flinched, before leaning forward and turning the radio off. She grabbed her phone from the centre console and plugged it in. Spotify flashed up on her screen. Fran slid her finger left, then right, until music filled the car.

Ruby tapped along for a few moments before she spoke. "Not a Delilah fan? I would have expected the opposite. I thought you worked with her?"

Fran gave her a slow nod. "I did, so I've heard her stuff a lot. Plus, things didn't end well."

Ruby sat up. "She wasn't great to work with?"

"She was at first." Fran took a deep breath. "I signed her, but now her immediate team has changed. It happens." Fran shrugged. "I wasn't that involved in her last album. The first one, though, was the two of us driving it from the start."

Fran cleared her throat, looking straight ahead. The traffic began to move, and she pressed the accelerator.

Ruby didn't want to pry, but her curiosity was piqued. She couldn't imagine being as big as Delilah, having her hits known around the world and playing to massive stadiums. It was never what she'd got into music for, but she'd love to experience it once.

However, Ruby loved the intimate connection with her fans. She usually gigged in places where she could see their faces. She even knew their names. Her hardcore fans came to most of her gigs when they could, and she often had a drink with them in the bar afterwards. She couldn't imagine Delilah being able to do that.

"I didn't realise you were so involved. That must have been exciting, being a part of a career that really blew up like that."

Fran didn't take her eyes off the road as they finally got over 20mph. She gave Ruby the faintest of nods as the snow fell that little bit harder. Seconds later, the traffic slowed again. "It was for a while."

There was an edge to Fran's tone that Ruby couldn't quite nail down. "Is it true she's queer? I've seen her out with guys and girls, but you never know what to believe. I'm nobody, but I've had fans question whether my flatmate and me are together." Ruby eyed Fran. "For the record, we're not. Tom is just as queer as me."

Fran gave Ruby a wide grin. But that was soon wiped off her face as a loud bang made them both jump.

Instinctively, Ruby turned around, but it wasn't on the inside of the car.

Fran turned the music down.

The car moved forward slowly with an ominous guttural sound. When she pressed on the accelerator, it sounded like the engine was eating itself. Either that, or Fran was the worst type of boy racer.

Ruby put a hand to her chest. "What the fuck is that? It sounds like something is dragging."

Fran winced then gripped the steering wheel, leaning forward as if searching for answers. "Not sure, but maybe something fell off the car?" She shook her head. "Fuck, my dads are going to kill me for not getting this serviced sooner."

The tops of Ruby's ears prickled. The noise wasn't letting up. "Do you think it's your exhaust?" It was just a guess; Ruby was no mechanic. She glanced out the window and pointed. "Look! There's an emergency layby just there, can you aim for that?" What a stroke of luck.

Fran nodded, then steered the car left.

They both winced again at the sound it made.

When they were safely onto the layby, Fran let out a relieved sigh. She flicked on her hazard lights. "Luckily, my parents buy me an AA membership for Christmas every year." Fran cut the engine and picked up her phone. "Let me see what the issue is, and then call them." She grabbed her coat and got out of the car, slamming the door. Then she disappeared out of sight.

Ruby twisted around, then back. She bit her lip. There wasn't much she could do. It began to snow more steadily, and the traffic started to inch forward again. She was glad they were tucked into an emergency layby and not just on the hard shoulder. She didn't fancy being there with cars whizzing by. They could be stuck for a while.

Ruby closed her eyes. She should have got the train. She'd bargained on two to three hours for this trip. However, now it could be double that. Ruby grabbed her phone and texted her mum to let her know what was happening. She got a sad-face emoji back, and a message that Mum would keep dinner for her.

The driver-side door opened and Fran sat back in her seat, rubbing her hands.

"It's bloody Baltic out there. I swear, it's not normally this cold at the start of December." She put her key in the ignition and jabbed the heater on, then breathed into her hands in a bid to warm up.

"What happened? Could you see?"

Fran nodded, still shivering. Her dirty-blond hair glistened with snow, as did her dark grey coat. "It was the exhaust. It's hanging off the car. I called the AA, and the bloke reckoned a bracket's come loose. He might be able to fix it roadside or he might have to tow us, but it's likely to be at least an hour until they can send someone, so get comfortable." Fran lifted up a bottle of water. "We have fluid. I also have wine in the boot if things get desperate."

"And I have Christmas biscuits. That's almost a party." Ruby gave her a grin. "If we have to eat my sister's present, so be it."

"Not Audrey's?"

"Are you mad? I value my life." Ruby tapped her fingers on her knees. Another hour in the car with Fran, maybe longer. This was going to be a challenge.

"How about we play a game. You ask me a question, then I'll ask you. It's how we used to pass the time on long car journeys when I was little."

Fran didn't look convinced. "So long as they're not too personal."

Ruby shook her head. "Not at all." She tapped her foot. "Let's see. What's your favourite colour?"

Fran threw her a withering look.

"Would you prefer to sit in silence?" Ruby was trying her best. "Work with me."

"Okay." Fran paused. "Yellow."

"Really? But you're always dressed in dark colours when

I see you." She wiggled her fingers in front of Fran. "Grey shirt, blue jeans today. You were all in black when I saw you at the pub the other day."

"You've got a good memory."

Ruby blinked. She did. "I look at people's clothes."

Fran shrugged. "Yellow is still my favourite colour, even if I don't wear it all the time."

"Do you have *any* clothes that are yellow?"

Fran turned to Ruby. "I had some yellow socks once."

Ruby laughed. "Daring. You need to get some colour into your wardrobe. It might cheer you up. Colour has an effect on mood."

"Is that right?" Fran tilted her head.

"Yep. I wrote a song about it. Called 'Multi-coloured Dreams'." Ruby paused. "Have you ever written a song, or do you just sell the music?"

"Isn't it my turn for a question?"

Ruby held up her palms. "My mistake. It is." Fran had flipped from being friendly Fran to spiky Fran. She clearly didn't deal well with motoring hiccups. Perhaps that's why her dads looked after her car for her.

"I got it." Fran pointed a finger in Ruby's direction. "Favourite band and album."

Ruby blew out a breath. "Impossible to narrow it down to one."

"Try."

Ruby shook her head. "I can't. But I can give you my inspirations. Janis Joplin, Joni Mitchell, Beth Orton, Rufus Wainwright. Also, George Michael. He's my mum's favourite."

"Your mum has taste."

"Plus the Indigo Girls, of course."

"Rite of passage," Fran replied. "Or should I say, *Rites of Passage*."

Ruby chuckled. "You know your Indigo Girls album titles."

"Don't sound so amazed." She paused. "And by the way, I'm a fan of all of those artists you mentioned."

A bristle of surprise ran through Ruby. Musical taste was important, and Fran had passed the first round. "Go on then, tell me yours." Ruby sat back.

Fran frowned. "It's a lot harder when it's me." She paused. "My taste is across the board. I love country old and new – Dolly Parton to Cam – as well as pop, rock, hip-hop and indie. Janelle Monae is a favourite. My dads are Tina Turner and Celine Dion fans, and the latter is one of the best concerts I ever saw. My parents took me to Vegas for my 30th and we saw Celine there. She was immense."

"I have no doubt," Ruby replied.

"I'm also a fan of the Wainwrights – Rufus and Martha."

Ruby hadn't expected that, either. "Sounds like you have impeccable music taste."

Fran eyed Ruby. "It sounds like we both do."

Ruby paused as she registered a slight shift between them. It was her turn for a question. Her mind was blank. "I can't think of another question."

"This was your idea." Fran glanced Ruby's way. "I've got another one. Signature dish."

A creative question. "That's easy. Chicken and mushroom pasta bake. I know it sounds easy, but trust me, it's delicious. The secret? A ton of parmesan and cream."

"Everything's better with parmesan and cream."

"Exactly." Ruby's stomach rumbled. "I could really eat a pasta bake right now. Warming. Tasty." She shivered. Outside, the snow was still falling.

Fran turned the heat to full.

Ruby adjusted her vent, then put her hands up to it like it was a roaring fire.

Fran laughed, then got on her knees and twisted round. Seconds later, she dropped Ruby's coat into her lap, before wriggling back into her seat, hugging herself. "You look cold, put it on."

Ruby glanced her way, doing what she was told. Gratitude tiptoed up her scalp. "Thank you." She buttoned up before she asked: "What about yours?"

"Mine?"

"Signature dish."

"I don't cook much. Perils of the job. I'm usually out at a gig or working late. Can I say Deliveroo?"

Ruby grinned. "You cannot. You must cook something." She twisted to face Fran. "Come on, you've got a date with a hot chick. She's coming around to yours. What do you cook her?"

"Panic on toast?"

Ruby smirked Fran's way.

"Okay." Fran paused. "Malaysian curry. My old flatmate taught me how to make that. It's surprisingly easy and never not impressive."

"There you go. Malaysian curry. If you fed me that, we'd definitely be off to a good start." It was only when the words were out that Ruby realised what she'd said. "Not that I'm coming around to yours for a date." Heat flooded her cheeks. "I mean, not that you're not datable, it's just…"

Now Fran twisted in her seat, a smile hanging from her lips. "You're right, this game was a good idea. Watching you squirm while we're sitting freezing on the side of the motorway has taken my mind off things."

Ruby wanted to curl up in the footwell, but one glance at the tiny space and her long legs made her reconsider. "Here to help," she replied.

Chapter 7

Ruby's face was still a picture as she tried to clamber over her awkwardness.

However, Ruby's flushed cheeks and stuttering had helped to ease Fran's funk about the car. It wasn't helping either of them. Plus, as she kept reminding herself, the whole point of this trip was to thaw the relationship with Ruby. Being snarly wasn't going to win Fran any popularity points. Perhaps sharing something of herself would make Ruby feel more at home. Who knows, they might even become friends.

"My Malaysian curry was a favourite of my ex."

Ruby stretched her legs at that. "You see, I told you it would lead to a sure thing." She smiled. "My ex was a fan of my pasta bake, too. Although she did constantly tell me I might die an early death if I kept eating it. Either from heart failure or obesity due to the amount of cheese and cream."

Fran glanced her way. "Seeing as your stomach is impossibly flat, the obesity dilemma seems sorted."

"You never know about heart failure, though, do you? You hear all the time about people who run marathons and drop dead."

"Don't run marathons. They bugger your knees and then you keel over and die."

"Good point." Ruby paused. "Are you cooking your curry for anyone at the moment?"

Fran shook her head. "I'm not. I broke up with my ex two years ago. I'm done with women." She snagged Ruby's gaze with her own. "What about you?"

"Confirmed singleton, too. Meal deals for one."

"Sounds like we both need to start a supper club. Or at least a meal exchange."

"Or just get laid." Ruby blushed again. She was cute when she blushed.

"Nah, I'm off that, too. After Delilah…" Fran stopped. *Shit*. She hadn't meant to blurt that name out. They'd never been out publicly, which was one of the reasons they'd broken up.

But Ruby was already staring at the mention of the name, her forehead furrowed as she pieced Fran's history together. "It was Delilah who ate your curry?" Astonishment tinted her words.

Fran bristled. "Is it *that* improbable?" She'd always worried she was punching above her weight. She didn't need it confirmed by Ruby.

Ruby shook her head. "I didn't mean it in a bad way. I'm just surprised she's actually gay. I'd heard rumours she was seeing someone, but we hardly run in the same circles. Now I find out it was you."

"It was me." There had been something there from the first moment they met. "I don't normally date musicians. Not because it's unethical — it happens all the time — but rather because I know it's a difficult road, with touring, fans throwing themselves at you, all of that."

"I don't get nearly as much of it as she would." Ruby

twisted her mouth one way, then the other. "I never saw you with her, though. How long were you together?"

"Nine months." They'd been split for a while now, and Fran was over it. But saying Delilah's name still cloaked her heart in sadness. She'd wanted it to work, but it hadn't.

"My dads knew, and my colleague, Damian. But apart from that, I was sworn to secrecy. It couldn't get out while she was trying to make it big, so we had to be super careful everywhere we went." Fran shook her head, remembering. "It was more than tiresome. Plus, I've been out and proud since I was 17. When you have two gay dads, you don't have to hide who you are. Going back into the closet was hard. My parents hated it as much as me. Plus, they could see that despite us getting along, it was never going to work. But I had to learn the hard way."

"I bet." Ruby paused. "No wonder you snapped off her music earlier."

Fran took a deep breath, then shrugged. "When we broke up, I asked to be taken off her team, and she endorsed it. But she's off on tour now, and things are really hitting the big time. I'm pleased for her, but she needs to be who she is. Come out as queer."

"Why wouldn't she, though? It's hardly taboo anymore. Maybe in the film or TV industry. But in music, people have always been able to be way more themselves."

"That's the irony, isn't it?" Fran was quiet for a moment. "Does whatever I tell you in this car stay right here?"

Ruby nodded. "Of course. You have my word."

Fran hoped she could trust Ruby. She was in the business, too, and she didn't strike Fran as the gossipy type.

"For Delilah, it's her parents. She might be the woman of the moment with chart-topping hits, but her parents are crazy-religious and she's not out to them. Until she does that, she can't be who she truly is." Fran shrugged. "Pop stars have hang-ups, too."

"More than most from the ones I've met," Ruby replied. "Wow, I can't believe you were with Delilah." She waved her hands at Fran. "Again, not in *that* way. I just thought she'd want a bit more of a starry girlfriend. Someone she could share the spotlight with."

"Nope. Delilah wants someone who she can keep in the closet. I did it for a while because she said she was going to come out eventually. But as time went on, it became apparent she was lying. That's when I realised it was never going to work. Doesn't mean it didn't hurt, though." It had hurt plenty. Still did sometimes.

"Makes my tale of woe about my ex being a different person to me pale into the background." Ruby paused. "Still, you've slept with a chart-topping artist. And she loved your curry."

"She did. She just didn't love me all that much. Or herself." Fran glanced in her rear-view mirror. No sign of a recovery truck. She wished it'd hurry up. Her stomach gurgled loudly.

Ruby twisted around, rummaged in one of her bags, then produced a neatly wrapped gift. She tore the paper without hesitation. "My sister won't miss these, and your stomach needs attending to." Ruby held up a yellow biscuit tin. "It's even your colour, so it's your Christmas present now. Just a month early." She grinned, giving it to Fran. "Happy Christmas. Have some vanilla and coconut whirls."

Fran took the tin. "Don't mind if I do."

They sat munching their whirls for a few moments. Then Fran's phone flashed. She picked it up.

"The AA man is 15 minutes away."

"It might be a woman," Ruby countered.

Fran gave her a pained look. "I don't know many women called Mike. Whatever, home should be within reach soon." She glanced out her window. "The traffic's moving faster now, too."

"We'll be in Mistletoe before you know it." Ruby grabbed another biscuit. "Are you still in touch with Delilah?"

"We still talk occasionally, but like I said, she's touring her new album now. She vowed she would keep in touch more, but she's busy. I get it. I've watched plenty of relationships between music execs and artists explode. I know the drill. You never think it's going to happen to you. But musicians are single-minded. They have to be to succeed. They're all about themselves and their careers." She glanced at Ruby, feeling the blood rush to her cheeks.

Fran sat forward, shaking her head. "Which I totally get, by the way. My job is important to me, too." She took a breath, trying to reframe her argument. "My point is, you can be career-focused, but also consider other people. Perhaps even have a relationship." Fran sat back. "I know I'm sworn off women, and that still stands. But in ten years' time when I'm ready again, maybe I'll go for a woman who's not even a music fan."

"You wouldn't last five minutes," Ruby replied. "You love music. It's in your bones, just like mine. It must be, or you wouldn't do the job you do."

"True. But right now, after Delilah, I am so done. So long as my next girlfriend eats my curry, I'd be happy if she works in a bank. Or a fishmonger. I've never dated a fishmonger."

Ruby raised an eyebrow. "Really? A fishmonger?"

"Think of all the cheap salmon and how healthy my skin would look." Fran could just imagine the glow. "Have you ever gone out with a musician? Or someone in the industry like me, come to that?" Fran's eyes widened. *Shit*. "Not that I'm suggesting…"

"A musician, yes." Ruby gave her an amused smirk. "Someone in the industry, no. Not really my scene. No offence."

"You know when someone says 'no offence', it means they're about to offend you, right?"

"You know what I mean. Music execs in general are just in it for themselves. Out to boost their careers. They're not interested in artistic integrity or in the artist's voice." She glanced at Fran. "In my experience," Ruby added hastily.

Wow. Ruby didn't hold back, did she? "You really don't have a high opinion of me, do you? At least I gave you the benefit of the doubt. I could have lumped you in with all other musicians, saying you're all as bad as each other. But I didn't." She glanced at Ruby. "Maybe I should have." She grabbed another biscuit from the tin. "Why are you so down on the music industry?"

Ruby rolled her shoulders and was silent for a few moments before she spoke. "Because I had a bad experience. I signed to a label when I was 21, and I thought that was it, that I had the dream ticket. But then they wanted to change my sound and make me more pop, more 'radio-friendly'. I went along with it because I was 21, but it wasn't me and I think listeners could tell. The music didn't sell. The label also wanted me to change my look, 'show more cleavage' I believe was the term used."

Fran winced. "I'd like to say I'm surprised, but I'm not." She'd heard that story too many times. "It's one of the things I'm most proud of with our new project, Fast Forward. They're a girl group, but a new style of girl group. No cleavage required."

"That should have been their band name."

Fran gave her a wry smile. "I did consider it."

Ruby shrugged. "But anyway, I didn't show more cleavage. It wasn't me. Then they tried to tour me, but they ended up putting me in the wrong venues and it was a disaster. My worst night was playing a rock club. I was pelted with beer cans and booed off stage. It's why I don't like playing venues bigger than around 100 people any more. Crowds behave better when they're not so anonymous. They're more my people."

Fran glanced in Ruby's direction. "I'm sorry that happened to you, but we're not all the same."

Ruby shrugged. "But money talks, doesn't it? When I stopped selling, the label dropped me, and every person I encountered was all about the bottom line and how it could work for them. I was never in the equation. It was a wasted couple of years and I had to start again from scratch."

"Have you ever taken the time to talk to music people, though? Really understand why they're doing their job?"

Even in the low lighting of the car, Fran saw Ruby's cheeks colour pink. "Nothing in depth," Ruby said, "but I know the type."

"Really." Fran turned her body towards Ruby, every fibre of her truly pissed. Maybe she shouldn't have offered her a lift, neighbour or not. "That type is me? Because I can tell you, I love music. My job is to get good music out into the world. The role I play is balancing the artist with what the label can offer, and it's all part of the creative process. Just like you making music is, too. But I care about my artists and I'm good at the business side." Was Ruby not listening to what she was saying on purpose, or had she just convinced herself that her beliefs were the absolute truth?

Ruby tucked her chin into her neck. The car was silent for a good few moments.

Fran cleared her throat as annoyance and frustration rumbled through her.

Ruby still didn't say anything.

Had Fran gone too far? She thought about it for a few moments, then decided she hadn't. Ruby had made assumptions about Fran and her career. She was wrong.

"It's the reason I tried to sign you. Because I think you're talented. Because I think your music deserves to be listened to on a much larger scale. I get that you want to help out your family at Christmas, but it's a big thing to put your career on hold for six weeks every year. Most people wouldn't do it, and if you want my professional advice, it's not the smartest career move. Wouldn't you rather be playing a gig that might get your music out there and open doors, rather than selling Christmas trees? If it's money you're worried about, you could help your family out far more when your sales go through the roof."

Fran wasn't done. "If you want my professional opinion, it sounds like you're making excuses to thwart yourself. Your family is a great excuse, and nobody is ever going to call you on it. But I see what you're doing. You're scared of trying, but even more scared of being a success." Fran winced. She hadn't meant to go into a rant, but Ruby had riled her.

She held up a palm. "I'm sorry, but I don't like being misrepresented." She held Ruby's gaze. "Also, I don't like wasted talent. It's part of my job to spot it."

Silence settled on the car. Seconds ticked by.

Ruby took a deep breath, then sat up in her seat. "Listen, Fran…"

But just then, the bright lights of the AA truck lit them up as it pulled in behind.

Both Fran and Ruby turned into the light, then squinted.

"Saved by the bell." Fran yanked open her door and got out, then flicked up the hood of her coat against the swirling snow. Only another few hours to survive with Ruby. She wasn't sure her plan of buttering Ruby up had gone that well. But frankly, when Ruby thought so little of her, did Fran really want to work with her anyway?

* * *

Mike couldn't fix Fran's car. "More than the exhaust," was his not-so-helpful assessment. He loaded it onto his recovery truck, with Fran and Ruby riding in his cab up-front.

When they arrived in Mistletoe an hour and a half later, the snow was still falling at a steady rate, and the village was picture-postcard pretty. The journey had been quiet, and luckily the traffic had eased. Fran kept her eyes on the road and her thoughts to herself. She'd avoided looking at Ruby too much. When she had, Ruby's eyes had been closed. Whether she was asleep or just attempting damage limitation, Fran wasn't sure.

As they both lived so close, the drop-off point was the same. Mike gave Fran a number to call to arrange a replacement rental while hers was being fixed. "Although," he said, looking into the sky, "if this keeps up, you might not be able to get it." The snow swirled around his face, like someone up there was grating the sky.

Fran shook her head. "I don't really need a car while I'm here. I'll follow up with the garage to see when they can get it back to me."

He nodded, then drove off.

Ruby stood as the snow fell, her numerous gift bags at her feet.

"You want a hand in?" Fran might still be annoyed, but she was polite.

Ruby shook her head, grabbing all the handles in her fingers. "I can manage." She took two steps, then a third.

Fran kept a narrowed eye on Ruby. She didn't look steady on the snowy ground.

On her fourth step, Ruby wobbled. On the fifth, she lost her footing, and almost in slow motion her right foot slid forward as her body jerked back. She landed with a dull thud on the pavement. Her gift bags scattered across the pavement, presents skidding out. A squashed "Fuuuuck!" escaped Ruby's mouth.

Fran stood still for a moment, biting down a laugh. Then she clicked into gear, rushing over to her fallen neighbour. She gathered the gifts back into the bags, stood them up, then offered Ruby her hand.

Ruby looked up, grimaced, then took it reluctantly.

When their hands connected, a sudden boom ripped through Fran's core. It wasn't subtle. It was seismic, shaking her from the inside out. It almost knocked her sideways. She squeezed her toes together and managed to stay upright. She clung on to Ruby's hand, willing her racing heart to slow down.

"After three," Fran said, ignoring the ricochets in her body. They couldn't be trusted. "One, two, three."

Ruby held onto Fran tight and heaved herself off the pavement.

When she made it to her full height, they stood facing each other. Ruby a few inches higher, her lips almost at Fran's eye level.

Fran hadn't considered Ruby's lips once in the car. At least, she didn't *think* she had. Ruby was attractive, but so were many women Fran came into contact with. She was used to attractive singers in her orbit. It was her world.

However, none of them had ever caused a mini-earthquake in her with a touch of their hand. Damn it, Fran *really* didn't need the one person who *did* to be Ruby. Not after the way their breakdown chat had turned so sour.

There must be something faulty in her wiring in Mistletoe. Something off. Maybe it was the snow.

She wasn't used to snow.

That was probably it.

"If it's any consolation, you went down with the grace of a top ballet dancer." Fran paused. "Will you accept some help to your front door, now? I promise, as soon as we get there, I'll leave and you'll be shot of this music exec."

Ruby grabbed some bags, letting Fran take some. She gave

her a weak smile. "Thanks." Ruby began walking, limping slightly. She glanced across at Fran, looking like she was about to say something, then didn't.

Fran let it go. "What are your plans for this weekend?"

It was still snowing, and every word Fran uttered was topped with wet snow. It settled all around her in thick layers.

"It's going to be a busy one," Ruby replied. "The start of December means the annual Christmas Tree Contest and Treasure Hunt, so this weekend is big news in Mistletoe." She flipped her head to the sky. "I just hope this snow, pretty as it is, doesn't cause an issue. Otherwise, there might be many furrowed brows in the village. Still, it's nothing we haven't dealt with before."

They walked down the drive to the farm in silence, battling the growing snow storm, Fran swallowing down many flakes by the time they arrived. She didn't have a hat or gloves. Her fingers were numb and her hair wet. She was sure she had a nose like Rudolph, too.

Ruby was just fishing in her bag for her key when the door swung open. Mary appeared on the other side, her cheeks flushed with warmth. It was in stark contrast to the pair of them. Chipper ran circles around them, jumping up at Ruby.

"Oh my goodness! Get in! Get in! You both look frozen!" Mary said.

"Hello, Chipper! Good boy!" Ruby flicked a worried gaze to Fran.

She didn't need to panic. Fran was happy to get as far away from Ruby at the fastest speed possible. "Thanks, but I was just giving Ruby a hand with her bags. Turns out she buys a whole lot of presents."

"That's our Ruby!" Mary took the bags from Fran's hands. "You sure I can't offer you a coffee or a hot chocolate at least?"

Fran shook her head. "No thanks. My dads are waiting for me. I better get home." She gave Ruby a tight smile. "See you soon."

Ruby dipped her head. "Thanks for the lift."

Chapter 8

Being woken at 7am and told she had to get up to help the village wasn't Fran's idea of the perfect Saturday morning. Especially not after the journey she'd endured last night, including a broken-down car and a spluttering friendship. Apparently, a siren call had gone out across Mistletoe this morning by text. Like it or not, Fran was part of the village now. She checked in the mirror, wiped the sleep from her eyes and splashed her face. Did she need to apply make-up? Who for? She didn't even know these people.

But she knew Ruby.

Fran pushed that thought to one side and trundled down the stairs, where her dads already had their coats, hats, scarves and boots on. They were Mistletoe-ready.

It was only now she did a thorough inspection of the hallway she took in just how all-in Dad and Pop had gone on the Christmas decorations.

Back in Surrey, they'd been far more reserved. The one thing her parents *always* made sure they had was mistletoe. Her dads had a thing for mistletoe. It was how they'd got together one snowy night in Soho some 40 years ago. They'd been inseparable ever since. Hence, when they'd seen a village in

Suffolk named Mistletoe, it had seemed like destiny. Resistance was futile.

Now, Fran took in the Christmas cards on strings and the tinsel on door frames. The fake snow on the window panes. She'd even spied Christmas tea towels hanging from the AGA last night. They hadn't even bought a tree or really got started yet. She blinked, gave them both a good-morning kiss on the cheek, then shrugged on her too-thin coat and inappropriate shoes. The clock had barely scraped past 7.30am when they opened the front door. There hadn't even been time for a cuppa.

When Fran walked out, the crisp, dazzling stillness tickled her cheeks and stole her breath. There was something to be said for being out this early. The holly bush had a brilliant snow jacket. The fir tree was majestic. The rest of the plants sported a snow trim. When Fran stepped onto the garden path — which Pop had semi-cleared — the thin layer of snow crunched underfoot. The best part of any snowfall was being the first one to tread in it. It never happened in London. It hardly ever happened in Surrey. But in Mistletoe? She could roll around to her heart's content and still have fields and fields of snow to go.

"Wow. I feel like I'm inside a Christmas card."

Dad nodded. "Isn't it magical? This is why we moved to Mistletoe."

Fran couldn't argue with that.

"We've done some fabulous bike rides around these roads and trails, too," Pop added.

"No doing that in this weather." When she heard the words, Fran rolled her eyes at herself. When had their roles of parent and child begun to shift?

"Yes, Mum." Pop gave her a wink.

They walked to Mistletoe Stores, the air so fresh Fran wanted to bottle it. She could make a mint selling it in London. They were silent, and the only noise was occasional bird song. Fran made sure her steps were small and heavy as her shoes had no grip. She'd seen what happened with Ruby last night, so she was taking no chances.

Signs along Farm Lane directed people to Mistletoe Christmas Tree Farm and the Christmas Tree Contest and Treasure Hunt. There was also a massive sign at the junction with Mistletoe Stores. Tall, elaborately decorated trees lined the route. Fran hadn't noticed them last night, in the snowstorm — she'd had other things on her mind. Now, she had no idea how she'd missed them.

When they arrived at Mistletoe Stores, they walked around a massive tree adorned with everything Elvis. It even had a sparkly jacket and a quiff. Fran wanted to stop and stare. Get her phone out and instantly Instagram it. However, everyone else took this tree in their stride, as if it happened all the time. Perhaps it did in Mistletoe.

She and her parents headed to The Bar. Outside the back door, a row of shovels were propped against the wall. Somebody had already been busy. When she walked in, Fran blinked again. The Bar was absolutely packed. She hadn't expected that.

There was barely space for them to squeeze in, but the villagers made room, slapping Michael and Dale on the back. The low hum of the coffee machine working overtime mixed with the chatter of the locals filled the air, along with the smell of freshly roasted beans. What Fran would give for a coffee.

However, to get there, she'd have to hurdle at least 30 people. She didn't want to come across as a pushy Londoner.

Fran spotted Mary and Paul behind the bar, along with Victoria and Eric who were doling out the drinks. Scott and Ruby were the other end of the bar, giving out mince pies and chatting with Sue and Penny. At the sight of Ruby, Fran inhaled a long breath. Ruby was deep in conversation, her face animated and alive. She looked happy. Fran hoped she'd get that version of Ruby today, rather than the spiky one. That they could get over last night and be civil to each other.

Mary checked her watch, then clapped her hands. Silence descended on the bar.

"Thanks everyone for coming at such short notice, and for being such phone addicts that you had them on in the first place!"

Chuckles from the audience.

"Also, thanks to OnePhone for providing service that can survive a snow storm. Remember that year we had to go door to door, knocking everybody up by hand?"

"Yes!" came the chorus from the front of the bar, followed by laughter around the room.

"Anyway," Mary continued, rubbing her hands through her short hair. It stuck up at all angles. "The village is looking picture-perfect this morning after all the snowfall overnight. But as you also know, picture-perfect means headaches for us. Especially this weekend for the Christmas Tree Contest and Treasure Hunt."

"Headaches for us all!" shouted Audrey. "How am I meant to get over to the supermarket to get my shop when I can't get the car out?"

Audrey was wearing what Fran could only describe as an artist's smock. It seemed wildly inappropriate for the weather. But then, Audrey was wildly inappropriate, so perhaps it suited her.

"You could always just buy from us at Mistletoe Stores," Eric said.

"When you start stocking my chorizo, passata and all the other goodies I get from Aldi, we'll talk."

Mary clapped her hands. "We don't have a lot of time, so if I could bring your attention back to the matter at hand. I've spoken to the council, and the gritters are already on the case making all the roads passable up to Mistletoe perimeter. I've got a cast-iron guarantee on that. I told them we can take the rest."

She paused. "As most of you know, our job today — as it has been every year when this has happened — is to make sure the pavements are passable, the farm is safe, and the Christmas trees scattered all over the village that are taking part in the competition are de-snowed, their themes visible. People will still come if they can drive their cars here, park it somewhere free of ice, walk on pavements that aren't skating rinks and most importantly, so long as they can see the trees to judge them.

"The forecast is good, there's no more snow, so let's give this a positive slant. The snow couldn't have come at a better time to make Mistletoe as Instagrammable as possible. Well, perhaps a day or two earlier, but let's not split hairs." Mary grinned. "The village is going to look gorgeous with your help. If we can all pitch in this morning, visitors will rave about our little hamlet, then come back next year. Pavements and trees are the priority. Everybody ready to ensure Mistletoe is open for business?"

The whole bar erupted into applause and whistles. Fran joined in the clapping, somewhat bemused.

"Order! Order!" shouted Paul, as if he was the Speaker in the House of Commons. "See Eric and Victoria over here for the duties we've assigned you. If you have a problem, speak to them, but hopefully everyone will be happy. Over 70s, you won't be shovelling snow, that much we can promise. Not after Norman's back went three years ago."

"I can shovel! I'm fit as a fiddle!" Norman shouted. He stood to demonstrate the point, waving his walking stick in the air.

Everyone ignored him.

"Tea, coffee and mince pies are on tap here to everyone helping. Take one before you go or come back afterwards."

Fran stood at the back as the crowd chatter filled the room once more. There was a swell to the front to get coffee and duties, then a slow dispersal as the villagers marched out, mission in hand.

Ruby's brother Scott bustled up, slapping Dad and Pop on the back. "Michael, Dale. You're both fit and able. I've put you two on snow-shovelling duty on the main road into town. You and six others. You should get it done in an hour or so, with luck. Shovels are stacked up outside. That okay?"

Both her dads nodded, puffing out their chests.

Fran suppressed a laugh. Her dads were fit, even though they were both in their mid-60s.

"As for you, Fran. I thought the best thing would be to team up with Ruby to get the farm gritted and the Christmas trees around it set for the treasure hunt and judging." He turned around, just as Ruby approached. "Here she is! I've given you Fran to help out. That okay?"

Ruby sucked on her top lip, then nodded. "Of course, that's great." Her tone was flat.

So far, this morning was going about as bad as Fran could have wished. She'd been hoping for a lie-in, followed by one of Pop's famous fry-ups. Then perhaps a spot of *Saturday Morning Kitchen* on the telly, where she could watch people cook food she would never recreate because she didn't have the time or the inclination.

Instead, here she was.

With Ruby.

Again.

It seemed like their lives were being thrown together whether they liked it or not.

Outside Mistletoe Stores, the snow was already grey and sludge-like from the early morning foot-traffic. Fran and Ruby set off down the road back towards the farm. A home they shared. Sort of.

"Seems like everyone's quite excited about this. They like being woken up early and giving up their Saturday." Fran was still a mix of perplexed and impressed.

Ruby shrugged. "Community is important around here. The village is important. It's one of the reasons I like to come home at this time of year, to feel that. It's why I value community in my music. It's not all about money for me."

Another dig at Fran. "You don't waste any time, do you?"

Ruby shook her head, then stopped walking. "I didn't mean it like that." She shoved her hands deep in the pockets of her thick coat, glancing Fran's way. "Look, I'm sorry about what I said yesterday. I was tired and hungry, but that's no excuse for tarring everyone with the same brush. It was unfair. Not all music execs are born the same, I know that. I wouldn't have liked it if you'd done it the other way around, but you didn't. I apologise." She stared at Fran.

Fran took a deep breath. "I apologise if I overstepped the mark, too."

Ruby shook her head. "I deserved it. Can we start again?"

Hadn't they started again a few times already, yet they always seemed to end up back where they started?

However, when Ruby's green gaze snagged Fran's, her doubts disappeared. Maybe they could. They should at least try. For the village's sake, if nothing else.

She nodded. "Let's put it all behind us. Clean slate. You've got yourself a deal."

Chapter 9

When they arrived at the farm, Ruby led Fran past the main house and down to the large courtyard behind. There was a wooden stage in the middle that Ruby had avoided singing on ever since Scott and her dad built it seven years ago. Firepits and picnic tables were dotted around the space, and a decorated Christmas tree studded each corner.

Flanking the courtyard stood three stone outbuildings that had been painstakingly renovated by her parents over the years. They now housed a café, a gallery that exhibited local art, and the all-important Christmas shop.

Apart from everything being covered in snow, the farm was ready for today. The four Christmas trees were the first they had to de-snow, so the contest could go ahead.

Three villagers — Roger, Betty and Joyce — were waiting at the nearest barn door. Ruby greeted them, gave them a bunch of keys, and they left.

"They're gritting the car park, then getting the café and food ready for later on." Ruby waved a hand around the courtyard. "These four trees are in the contest. There are 38 trees scattered about the village, decorated and ready for judging. It's the most we've ever had in one year."

Fran was standing next to one of the courtyard trees,

sniffing one of its branches. "It smells like Christmas." She spread her arms wide. "It's making me feel all warm inside, even though I'm bloody freezing." Fran shook the tree. Snow cascaded onto her. She scrunched her face and blew it off.

Ruby could do nothing but laugh. "You need a thicker coat before you do that again."

Fran wrapped her arms around her torso. "Tell me something I don't know." She stared up at the tree. "The theme for this one is Scotland?" The tree was wearing a kilt with a tartan hat on top, and had an inflatable bottle of Glenfiddich in its branches. Heather peaked out of its pines, too, and a laminated life-size bust of Rod Stewart hung from its right side, a scaled-down Nicola Sturgeon stared from its left.

Ruby nodded. "Well done."

"I saw the tree at Mistletoe Stores. That's my favourite so far."

Ruby grinned. "Victoria is responsible for the Elvis tree. But it can't win, seeing as we're running the contest. Victoria's still pissed."

"I would be, too. But I can already see there's stiff competition. Who knew a Christmas tree could be Elvis?"

They crossed the courtyard side by side.

"How does the contest work?"

"Local businesses, charities, and families pay to enter their trees into the contest. They get a pot and a location. They buy a tree from our farm, plant it, decorate it with a theme, then write the theme on a card under their tree."

Ruby pushed open the tall Christmas Shop door and invited Fran in. "Then people pay to buy a Treasure Hunt map from the store and the challenge is to hunt down all the trees in the village and surrounding roads, write down each tree's theme, then pick your top three."

Ruby was so used to the wealth of festive paraphernalia on offer inside, she didn't even pause as she entered.

But Fran did. "Blimey. It's like someone vomited Christmas in here." She stamped her feet.

Ruby glanced down: she bet Fran's toes were numb. "That won't be our new slogan in case you were wondering."

However, Fran was right: this shop was a love letter to Christmas. The farm was competing with local garden centres, so it had to be. Festive-themed soft toys, tree ornaments and baubles in all shapes and colours stood to Ruby's right, along with tinsel, tree beads, and tree-toppers. To her left were the greener options, including wreaths, poinsettias and a vast range of festive plants. The back wall was full of chocolates and confectionery, along with stocking fillers as far as the eye could see. If you wanted a Christmas tea towel, mug, wine glass or tin opener, you were in the right place.

Ruby walked over to the till area, leaned down and grabbed a wedge of paper. "These are the Treasure Hunt guides, listing the locations of every tree in the village. A committee makes up 50 per cent of the judging — basically, our family, as we run it — and then everyone who pays for a treasure hunt gets to judge the entries, too. The judging takes place over today and tomorrow, then we announce the winner on Sunday at 4pm. All the money collected from the entries and the treasure hunt goes to charity, and the top three winners get prizes donated by local businesses."

Fran shook her head. "I absolutely love that, it's so creative."

"It is. I love coming back for it every year. Scott's trying to get digital ads up and running for the farm as well, and it's working. But the contest and treasure hunt drive people to the village, get them to the farm and hopefully they then spend money and buy trees."

"Who came up with the idea of the contest in the first place?"

"Mum and Dad did when the business needed a boost after big shops started selling Christmas trees. We're not all country bumpkins selling eggs from the side of the road." Ruby banged her hands together. "Ready to do the treasure hunt before anyone else and de-snow some trees?"

"Can we get coffee first? It's still early and fucking cold, and I didn't get one in the stampede at The Bar." Fran walked up to the large rack of Christmas crackers by the door. She picked up a box. "Also, I like these."

Ruby walked up beside her.

Fran turned and their gazes met.

Ruby shivered, even though she wasn't cold. The blue of Fran's eyes seemed richer than before. Her skin glowed. Ruby couldn't quite make sense of the way her heart began to thud in her chest. She focused on the crackers, not the fact that she was going crackers.

"Mum and Dad have been making them for the past month. It's their big hope for this year. They're pretty cool, and the presents inside are actually things you might want. You should see the spare room, it's stacked with them."

"They should stock them in Harrods, they'd make a killing. Double the price, too."

Ruby laughed. "If you know a buyer for Harrods, do let

me know. Mum and Dad would be well up for it." She gave Fran a Treasure Hunt map. "Here you go — pirate treasure in tree form. We'll call in at the café, grab a coffee, grit the yard and surrounding paths, then tackle the trees. Ready?"

Fran stamped her feet and shivered. "Ready."

But Ruby shook her head, then frowned. "You know what we have to do before we do anything else? Get you a proper coat and boots so you don't freeze to death today. Fashion shoes and your thin jacket won't do. It's a criminal offence not to have the correct footwear and jacket in Mistletoe. Even when the rest of the country has no snow, Mistletoe is often the blind spot."

"Next you'll be telling me Santa makes a special stop on his sleigh here, too."

Ruby gave her an exaggerated shrug. "This is where he refuels, of course." She leaned in. "He even gets his tree from Mistletoe Farm. We give him a discount, naturally. We're not mercenaries." She tilted her head towards the house, her eyes stuck on Fran. "Enough chat. Let me give you some proper boots, at least. What size are you?"

"Six," Fran replied.

"Perfect. Mum has boots for every occasion, and she's a six. She also probably has a spare coat, too. You'll thank me later."

Chapter 10

Their first job was to grit the paths in and around the farm. Fran got the hang of shovelling grit pretty quickly after Ruby kept shouting at her to "just fling it!" However, Fran had a different method than flinging. She preferred to drizzle. The trick was to get as much orange grit on your shovel as possible, and then shuffle the contents liberally on the ground. Gritting was also a surprisingly good workout once you got going. Fran's hips hadn't moved this much since she was… well, since Delilah. Too long ago.

"You're creating some lovely patterns in the snow." Ruby put a hand on her hip and assessed Fran's handiwork. "You're wasted in the music business. You clearly should have been an artist."

"I did two years of an art degree."

Ruby's eyebrow lifted in surprise. "You did?"

Fran nodded. "I never said I wasn't creative. You assumed that. I just favoured going the business route. But like I told you, that can still be creative."

Ruby winced. "You're right. I did assume. I promise I'm going to stop doing that."

Fran hoped that was true. She let it go.

Once the farm's courtyard, drive and paths were gritted,

Fran helped Ruby clear up the rest of the courtyard trees. The other three had themes of Madonna (the pop star, not the mother of Christ), love, and Italy. Fran had never seen a tree decorated in red, white and green dried pasta before, along with a pizza tree-topper, but there was a first time for everything. The Madonna tree won this round, though, with its mix of lace, leather, leotards, cowboy hats and pointy bras. Whoever was responsible had covered all of Madge's key eras.

Once the courtyard trees were done, there were four more nearby to clear. As they walked, Fran flexed her toes to keep her blood moving. Her warmth factor was infinitely better than it had been at the start of the day. Ruby had been right — getting a pair of Mary's boots had been a smart move. She'd also accepted a bright pink ski jacket, scarf, and bobble hat. She'd have frozen to death by now in what she had been wearing. Her mission when she got back to London was to get all-new outdoor wear and be Mistletoe-proofed.

Ruby took Fran's gritting shovel and stowed it with hers by the farmhouse front door.

"I just need to check something at the café, then we'll go."

Fran nodded, then blew out a breath. It froze in the cold morning air. It was still only 10am, but they'd accomplished so much. Fran's days were always busy, but some whistled by and she had to think hard about what she'd accomplished. It wasn't like that in Mistletoe. The jobs were tangible. Grit the yard. Bake the pies. Shake the trees. There was none of the ambiguity of modern life. The feeling of accomplishment was on a different level.

She took off a glove and held it between her teeth, the ends of her fingers still numb as she prodded her phone. She asked her dads how they were getting on. They replied almost instantly that they were nearly done, and heading to The Bar for coffee and refreshments in half an hour. She told them she'd meet them there.

Five minutes later, Ruby's voice carried in the air. Fran turned as she strode towards her. There was no doubt about it, Ruby *did* stride. She looked so at home in this environment, too, which was such a long way from Fran's comfort zone. She was wearing black jeans, a black Berghaus jacket ("built for warmth" as Ruby had told her before), plus a thermal hat and gloves. She didn't have any make-up on, but her skin was unblemished and naturally rosy.

Ruby fitted here.

Fran had admired Ruby's style from the moment they met. It suited her and her music. How was it possible this country-living style suited her, too?

The farmhouse keys dangled from Ruby's fingers. "You want to come in and get a blast of warmth while I pick up the food mum's done for the hungry workers? We'll do the tree inspections on the way."

"Sure." Fran followed Ruby into the house. As soon as she stepped through the door, her senses were overcome by the smell of baking. "Your house smells like Christmas."

Ruby turned and gave her a grin as she dropped the keys on the table. "That's why I like to come home. Mum was up at 5am. There's nothing like waking up to the smell of fresh baking in the morning. Do your dads bake?"

Fran nodded. "They never used to, but now they're living

in Mistletoe, so much has changed. Every time I walk into the kitchen, they're whipping up batches of scones and mince pies."

Ruby grabbed a couple of tins from the table, and lifted the lids to check what was inside. "I challenge them to make them as good as these." She closed the lids and walked towards Fran. "Can you take these?"

Fran held out her arms and Ruby plonked the tins into them. "Mistletoe will work its magic on your dads, mark my words. Before they know what's happening, they'll be putting on a Santa outfit and eating mince pies at every meal."

She and Ruby ferried three tins of pies to the van, putting them on the front seat. Fran slammed the door, and when she looked up, Ruby's brow furrowed.

"You know what, on second thoughts." She held out a thermal-gloved hand, and grabbed Fran's arm in her grip. "Let's go and see the trees now. You got your map?"

Fran patted her jacket pocket. "Never leave home without it." She was trying to ignore the warmth racing up her arm, emanating from where Ruby was touching her.

"You're a natural at this, London girl."

Ruby threaded an arm through Fran's and together they crunched down the farm pathway, stopping at the first tree which was 50 metres ahead. Ruby spread her arms before giving Fran a "ta-da!", along with a broad smile. "This is Mistletoe Farm's entry."

Fran peered upwards, in awe of the tree's height. It had to be at least 20 feet tall. "It's wonderful. I love the candy canes. It reminds me of *Elf*, the one Christmas film I like. What's the tree theme?"

"The O'Connells." She pointed at a bauble. "See this? It's me, aged nine, the first year we moved here which is when Mum began the tradition." On the front of the bauble was a tiny girl with a wonky fringe, standing proudly next to a snowman. Ruby twizzled it around to see the number nine stamped on the other side. "Mum and Dad got a bauble done of each of us for every year of our lives when we bought the farm. Luckily, the tree's pretty tall, and we have another one inside, otherwise we might run out of branches."

"I never even knew personalised baubles were a thing."

Ruby quirked an eyebrow. "So much to learn about Christmas."

Never a truer word spoken. To Fran, Christmas was an unnecessary pause in her work calendar. She tolerated it because the final quarter sales were always the best, but she didn't always celebrate it. Didn't always come home for it. Whereas, the O'Connells embodied Christmas. "Do you still get the baubles done?"

Ruby nodded. "Every year. Plus, me, my brother and sister decorate this tree every year. I finished my part at 6am this morning. Scott and Victoria did their bit earlier in the week. It's another reason I can't stay in London around the festive time. We have traditions I can't walk away from, you know?"

Fran nodded, staring into Ruby's eyes. "I'm kinda getting that impression."

Ruby held Fran's gaze for a beat, then shook her head. "Who knows, maybe Hollybush Cottage will enter a tree next year?" She gave Fran a smile. "And by the way, *Elf* is one of my very favourite movies. Never trust anyone who doesn't like it. But there are plenty of other Christmas movies you really need to watch, too."

Warmth coated Fran's insides. Was Ruby offering to show them to her? Perhaps this morning had begun to turn their relationship around. "I'd love to get Christmas-movie schooled if you're offering." Fran scrunched her forehead. "That's a sentence I never saw leaving my lips. Who am I in Mistletoe?" She'd been here less than 24 hours.

"Someone who's discovering their Christmas soul." Ruby reached out and shook her family's tree. A mini-avalanche ensued, and Ruby jumped back seconds too late. She took off her bobble hat and shook her head, then gave Fran a grin. "Remember: snow looks pretty, but it can be bruising."

They cleaned up the O'Connell tree, then walked to the top of the farm's drive and turned right, just as they had a few months ago when Fran first arrived in the village. Then, she'd thought Mistletoe Farm was a little unkempt, a little rough around the edges. She no longer thought that. Plus, somebody had touched up the sign, and it looked good as new.

On top of that, Fran and Ruby's initial war seemed to be ebbing away, and after a morning spent working together, the barriers were down. Now, Fran almost went to bump Ruby's hip when she made a joke. Which was all sorts of weird. Fran didn't even do that with her friends.

They walked up the road towards the store. They'd cleared this path earlier, too, piling up the snow into the ditches. The grit was doing its job. Now Fran understood the contest, she saw the trees in a whole new light. These ones didn't have lights, but they had tinsel, baubles and strings of gold beads around them, as well as weather-resistant ornaments, visible when you were up close. Fran touched one of the ornaments, a polished wooden horseshoe. *Anna, will you marry me? Love, Richard x* was engraved on it.

She turned it towards Ruby. "When was this done?"

"The second year of the festival, so 11 years ago."

"Did Anna say yes?"

Ruby laughed. "She did, otherwise we might have taken that down. Anna is now a Beverton, and the Beverton family do this tree every year." She pointed to the pot at the bottom of the tree. "You see the theme at the bottom? Horses." Ruby pointed upwards. "Also, the saddle and riding crop on the top is a bit of a giveaway. Three years ago their theme was London and it won. They went to town with tiny black cabs, The London Eye, Buckingham Palace, every royal figurine they could lay their hands on. Their granddad even made a Tower of London for the top."

Fran grinned. "I love themed trees. They should be everywhere!" She gave the nearest branches a shake, and snow fell off. It didn't need much. This tree was weather-ready. Well done to the Bevertons. This was not their first Christmas tree rodeo.

"You should see my favourite. It's tucked away behind Mistletoe Stores. The theme is Downhill Skier. It's by the local printing company, and they've turned the tree into just that, with skis, a face, even goggles and crazy hair. I saw it this morning. It's amazing."

The next tree — with a theme of film — needed more work. Ruby shook it vigorously, got covered again, then together they cleared the branches as high as they could reach. Fran stood back as Ruby gave it one last shake that dislodged the snow from the clapperboard tree-topper. Luckily, the tree-topper stayed attached. After they'd tackled tree four (theme: wine), and Ruby had ticked it off her list, she messaged her brother to see if anything else needed to be done.

His message back was quick. Ruby let out a cute bark of laughter.

Fran frowned. Cute? Since when was Ruby's laugh cute? Since now, apparently.

"Scott says to bring the food." Ruby went to walk right, then stopped and hit her forehead. "Shit, I was about to walk. I forgot we need the van." Ruby nodded towards the farm. "Shall we?"

Fran twisted on her foot and walked back down the slight incline, tilting her head to the clear sky above. Everything about Mistletoe was bright white, like someone had just applied a fresh coat of emulsion. The roads, the trees, the houses, the sky. Even the sharp air around her ears crackled white. The stillness was what got her, too. Her dads had said it had taken some getting used to, but now, they slept like gods.

They crunched back towards the farm.

Fran walked past the farm's hedge, which was handily at hand height. Before she knew what she was doing, she reached out and scooped a pile of snow into her gloves. It packed down easily. Then she turned, and flung it at Ruby. It hit the back of her head.

Ruby stopped walking, put a hand to her hat and turned. She shook her head. "Did you just throw a snowball at me?"

Her tone was incredulous. "You, the townie, want to take on the country girl?" Ruby raised an eyebrow, then ran to the other side of the road and grabbed some snow. "Big mistake, townie. Big mistake."

Before Fran knew what was happening, a snowball hit her head. Then another. She rushed to make some more, but Ruby was on a different snowball-making level to her. For every one Fran made, Ruby made three. Possibly ten. Shit, Fran was buggered, wasn't she?

Her only choice was to run. She broke into a jog, as snowballs hit her back and neck, cold penetrating to her skin. Fran shivered.

"No running! Against the rules!" Ruby shouted.

Ahead was the farm's entrance, where they'd piled the big mound of snow earlier after clearing the paths. Fran reached it just as she heard Ruby's footsteps screech to a halt behind her. Before she knew what was happening, Ruby's arms were around her waist.

Fran wasn't prepared for this to be a contact sport and fell sideways into the mound of snow.

Ruby fell on top of her with an audible 'oomph'.

There was silence as they both lay there, on a duvet of snow, with body warmth alone for heat.

Fran opened her eyes.

Ruby was staring at her, a surprised look on her face. Her eyes travelled down Fran's face, then her breath stilled.

A little like the moment between them.

A jolt of feeling hit Fran in the chest and melted through her veins, until it landed heavily in her stomach. She took in Ruby's rosy cheeks and her sparkling emerald eyes, before dropping to her lips. They were oval, glossy and inviting. If she pushed herself up, she could press her lips to Ruby's. Fran bet they tasted divine.

But then she blinked. What the hell was she thinking? She shook herself internally, ground her teeth together and flicked her gaze away. To anywhere but Ruby's face.

Ruby might be beautiful, talented and lying on top of her, but kissing Ruby was *never* going to happen. It couldn't. They'd only just got back on an even keel.

Plus, Ruby was the enemy.

A singer.

Only, with her full weight on top of Fran and a hungry look in her eye, Ruby didn't feel like Fran's enemy. Plus, was Ruby's gaze lingering on Fran's lips, too?

It was all far too confusing for this early on a Saturday morning.

"You know that falling over is conceding, right?" As Ruby tried to get up, she leaned in that little bit closer to get her balance right. As she did, her mouth stopped inches from Fran's.

Something flickered on Ruby's face.

Something Fran couldn't quite work out.

Was it the same thing still flickering inside Fran? She closed her eyes and hoped it would make her brain quit working overtime.

Ruby took a deep breath and pushed herself up. Then she held out a hand.

Fran took it, then a zap of heat fizzed up her arm. She ignored it, along with the slight shake in her body. Instead, she hauled herself up and brushed herself down. The cold wasn't bothering her anymore. Not now her internal flame was firing on all cylinders.

Ruby nodded towards the van, avoiding Fran's gaze. "Shall we get the food to the hungry hordes?"

Chapter 11

"What about this one?" Dad stood in the Christmas tree barn, next to the tree of his choice. He grabbed one of the branches and rested it above his eye, then wiggled it up and down. "Does it look good on me?"

Pop laughed. "Like you were made for each other." He turned to Fran. "What do you think?"

Fran was really trying not to roll her eyes. She wasn't too old to be embarrassed by her parents. "It's green and looks like a tree. If you like it, get it."

Dad shook his head. "Where did we go wrong, Dale? We raised a loving, caring, creative daughter, and then she ran off to London and came back impervious to Christmas or Christmas trees." He put both hands to his chest, then doubled over. "It's like a dagger to our gay hearts."

Pop pouted. "I agree with your dad. A Christmas tree is not just a tree. It's a family member. A choice. It's a feeling."

Fran widened her eyes. "Have you two been drinking?"

"Nope. We just spent yesterday shovelling snow with Scott, and he schooled us. Plus, we live in Mistletoe now. You have to love Christmas and everything about it." Dad stood straight, and put his arm around the tree. "So, I ask again. Me and Clarice the Christmas tree. Love match, or not?"

Fran couldn't help laughing. Her parents were so much more playful since moving here. She liked it. She wasn't going to stand in their way. "Definite love match."

Dad gave her a grin, Pop put his arm around her, and together they carried the tree over to the checkout, currently staffed by Mary. The back barn that housed the trees was a mass of activity, showing the Tree Contest and Treasure Hunt had worked their magic. When Fran looked left, Eric was chatting to a family about their tree. Over towards the back, Paul patted a particularly statuesque variety: the Peter Crouch of trees. Fran scanned the rest of the area, but she couldn't spot Ruby.

Fran was heading back to London tomorrow. By train, as her car still wasn't ready, and the garage couldn't say when it would be.

Fran would never admit it out loud, but she was sad to be leaving. This weekend had been a case study in community and team spirit, something London was severely lacking. Yes, Mistletoe didn't even have a pub or a restaurant, but it had heart and it had soul. You couldn't buy that.

It also had Ruby, who Fran had woken up thinking about this morning. Who had kept jumping to the front of her mind when her dads made her breakfast, and chattered excitedly about their festive plans. Fran had made the decision not to come home this Christmas. To stay in London and catch up on work. However, now she'd immersed herself in Mistletoe, she was beginning to question her logic. Was work the most important thing? Her dads didn't seem to think so, even though they were being understanding. They always were.

Ruby certainly didn't think work came first.

Fran wanted to find her to say goodbye. To tell Ruby she was starting to thaw towards Christmas, and towards her. However, she was still having trouble processing that in her own mind. She glanced around the barn one more time. Still no Ruby.

"Hello, lovely neighbours!" Mary took the tree from Dad like it weighed nothing. She gave it a forceful shake, and some pine needles fell to the floor. "The classic Norway spruce, good choice. It's already been through the tree shaker to get rid of any creepy-crawlies, but I like to give it one last go." Mary grinned, then heaved the tree into the netting machine.

Dad hurried around the other side, before pulling it out and hugging it. "We've called her Clarice. Good name, Mary? What do you think?"

Mary took Pop's money, and gave Dad a smile. "I was just going to say, she looks like a Clarice. She's going to be a wonderful addition to the family."

Fran bit down a comment. Everybody in this town was Christmas crazy. It was an epidemic.

"Ruby's in the barn shop, in case you were wondering," Mary told her.

Could she read Fran's mind? She was in trouble if Mary could.

"Great," Fran replied, like it meant nothing.

"Come along to The Bar later if you're free and still here? There's a village drinks as soon as the festival's over. Everyone should be there by seven. I've made more mince pies."

No doubt Mary was up at 5am again. That seemed to be standard in Mistletoe. Her dads had been up for two hours

94

when Fran appeared this morning at 9am. "Country air, makes you want to make the most of it," Pop had told her.

"We'll try to stop by." Fran glanced at her parents. "I'm leaving tomorrow morning, but there's time for a drink."

"Always time for a drink with friends," Mary said, glancing at the next customer who'd just walked up behind Dad. "Don't forget the Christmas Tree Contest ceremony at 4pm in the courtyard!"

"Wouldn't miss it for the world," Dad replied.

* * *

Twilight had arrived by the time of the contest winner announcement, but that only added to the farm's atmosphere. Santa was drinking a hot chocolate by the stage. Fire pits made out of old washing machine drums were scattered around the courtyard for warmth. The mulled wine and hot dog stands helped with that, too. Meanwhile, every fairy light in the country appeared to have got the invite, and the Christmas trees in each corner were working their magic.

In the centre, Paul was on stage, microphone in hand. "Testing, testing." He tapped the top of the mic. "One, two, Mistletoe."

Fran had heard many soundchecks in her life, but never one like that.

Ruby rolled her eyes, but she was smiling. "He does that every year. I used to get so embarrassed as a kid. Now, when I'm mic-checking, it's what I do, too. Testing, testing. One, two, Mistletoe."

"I'll remember to look out for that at your next gig." Fran stamped her feet against the cold. When they'd been busy earlier, the cold had been kept at bay. However, standing around was a different story.

Ruby glanced at her, went to say something, then stopped. She bit her lip, then took a breath. "Are you coming to The Bar later? Mum's made mince pies. Audrey's made sausage rolls. It's going to be a spread of beige food, the likes of which would cause London to have a cardiac."

"We're coming. Your mum told us about it earlier."

"Great."

Fran moved her mouth left, then right. "Who's won, by the way?"

"I can't tell you that. Let's just say, it's not a million miles away from my favourite. In fact, it might even be that one." She leaned in closer, putting her mouth by Fran's ear. "The downhill skier," she whispered. "But you didn't hear that from me."

Ruby's breath tickled Fran's ear, and the tingle that ensued zipped down her body. Fran kept a straight face, then mimed zipping up her lips and throwing away the key. Her heart clattered in her chest. Fran just about held it together, pulling her shoulders back to stand as tall as she could muster. A little like a baby Christmas tree. "Just as a matter of curiosity, what's the punishment of giving away the result? Has anyone ever done it?"

Ruby grinned. "Mum did once. She was chatting to a customer, and it just popped out. Dad didn't speak to her for two days. Just tutted. If you want to avoid Paul's tutting, best to play dumb."

"Gotcha." Fran nodded towards the mulled wine stand. Her pulse was still thumping. "Can I get you a mulled wine? Or is drinking on the job discouraged?"

"When I'm not being paid, I make my own rules. I'd love one."

Fran nodded. "Two mulled wines, coming up."

* * *

"Another beer, Michael?" Sue asked.

Dad glanced over to Pop, then at Fran. "Can we stay for one more?"

Fran nodded. "Have another beer." She should go, but she was having a good time. Plus, her dads didn't have to rush home for anything. This was what they'd moved for. Community and a more relaxed way of life.

"Two more beers for Michael and Dale, please Eric!" Sue shouted over to the bar.

Plus, Fran was sat next to Ruby, with the warmth of Ruby's thigh seeping through Fran's jeans.

Fran glanced down the bench, checking the space available. Yes, there were four of them sitting on it, but it was plenty big enough. Ruby didn't have to sit this close to her, but she chose to.

Her proximity made Fran's stomach tighten. She had no desire to stop this night, or this whole weekend. She wanted to stretch it out like a hot marshmallow. Tomorrow she had to go back to London. She didn't want to think about it.

"Did everyone get their crackers this weekend, too? Because we sold out, did we tell you? All that slave labour from your children paid off, didn't it, parents?" Victoria took a slug of her lager and lime.

"It did." Paul raised his pint of Guinness to her. "I hope you're looking forward to making more."

"I got my crackers," Audrey said. "I hope there are some good gifts in there. Not just a nail file or a pack of tiny cards. I want a mini vibrator or a glittery pan scourer. Something practical I can truly use."

Ruby spluttered into her wine.

"Don't get those two mixed up, Audrey," Mary said. "Could lead to all sorts of injuries."

Ruby got her breath back. "Stop it, you two. I needed to swallow, not spit."

Now the whole table collapsed in giggles.

"Honestly." Ruby rolled her eyes. "You're all terrible." She gestured towards Dad. "Michael bought two packs of crackers, along with a gargantuan tree. Looks like you're going all out for Christmas."

Dad nodded, making room for Eric to put their beers on the table. "We are. My sister might be coming with her two daughters, but she's still in two minds. Now, if we could just persuade Fran to be there, too, it would be complete."

Fran wriggled in her seat. "It's why I'm here this weekend, because I said I'd work through Christmas. You said you were fine with me not being there."

Mary was having none of it. "Francesca." She turned to her dads. "Do you call her Francesca when she really needs to listen to you?"

They both nodded.

"In that case, I'll carry on. Francesca." She reached over and took Fran's hands in hers. "I know we had this chat once before. But that was when you first arrived. Now, I hope you understand Mistletoe that little bit more. We're about sharing Christmas. About everyone mucking in and helping out. Family and friends. It's not just another day. It's a time when we all get together to celebrate our year and feel the love in the room. You should come home. We've only known you for a couple of months, but it won't be the same without you."

Fran gulped, as eight pairs of eyes fixed on her.

She took her hands back as Mary released them. A flush started in her core, and worked its way up her body. Fran chewed on the inside of her cheek.

The problem was, her new friends didn't know her work commitments. She had so much to get through before Christmas and beyond. Plus, she'd promised her boss she'd make a start on next year's plans over the festive break. She couldn't change now even if she wanted to. From the mix of emotions churning through Fran's body, part of her clearly did. This village dream wasn't only pulling at her parents' heart strings.

Fran was about to reply when a warm hand took hers under the table and squeezed.

She froze, her neck rigid.

The hand was attached to the person on Fran's left.

Either that, or Audrey has freakishly long arms.

But no. The hand was Ruby's.

Ruby was telling her it was okay. That she understood.

In that moment, it meant so much.

Fran gulped again before she spoke, keeping hold of Ruby's hand. It was a welcome anchor in a choppy moment.

"I do understand what Christmas means around here. I can feel it, too. But I've got a lot of work to get through right up until the day and beyond."

"And we totally understand." Dad gave her his

understanding smile. "But do think about coming home. Even on Christmas morning if you have to."

Fran nodded. "I will."

Under the table, Ruby squeezed her hand and let go.

Fran quivered, but didn't dare look Ruby's way.

"It was a good job the crackers sold, but the trees didn't move quite as well as we wanted." Paul sighed as he sipped his pint. "I blame Ikea."

"What's Ikea done?" Fran wanted to get the conversation moving again. Away from her.

"Last year, they built a store 15 miles away, and offered customers a £20 voucher if they buy their tree from them for £30. That makes the tree a tenner, and we can't compete with that. The festival was always our biggest-selling weekend of the year until Ikea opened. Our sales were down 25 per cent last year."

"Still, it'll all work out. We've been through worse!" Mary gave the table a decisive nod. "I believe in the power of community. We told enough people today to tell their friends to come to us. Hopefully, the word will get out and that will happen. I have faith."

"Or people will give all their money to Ikea," Audrey chimed in. "The coffee's cheap, too. And the cinnamon buns are delicious."

"Audrey Parrot! Tell me you didn't buy your tree there?" The vein on the right of Mary's neck began to throb.

"Of course I didn't! What do you take me for? I just go there for tealights and kitchen goods. Also, for the cinnamon buns."

* * *

Two hours later, Victoria and Eric turned out the lights, and the O'Connells and the Bells walked home together. The Christmas trees lining Farm Lane rustled in the breeze as they passed. It was still freezing, and Fran had her coat back on which wasn't a patch on Mary's. The first thing Fran was going to do in London was buy a better winter coat.

They arrived at Mistletoe Farm in five minutes. Mary and Paul hugged everyone, as did Fran's dads. Their respective parents left, leaving Ruby and Fran together.

"No chance I can persuade you to come back to London and do the gig on the 22nd at The Pennywhistle?" Fran took a gamble. "There's still a slot on the bill and you'd be perfect. Great way to showcase 'Pieces Of You'."

Ruby smiled, but shook her head. "I'm in Mistletoe for the season. I told you that; my family needs me. Plus, The Pennywhistle is hardly my crowd. You know my gig rules."

"I disagree. It's under new management and they've mixed things up. Plus, rules are made to be broken."

Ruby ignored her comment. "I should be asking you the same question. No chance you'll be coming back before the end of the year?"

"Not unless something drastic happens. My schedule doesn't permit it." Fran got caught in Ruby's stare.

Something boomed in her chest, and Fran was taken right back to the hand holding earlier. She wasn't sure what to do with these new emotions. She stuffed her hands deep in her pockets.

"Have a great Christmas. I'll see you in the New Year?"

Ruby's gaze dropped down Fran's face, before returning

to rest on her eyes. "I guess you will." She gave her a nod, then walked down the drive.

Fran watched her go. Half of her wanted to walk with Ruby, to keep chatting. She was enjoying their time together. Enjoying this new level of friendship they seemed to have encountered. However, Fran's sensible half knew she had to go.

Back to her normal life. Back to work. Back to reality.

She was just about to do just that, when Ruby stopped, then turned back to Fran.

When she saw Fran was still there, Ruby smiled.

She gave Fran a half-wave.

The world stood still for just a few seconds, the moonlight bathing the pair of them.

Fran sucked in a deep breath.

Then Ruby turned back, and walked to her front door.

Fran exhaled, then did the same.

Chapter 12

Ruby walked up the farm drive the next day. The pile of snow was still there, but the imprint of Fran's body where she'd fallen had gone. It had snowed again overnight, and the air was icy on Ruby's face. She could still picture Fran's piercing blue eyes. The beat of her own heart. Had the surprise of her emotions shown on her face? She hoped not.

Ruby was still trying to work out her feelings towards Fran. It had been on her mind this morning, all through the voice coaching lesson she'd given on Zoom. Ruby had gone from being irritated and annoyed, to now sad she'd left? That was even after Fran kept pressing her to play some gigs. Ruby hated being challenged about that. She should have got straight back out there and played bigger venues. She knew that. Now, every year that went by, the fear just got bigger.

Ruby shook her head, and walked down Farm Lane. It was a lot quieter today after the hustle of the contest over the weekend. Now, the roads were clear, and the sky a brilliant white. When Ruby breathed out, she could see her breath in the air. Their gritting efforts over the weekend were already snuffed out with a new layer of fresh snow coating the village. It looked gorgeous, but it wasn't good for business. Ruby had spent a lonely morning in the café with a steady trickle of customers. Still, it was only a Monday. Hopefully the week would pick up.

She breathed in the smell of Mistletoe Stores' Christmas tree as she passed it — the Elvis Nordmann fir. Ruby waved hi to Henry who lived down the road, walking back with a bag of firewood. The bell over the shop rang as Ruby walked in.

Victoria popped up from under the counter.

Ruby let out a yelp as she clutched her chest. "What the hell are you doing, scaring me like that?"

Victoria grinned. "I didn't mean to. I was trying to rescue a 10p, but it's gone to the under-counter god, and shall never be seen again. When I die and they take this counter out, you'll find riches underneath. It could pay off your mortgage."

"Like I'm ever going to have enough money for a mortgage." Ruby walked behind the counter and gave Victoria a hug. While Ruby had fiery-brown hair and emerald eyes, Victoria was fair-haired and blue-eyed. Nobody could ever believe they were related and came from the same parents, but they were. They shared the same wide mouth, inherited from their mother, but apart from that, the two sisters looked nothing alike. Plus, at 5ft 3, Victoria was a short-arse.

"To what do I owe this honour? I thought your plan today was to flog Christmas trees?" Victoria asked.

"That's still the plan, but we need milk. We've run out at home, and Mum doesn't want to eat into the café stock, just in case we have a mad dash on coffee later. I can't see it happening, but Mum doesn't want to tempt fate. Plus, we're out of cheese. Which is an emergency in our house, as you well know."

Victoria walked around the counter and to the fridge, bringing back a four-pint of milk and some Cathedral City, their dad's favourite cheddar. "Do you have a lot of collections tonight?"

Ruby nodded. The farm had a couple of open days during November, where customers could walk the tree fields, then tag and pay for the one they wanted. They then arranged to pick it up on a specified date. The first week of December was a popular collection week. "A fair few. But we also need to shift the potted trees, plus all the mistletoe, wreaths, all that gubbins. You'd think people would want to come to Mistletoe Farm for their mistletoe, but when Sainsbury's sells it for a quid a sprig, it's tricky to compete."

"I've been sending people your way this morning, so fingers crossed it picks up." Victoria put the groceries on the counter, then glanced at Ruby. "While you're here, can you give me a hand putting up the Christmas stuff in the window? I need to get up on the ladder, but you know I hate doing that."

Ruby grabbed the stepladder from the back. This had always been her job in the family ever since she was little. Chief getter of things from up high.

Victoria pointed. "I want to put up a display with panettones, crackers, and Christmas puddings. The hampers are selling like hot cakes, so they were a great idea."

"Good." Ruby steadied the ladder. "You got the stuff to give me?"

Victoria disappeared, before reappearing with boxes of Christmas supplies.

Ruby climbed four steps, then turned around, bending her knees carefully, hands out.

Victoria began passing mini Christmas puddings up for the festive shelf, which was suspended over the window display with two chains, like a massive swing.

Ruby took three puddings and began to juggle them. She was a champion juggler. Also, a champion sibling annoyer.

Sure enough, Victoria tutted. "No theatrics, thank you. I'd like the display finished today."

"Where's your sense of adventure?"

Ruby juggled for a few seconds, then put the puddings on one of the ladder's steps, giving Victoria a bow.

She got an arched eyebrow in return.

Ruby picked up the goods with a smirk, then missed her step on the next rung. Her heart dropped as she crushed her weight into the ladder to steady herself, the puddings clutched to her chest. She didn't drop one. She never did. Ruby was rock-solid on a ladder. Even when she was a little too big for her boots.

Victoria gave her a stern stare. "Fucking hell, that was close." She gestured with her hand. "Put it on the display shelf, please."

Ruby's heart was still racing. She did as she was told, then took four more puddings and did the same.

"The contest went well, didn't it? Dragged the crowds in, despite the snow."

Ruby nodded. "We could just use another push. It's rough having so much of your money earned in a single month."

Victoria grunted.

It wasn't a new issue.

"How were things with Fran when she left? You two looked like you were getting on better than when she spat her sausage roll on you." There was a smile in Victoria's voice as she spoke.

"It could only really get better from there, couldn't it?"

"That's a hard yes."

Ruby took a fruit panettone from her sister and put it on the festive shelf swing. "Did Eric do this?" Ruby patted it. The shelf bobbed from side to side, the chains clanking.

"He did. Very happy with himself."

"I can see why." Ruby took another panettone, then another. "Do people actually buy these?"

Victoria nodded. "They do. Whether they eat them or know what to do with them is another matter. Audrey said she bought one last year but was baffled by it. She was thinking of using it as a small stool." Her sister laughed. "Might be the last Christmas we sell them with Brexit looming."

Ruby harrumphed. "Next year, it'll be suet pudding and other grimness. Back to the 40s. I've never eaten panettone. Maybe I shouldn't try, in case I love it and then I can never buy it again."

Victoria made a face, and passed her more Italian cakes. "Anyway, back to Fran. You two were working together at the farm on Saturday, weren't you?"

Ruby nodded. "We were. It was a little rocky to begin with. She doesn't trust singers because…" Ruby paused. She'd made a promise not to say anything about Fran and Delilah. "She's had her heart broken before. I don't trust music execs because I've had my trust broken before. We had some hurdles to overcome. But once we did that, it was fine."

More than fine, but Ruby wasn't about to tell Victoria that. Her sister had a way of running her mouth off to their parents. Ruby was still processing what had happened between her and Fran. The last thing she needed was Mum and Dad's curiosity piqued.

"Is she dating?" Victoria's tone was light, but Ruby knew the question behind it.

"She's not. She's single and happy with that."

A pause, some rustling, then Victoria passed Ruby two packs of Florentines. "Can you put them at the front? I've got some tinsel to pack around it all, too."

Ruby held the display with one hand and arranged the festive treats.

"She's gay, though? I mean, she didn't come out and say it, but I got the impression she was."

"The impression?"

"Yes," Victoria replied. "Just something about her. Plus, she was wearing those cool, arty shoes."

This was new. "I don't wear those, and I'm gay."

Victoria waved her hand. "Yes, but you're a musician. You wear all manner of weird and wonderful things and nobody bats an eyelid. Fran, on the other hand…"

"Looked like a hipster? Those shoes are in."

"Not in Mistletoe," Victoria replied.

"Last time I checked, our little town was not the height of fashion. Or did I miss something? Is Milan planning to forego its slot on the European fashion circuit and base it here instead?"

"It would be a great plan for getting customers to the village year-round."

Ruby snarked an eyebrow. "If you're asking is Fran gay, the answer is yes. At least, her last relationship was with a woman."

Victoria gave Ruby a wide smile. "You see, I can still pick them. I may be boring and married to a man, but I'm still up on the game."

"So long as you're not on the game."

Victoria slapped her leg.

Ruby grabbed the top of the step-ladder, then steadied herself. "Ow! You really need to treat your unpaid help a little better."

"Yeah, yeah. Anyway, back to you. Fran is gay, queer, whatever. She likes the ladies. You are queer and also like the ladies. So perhaps there's something there?"

"Just because we're queer does not mean we will automatically fall into each other's vaginas. It's not how it works, Vicky. I thought we had this discussion when I came out ten years ago." Ruby purposely used the shortened version of her sister's name, knowing she hated it. It was only ever Victoria.

"Less of the Vicky, thank you." Victoria scowled as she passed up some green tinsel, along with some foam Santas and reindeers. "Hang this lot from the chains, please. And you know what I mean about Fran. You said yourself you got on. Didn't you?"

Ruby smiled. In the end, they had. Even had a laugh together. They'd made trees look pretty. Fallen in the snow. Plus, Ruby couldn't deny that Fran had stirred something inside of her. That she'd let her eyes trail Fran's lips and think about kissing them. What's more, Ruby had clutched Fran's hand at the bar.

Ruby scrunched her forehead as the memory popped into her mind. She tried to push it away. It didn't work.

109

Standing on the ladder in Mistletoe Stores' shop window, her pulse quickened. It was almost like she was next to Fran again, her leg pressing against hers, their hands joined. Ruby couldn't say why she'd grabbed Fran's hand. In the moment, it had felt like the right thing to do. To support her. Londoners had to stick together in the face of country folk who didn't understand their world, even if Ruby had a foot in both camps.

And yet. There had been something more to it, hadn't there? Something Ruby had seen in Fran's eyes when she'd landed on her in the snow. Something Ruby had felt in her bones when she had to say goodbye to Fran last night.

Ruby missed Fran. Despite their initial differences, they had a lot in common: a love of music, family, London, Mistletoe. Ruby missed their chat. Their connection. Fran's smile.

Am I seriously thinking about the smile of a music exec? She needed her head examined.

As the image of Fran's radiant smile filled her head, Ruby wobbled. Her body shook. Then she fell sideways, dropping through the air, to land squarely on a box of Florentines which now might have to be marketed as 'broken but edible'.

"Ruby!" Victoria's voice scratched the air as she smothered Ruby, pushing her sister's hair back from her face.

Ruby winced. Her knee throbbed. Her hand was grazed. Her shoulder was hot. But she was okay. She sat up, and rubbed her shoulder with her other hand.

"What the fuck? You never fall. Did you black out? Should we call a doctor?"

Ruby shook her head. This was normally true. But since she'd met Fran, she'd fallen twice. Was she falling for her, too? Ruby's throat went dry. "I'm fine. I just zoned out for a moment, then I was on the ground." She staggered upright, the heat of embarrassment crawling up her cheeks. She wanted to get out of there as quick as she could. She didn't need an inquisition from her sister.

"Are you sure? You don't feel light-headed?"

Ruby shook her head, brushing herself down. She glanced at the Florentines. "Sorry about those."

Victoria grinned. "Eric will be thrilled. He loves them. Now he can have a box all to himself." She put a hand on Ruby's shoulder. "Are you sure you're okay?"

Ruby stepped back onto the ladder. There was nothing medically wrong with her. She wasn't going to tell her sister she'd zoned out thinking about Fran, the very person she'd just told her she wasn't interested in. The best way to avoid more chat was to finish her display and get back to the farm.

Chapter 13

Fran twisted in her office chair and stared at Damian. His mouth was full of Double Decker, and he was trying to get her to place a bet on whether it was going to be a white Christmas, as well as what song would take the coveted Christmas number one spot.

"The forecasters are predicting snow." Damian wiped the side of his mouth.

"That's not a stretch, seeing as it's been pretty snowy already."

"Stick 50 quid on and you could easily double your money."

"Or lose it all." Fran wasn't keen on predicting the weather or the charts, especially when they had skin in the game with Fast Forward. The band had just released their Christmas single, and the next couple of weeks would be the big push to get them as close as possible. Top five would be a result. Top three, even better. Number one was the dream. But their main aim was to get the song into the heads of all the teenagers out there, so they'd be streaming it throughout December and beyond.

"Let's look at the number one contenders apart from Fast Forward," Damian said. "It could be any ex-member of Boy Wonder. They've all got their solo albums out, but who will fans pick? The ballady one, the wholesome one, or the sexy one who can't sing and is about as interesting as a cupboard?"

Fran tapped some keys, then pushed her chair back. "Cupboard Boy will walk it. But there's also the big one from Julia Hewson. Fast Forward have got a fighting chance if they can stand the heat. But you know what I think about betting. You might as well burn your money in a firepit. At least you'll get some heat."

When Fran thought about a firepit, she was immediately transported back to Mistletoe. To the weekend when she'd drunk hot chocolate, sung Christmas carols, and watched as Ruby mouthed the words to them beside her. When she'd asked her why, Ruby said it was best not to sing if you were a singer in real life. People thought you were showing off. Same with karaoke. Ruby avoided it at all costs.

Her weekend with Ruby had been unexpected. Just like the pangs she'd felt for Mistletoe and its inhabitants ever since she'd come back to London. Where else had Christmas trees dressed as countries or pop stars? Something had shifted inside her. Mistletoe was like a world she'd only believed existed in the movies. But it was real, and it had been living right under her nose all her life. Now, not going back for Christmas was a decision that was gnawing at her from the inside out.

"Actually, if I was going to put money on a Christmas number one, it would be on that YouTube bloke," she said. "The impossibly skinny one with the floppy hair who sings that novelty song about wheelbarrows. He was having a right old time in the press room when I saw him the other day. He might make Cupboard Boy cry come December 25th."

Damian wagged a finger at her. "You might be onto

something there. And if Skinny Boy can make Cupboard Boy cry, imagine what he can do to Fast Forward."

Fran grimaced. "Their song is so much better. They deserve it. But Christmas number ones are all about novelty, so Skinny Boy might win."

"You've got me feeling sorry for Cupboard Boy now."

Fran scoffed. "Don't feel too bad for him. He left Boy Wonder with £25 million and the status of sex symbol, so things could be worse."

Fran's phone began to ring on her desk. She strained her neck to check the caller. Dad. She grabbed it.

"Hey, how are you? Did you miss me too much already? I've only been gone three days."

There was a pause on the line. Too long a pause. "Listen it's nothing to worry about, but Pop's in hospital."

Fran sat up straight, a shiver running down her spine. "What's he doing there? What happened?"

Damian scrunched his forehead, before wheeling his chair back to his desk.

"He had a fight with some ice when he was riding his bike, and the ice won. It's not serious, but he's broken his leg and buggered his shoulder a bit, so they're keeping him in as he needs surgery. I know you're busy, so don't worry. Just send him a text, I'm sure he'd appreciate it."

Fran's stomach dropped. What had she told him about being careful on country roads? However, now was not the time for lectures on road safety. The damage was done. "Don't be ridiculous. I'll see if I can juggle my work schedule."

"Okay, honey. But your job's important. We both know that. See what you can do."

Maybe her job was a little *too* important.

Fran hung up and turned to Damian. "If I pay for you to have a bet on Skinny Boy beating Cupboard Boy, can we chat about this week and juggling schedules so I can go home and work from there? My dad's in hospital."

Damian's face fell. "Shit. Is he okay?"

Fran nodded. "Broken leg, but he'll survive." She paused. "What's it going to cost me?"

Damian cocked his head. "£25 each way on Skinny Boy and I'm all ears."

Chapter 14

Fran backed her dad's car into her parents' driveway, and shut off the engine. Surgery had gone well, and Pop had been kept in for observation overnight. He looked battered, too, his face a mass of red marks and cuts. She could tell Dad was just as shook up as Pop. It was often like that — the person left holding the fort was just as affected, sometimes more than the patient. She'd left Dad at a pub near the hospital, as he wanted to stay close by and had snagged an overnight room. Fran had promised to drive back and bring them home tomorrow. It had been a stark reality check for her, too. A flush of doing-the-right-thing energy travelled through her.

At times over the past few years, Fran hadn't gone home as much as she should, and that was on her. However, now, her parents needed her. Could she work the next little while from their cottage? Maybe. Plus, her boss was being sympathetic and Damian was picking up the slack, so there was no need to hurry back at least until after the weekend. Four days away. Being here also meant she could hassle the garage about her car. Their answers so far had been vague and involved the words 'part from Swindon, possibly Japan' and 'could run to after Christmas or the New Year'. She knew things worked on a different time frame in the country, but three or four weeks? Fran made a note in her phone to get on their case.

She got out of the car, admiring her parents' frosted front garden again, with its holly bush and array of plants. She stopped beside the garden's mature fir tree and breathed in the pines. Was there a better smell in the world? The fir tree had a fresh layer of snow on it again. Did it always snow like this in Mistletoe?

This time, however, Fran was prepared for the weather. When she'd got back to London, she'd gone shopping and bought a bright yellow winter coat that came past her knees, along with new gloves, thermal-lined boots and a hat. She'd also bought some more colourful clothing after Ruby's comments. A baby-blue shirt. A mustard top. Dusty-pink trousers. Never let it be said Fran Bell was averse to change. She was far more flexible than most people gave her credit for.

She let herself into Hollybush Cottage, then shivered. It was freezing. She took off her gloves and touched a radiator. Stone cold. Fran prodded the heating control until she heard the boiler fire up. Then she grabbed her suitcase and pulled it up the stairs and into her new room. Immediately, she saw that view again, and she was at peace. What was it about this place?

As the train had unzipped the surrounding fields on the way over, Fran had simply sat and watched, transfixed. Fran didn't do that. She was always on. If she was travelling somewhere, she never *just* travelled. She was either answering email, listening to a new artist or reading a business book. But on the way to Mistletoe, she'd just sat, soaking in the surroundings.

Fran opened her suitcase and stashed a few items in her old chest of drawers. Not everything had made it in the move, as her parents had downsized. Fran had been sad to see her dressing table and mirror go, along with a bookcase from her old room. But really, she didn't miss them. Her dads were here. Fields were here. Christmas was here. A warm, fuzzy feeling ran through her. She wasn't in London, and already she could breathe better.

What the hell was that?

It felt dangerously close to contentment.

Fran flicked away her thoughts as she lifted her laptop and pressed the on button. She searched for her parents' Wi-Fi, and then tried to connect.

No dice. Immediately, her muscles tightened.

She frowned at the screen. *Come on.* She had work to do tonight. It was the first week of December and she had a stack of emails to answer and meetings to virtually attend over the next few days.

She fiddled with the settings, and turned her laptop on and off again, which was normally the magic bullet. Still no go. She grabbed her phone, and tried to get the hotspot to work, but the universe was against her tonight.

Fran sighed, glancing out of her window. She checked her watch. Just gone 7pm. The farm would still be open and hopefully busy now they'd hit December. Perhaps she could work down there for a couple of hours? She could buy a coffee and a sandwich for their trouble.

Plus, she'd get to see Ruby, who'd been pressing on her mind for the whole day. Just to say hi. Let Ruby know she was back. Nothing more.

Making the decision and not second-guessing herself, Fran stamped down the grey carpeted staircase and wrapped up again.

Minutes later she walked down the farm drive, her laptop bag hanging from her thermal-gloved fingers. The farmhouse lights were off, but the main courtyard lights were blazing. It was Thursday, December 6th. Not long until Christmas. The courtyard was busy with customers shopping, eating and drinking at the picnic tables, and carrying trees to their cars. Fran popped her head into the café and the shop. They were both bustling, but no Ruby. She walked through to the Christmas tree barn.

Ruby was serving a customer. Her hair was tied up today, put under a thick Mistletoe Farm beanie, complete with mistletoe knitted into the design. She was wearing blue jeans, scuffed Doc Marten boots and a coat that looked like it had its own central heating system. Standing in a barn open to the elements all day long, Ruby needed it.

Fran arrived at her till just as Ruby finished serving the customers.

"It's a Noble fir, so non-drop. Pots are in the shop on the way out, as are stands, wreaths and mistletoe. Don't forget the mistletoe. Who doesn't like a kiss at Christmas?"

The couple chuckled at Ruby's joke, and thanked her.

Ruby ripped the receipt from the credit card machine. When she looked up, her smile grew wider as she clocked Fran.

Ruby said goodbye to her customers before addressing her. "If it isn't the Londoner returned. I guess you're back to see your dads don't break any more bones."

"That's the idea, but boys will be boys. Even when they're in their mid-60s."

"My dad's the same. Although I fell off a ladder the other day, so there's an epidemic of clutz around." Ruby's cheeks coloured red.

Fran stepped forward. "Are you okay?"

Ruby shrugged, snagging her gaze. "I'm fine."

Fran saw Ruby's lips moving, and tried not to stare. She failed. Suddenly, she'd forgotten why she was there and what she was meant to be doing. Ruby was having a detrimental effect on her ability to go about her daily life.

"I liked your joke about kissing." Had that really just jumped out of Fran's mouth? Apparently, it had.

Ruby blushed a little more, and stuck her hands in her pockets. "It's Mistletoe. Gotta give the punters what they want, right?" She paused, looking Fran up and down. "Do I spy a new, more Mistletoe-appropriate coat? And a yellow one at that?"

Fran did a twirl. "You do. The city girl splashed some new colour into her wardrobe. Somebody told me colour affects your mood, so I thought I'd buy a coat of my favourite shade." She grinned. "I bought some new clothes, too." Fran patted her head. "Do you like my new hat and gloves?"

Ruby gave an approving nod. "Very much."

"Plus, I bought some fleece-lined boots. I am ready for the season. No more freezing my tits off."

"Tits are important, so it's a good move." Ruby cleared her throat, then shifted her gaze to the floor. "How long are you staying?"

"At least until Sunday. Which is why I'm here. My dads' Wi-Fi is down. Is yours working?"

Ruby nodded. "It is." She fished in her pocket for her keys. "You want to take these and work at the kitchen table? Nobody's in the house, but you're welcome."

Fran shook her head. "No, that would be weird. I thought I could just sit in the café and work there?"

"Be my guest. Joyce is working tonight with Ben. Just tell them not to disturb you."

"Thank you. Hopefully tomorrow it'll work again."

Ruby wrinkled her nose.

Fran fought the urge to tell her she looked cute when she did that.

Be cool.

"If it's not, you could use The Bar. It's free until it opens at six and the shop has good Wi-Fi. I'm sure Victoria wouldn't mind. That way, you get your own office of sorts."

"That would be a lifesaver if it's still down."

"Leave it with me and I'll ask."

"Thank you," Fran said. "By the way, I love your hat. Very on-brand."

"That's me. I'm not a singer while I'm here. Just a Christmas-tree seller."

More customers approached Ruby.

"I don't think you're 'just' anything." Fran pulled her hat further down her forehead. "I'll see you later."

Ruby captured her gaze. "You will."

* * *

Fran woke up the next morning to a text from Ruby: 'The Bar as your office is go. Just go to the store. Victoria's expecting you.'

She grinned at her phone: at least that was working, even if the reception was patchy. Once she'd picked up Dad and Pop from the hospital and settled them back here, she could work at The Bar this afternoon. At least then, the time in Mistletoe wouldn't be such a bust.

Three hours later and after lunch with her parents, Fran walked up Farm Lane, nodding at the horsey tree, then the Elvis tree, before she reached Mistletoe Stores. The trees were already such a part of the village and her daily life. She was going to miss them when they were taken down. Dad and Pop had been so thrilled to see her this morning. Bringing them home and making lunch of toasted tuna sandwiches (Pop's favourite) and strong coffee had made them wildly happy, too.

If Fran was being honest, it had done the same for her. These daily pleasures of just sitting and having lunch with her parents was something she didn't do often. When she came home, it was often just for 24 hours on a weekend, and she was always rushing, meeting someone else or checking her phone. In Mistletoe, Fran slowed down.

Now she stood outside the store, admiring the window display. Panettone, Florentines, and those German gingerbread biscuits she loved. She hadn't expected that here. They were mixed in with more local biscuits, Christmas puddings, and yule logs. Her mouth watered as she pushed open the door to the shop. She had to buy a panettone. It was one of her go-to Christmas treats.

"Hey Fran! How are you? How's your dad doing after his fall?"

Fran approached Victoria who was behind the counter.

She really did look nothing like her sister. "Doing well, thanks. Just brought him home this morning, so I've left them both on the sofa with a Christmas movie. They do love a festive film."

"Who doesn't?" Victoria motioned with her hand. "Come behind the counter. We have a secret door to the bar from here. I've put the heater on, and help yourself to a coffee from the machine. The cups are behind the bar."

Fran followed her through as Victoria hit the lights. The bar looked a lot bigger now it was empty of people. "I really do appreciate this, you've no idea. I'll leave some money for the coffee. Also, I want to buy some panettone and Florentines while I'm here. I love your display, very festive."

Victoria gave her a smile. "You're welcome to use the space whenever. It's just sitting there otherwise. Plus, you're a local now. In Mistletoe, this is what we do."

Fran was discovering that.

Chapter 15

It was just after 8pm when Ruby arrived at The Bar. She'd been in the Christmas tree yard for 12 hours, and she needed a break. When she walked in, a rousing rendition of 'White Christmas' was underway, with Audrey, Sue, and Penny all in fine voice. They'd clearly been here since the place opened at six. What Ruby hadn't expected to see was Fran in the middle of them, dressed in her regulation black. She must have worked here all day, and then stayed. Fran was truly turning into a local. That thought made Ruby smile.

"Ruby!" Audrey jumped to her feet as the chorus kicked in, shouting. "Your new friend is proving herself an asset to the community. She knows all the words to 'White Christmas', along with many other songs. Apparently, she works in the music business, did you know?"

Ruby was pretty sure Audrey knew that already, but had forgotten. It wasn't unusual.

"I told her she has to help with your music." Yup, she was still shouting. "I mean, Fran's in London, you're in London. It could be a good match, right?" Audrey tapped the side of her nose with her index finger and gave Ruby an exaggerated wink.

Ruby walked to the bar, giving Fran a slight wave.

Fran waved back, also miming the words 'help me' to Ruby.

Ruby shook her head. Fran was going to have to get out of this one herself.

Five minutes later, Ruby pulled up a chair and joined the group.

"Is it a bad sign you're in here when the farm is still open?" Sue put both elbows on the table, her chin in her palms.

"It's been pretty busy today, so the lull isn't unwelcome. Plus, there are still a bunch of staff working, so things are okay." Ruby glanced at Fran. "Did you get your work done?"

Fran nodded. "I did. I've been trying to go home since six, but everyone keeps telling me I have to stay. Particularly since Victoria put the Christmas hits on, and the singing commenced. Any tips on making a great escape? I've messaged my dads, but they've ordered Thai food and told me I could stay as long as I want."

"The Bar can do that to you," Ruby replied. "It can suck you in like a vortex, and in the end, you're not quite sure what day it is or what your last name is. How many times have you woken up asleep on the sofa over there, Audrey?"

Audrey waved her hand. "Who's counting?" She gave Ruby a grin. "More than you, but less than Norman?"

"Which is pretty bad, considering you live four doors down."

"I still look good on it, don't I?" Audrey gave Ruby her side profile. "Unlike Norman over there, who's got a face like a dropped pie. Plus, it's your sister's fault. She shouldn't have such comfy sofas, should she?"

All of a sudden, the music was turned up.

Ruby turned her head.

Victoria had a grin on her face. "Come on, little sis."

Ruby shook her head. "Uh-uh. You know my thoughts about karaoke."

"This isn't karaoke! This is you singing in your sister's bar with a tiny audience of," Victoria glanced around the bar. "Seven people. Eight if you count Norman, but he's asleep in the corner. Plus, Fran's never heard you sing this song." Victoria waved her hands. "Sing up! I'm going to put it back to the start." She pointed. "Pick up Sue's empty bottle of Peroni: instant makeshift microphone."

Sue passed the bottle to Ruby.

Ruby took it, every inch of her tight as she took a breath. But maybe she should lighten up. Her sister was right. This wasn't karaoke. It was almost like singing at home. She did that all the time. Ruby pushed the negative thoughts from her mind and took a breath, before starting to sing along with the Wham! classic, 'Last Christmas'. As she hit the first chorus, the whole table joined in, Audrey waving her hands in the air, getting the words wrong just like every year.

But what wasn't like every year was Fran's eyes on her.

Ruby moved through the chorus and the second verse with silken ease, wrapping her mouth around every lyric. This was the song of her childhood, the song that she and Victoria had sung almost since birth. No Christmas was complete without it on repeat.

As they hit the final chorus, Ruby turned her head to Victoria. She was kneeling on a bar stool, arms in the air, eyes tight shut.

Ruby spun around and clocked the group at the table,

blissed-out looks on their faces, belting out the song like they'd written it themselves. Ruby's gaze stopped moving when she got to Fran.

She was still watching Ruby, a soft smile on her face, head tilted to the side, her blond hair a little messy from her hat.

Fran wasn't singing.

She simply stared.

A fire heated inside Ruby and rushed up her body, from the inside out. She gathered up all her breath to finish strong. She held Fran's gaze as she hit the final note, pouring everything into it.

When the song finished, everyone clapped and cheered.

Ruby's skin tingled as she dropped Fran's gaze, then scanned the room. It was as if she'd been in a daze. She cleared her throat and painted on a smile.

A searing whistle broke the applause.

Ruby turned. Norman was awake, rubbing his eyes. "I can't think of a much better way to be woken up than with Ruby's angelic voice," he said. "Pint of bitter, when you're ready, Victoria."

"You old sweet-talker, Norman." Ruby swept her gaze back to the table, being sure to avoid Fran.

Sue patted her on the back. "You're destined for big things. I've always said so."

Ruby's smile tightened. She heard the same thing every year. "Thanks, Sue."

"I told Ruby the same when I first saw her earlier this year," Fran added, getting nods from the crowd. "But while you were singing, I had an idea." Fran caught Ruby's gaze. "And before you say no, hear me out. Have you ever thought of putting on a gig at the farm to get people to visit and buy a tree, or better yet, order one for next year?"

Panic ran riot inside Ruby. "I told you, I don't do bigger gigs. I like more intimate stuff."

"But this would only be a few hundred, max. Plus, surely Mistletoe is the exception?" Fran's face was a question mark. "It's your home town. *Everybody* wants you to do well. It would be the equivalent of singing to an audience of super-fans. You've just sung to us, and you told me you didn't do that. Why not break all the rules this year? Feel the fear and do it anyway. Who knows what might happen?" Fran's words held a challenge.

A tremble ran through Ruby. It wasn't that she didn't *want* to. It was just that, it wasn't what she *did*. But maybe it *could* be what she did? After all, she dictated her own career.

"Think about it," Fran continued, her hands animated. "You could do a big festive gig. Invite local crafts people to exhibit their wares. Get people buying everything you've got for sale already, too."

Victoria snapped her fingers at the bar, making Ruby twist around.

"She's got a good point. You've always said you'd do a gig here, but you never have. The stage is already set up. The villagers would love it, as would everyone else. We could put on a bar and do food, too."

Ruby frowned. "Christmas is nearly here." She checked the calendar on her phone. "Plus, we couldn't do the weekend before Christmas, it's too close. Which means it would have to be next Saturday. A week tomorrow." But she'd done quicker gigs in London. Could she do it here, too, without her infrastructure around her?

"Would the musicians who play with you make the trip?" Fran asked.

Ruby rocked her head from side to side. "Not sure. If they were free, yes. But I know a few people around here who could fill in if necessary. Eric for one, right?"

Victoria nodded. "He could be your guitarist, no problem."

Ruby's body fizzed with excitement and fear. She'd always harboured a secret dream of doing a gig in Mistletoe. But what if nobody came? What if everyone was polite, but they hated her music? She wasn't worried about flying beer bottles. In Mistletoe, she was worried about the people she loved the most loving her back. But also, of trying something new. What if she failed? Or what if she succeeded?

Fran stared right at her. Fran was pushing Ruby out of her comfort zone and she had no qualms about doing it. Fran made Ruby nervous. She also made her think. On top of that, she was giving Ruby a heated stare that made her truly reconsider their relationship. One that made Ruby's heart pound in her chest.

"You could even play Ikea at their own game. Offer people something free if they place next year's order now. A free mulled wine or sprig of mistletoe. Free kiss from Audrey or Norman." Fran grinned. "I could help with the marketing."

Audrey beamed. "I'm in! So long as I don't have to kiss Norman."

Ruby ignored Audrey, still staring at Fran. "I thought you were going back to London?"

Fran nodded slowly. "I am, but I might be able to switch

some things around, particularly now my parents need me. No promises, I'd have to check my schedule, but if I can make it work, I will. Also, I'm a local now, aren't I? I'm invested in whatever happens here. I have experience of digital marketing. You might as well put me to good use."

Fran was planning on sticking around?

"What do you think, Rubytubes?" Victoria asked from the bar. "Can we turn this around in a week?"

"We did far more than this back in the war, Ruby!" Audrey told her.

"You're 72 years old, Audrey," Norman piped up, as Victoria delivered his pint to his corner table. "You weren't even born in the war, so stop trying to tell us you were."

"I've read books!" Audrey's tone was incredulous.

Ruby rubbed the back of her neck. "When you're finished debating history, let's get back to the matter at hand. Let's say it's a tentative yes. The community pulled together for the festival. We can leave the trees up and do this, too. Anything for Mistletoe Farm. But you have to promise to cheer when I'm on stage, okay?" Ruby's gaze travelled around the table.

"Of course we will!" Sue replied.

"Try to stop us!" Penny said.

"Cheer?" Audrey added. "We'll do more than that. We'll raise the bloody barn roof off!"

Ruby glanced at Fran, who gave her a delicious smile.

Ruby's stomach flip-flopped. She might have just dropped herself in it big time, but Fran's smile was worth it.

Chapter 16

Ruby waved Norman off, then zipped up her jacket against the cold.

It was the third different jacket Fran had seen her wear. But at least Fran had one to rival it now.

Ruby glanced at Fran's loaded bag as they left the bar, the last to leave. "You bought some panettone. I was just wondering who did in Mistletoe. But Victoria says it's a hit in the shop."

"I love the plain one, where you shake the icing sugar over it. It's delicious. Not so keen on the one with the candied fruit in it. A little like Christmas pudding and Christmas cake, I give that a swerve."

Ruby pulled the door of The Bar shut, turned the key and gave it to Fran. "You don't like Christmas pudding? Perhaps we can't be friends anymore."

"More for you to have, look at it that way."

Ruby smiled. "Good point."

Fran put the key in her bag, and they fell into step, walking away from the shop.

"How's your dad doing?" Ruby asked.

"My Pop," Fran replied. "Sorry, I don't expect you to know that, but I call them Dad and Pop. It's been that way forever."

Ruby shook her head to tell Fran it was no problem. "How's your Pop doing?"

"He's okay, being brave, but I can tell being in plaster is messing with his village dreams. I'm spending the day with them tomorrow as I've been busy working. It's Saturday, so I promised. I'm going to cook them dinner, too."

"Daring after what you told me."

"It's my Malaysian curry. Nothing too fancy. I'm thinking a bottle of wine, some hopefully edible food, and then maybe watching *Elf* to get us in the festive mood."

"Sounds great, what time do you want me over?" Ruby gave her a wink.

"Can I take a rain check?"

Ruby nodded. "A Malaysian curry rain check is my very favourite kind." She paused. "But that's good you've come around to the dark side and are taking some time to be with your family. You came back, too, after saying you couldn't. I'm impressed. You dropped everything when they needed you. You didn't put your job first. You're fooling me into thinking you have a heart." Ruby bumped Fran's hip as she spoke.

Warmth thundered through Fran, which was bonkers as it was hovering around zero. Being around Ruby did something to her. "I do have a heart, it turns out. It was buried, but I found it." Fran gave Ruby a grin. "But you're right. It's good I came home, especially as I have The Bar to work from. Thanks again for coming to my rescue with that." Fran shook her head. "Can you imagine that ever happening in London? You just gave me the keys to a bar. I might go in there tomorrow and drink the place dry. But you trust me."

"We know where you live, so if you do go mad on the

Aperol, we can hunt you down and force-feed you Christmas pudding."

Fran's laughter shook the air. "The very worst kind of punishment." She took a deep breath before she continued. The night was cold, and the air was sharp as it made it to her lungs. "I don't know what it is about this place, but it's giving me something I never even knew I needed. Community. Laughter. Relaxation. Who would have thought I would do such great work in a bar in Suffolk? But today I was focused, and I got loads done. And then the village arrived and we had a drink and sing-song. It was weird, but kinda lovely."

Ruby reached out a hand and put it on Fran's arm.

Fran's whole body tingled at the connection. She knew why, too. It was to do with Ruby's intense stare, the way her lips had parted slightly, the way her gaze now caressed Fran's face, all the way down to Fran's mouth.

When she got there, Ruby froze, took back her arm and looked away.

Fran bit her lip, then cleared her throat. That hot feeling inside her was still there. Ruby had been checking her out.

The weird thing was, Fran had no qualms with it happening. She began walking again, clearing her throat, her brain stuck on repeat.

I like her. Even though she's a singer.

That was the thought that was flashing on and off in her brain, like a faulty neon sign.

She couldn't *like* Ruby. She didn't need another singer in her life. She had enough of them at work.

Ruby wasn't like the others though, was she? She wasn't chasing fame. She wasn't trying to make up for all the attention she never got in her childhood. Ruby came from a loving family. She could sing. She wanted to do it for the art itself.

"You're not the first person to ask what it is about this place. Mistletoe holds magical qualities. But it's not the place that makes it. It's the people. Even Audrey." Ruby's tone held a smile.

"Especially Audrey," Fran laughed. "Also, I wanted to ask: are you okay with the gig idea? I really do think your home town would love it." She stopped walking. "But I also know I was probably over-stepping the mark when I mentioned it. It's a speciality of mine." She waited for the answer.

Even though, now she thought about it, she was pretty sure Fast Forward had something next weekend. An appearance or an interview, perhaps both. Shit, how could she have forgotten that? She gulped. But this gig was important for Ruby and the village. She'd have to check her calendar and speak to Damian. Maybe she could do both? But she wasn't going to worry about that right now.

Ruby studied her, blew out a deep breath and shook her head. "Strangely, I am okay with it. Mistletoe hasn't seen me perform, and this is the perfect way to do it. I won't lie, you are tipping me out of my comfort zone. But if it helps the farm, that's a good thing. Plus, I didn't come up with it. You did. It makes me look like less of a diva that way."

Now it was Fran's turn to shake her head. "You're the least diva-ish singer I know."

Ruby's gaze snagged hers in the darkness. "I think there's a compliment buried in there somewhere."

Fran nodded. "There is. Anyway, I'm glad you're not angry." Fran carried on walking, every muscle clenched, breathing out.

"I'm not," Ruby said. "Plus, some of what you said was true. I should have played to bigger audiences by now, and I'm not going to get a more receptive crowd than Mistletoe. Nobody's going to pelt me."

"Only with love," Fran replied.

Ruby's breath caught at that, and she stared at Fran. "Where did you come from?" Ruby shook her head and they carried on walking, past two Christmas trees, and then Ruby repeated her actions of the other night. She took Fran's hand in hers and tugged her across the road and down a tiny lane. "I've got something to show you."

Adrenaline surged through Fran at their contact. "Where are we going?" She could hardly see a thing because the lane was narrow and covered by thick hedges on both sides. "Should I trust you?" Fran smiled as she spoke.

Ahead of her, Ruby chuckled. "I think you know the answer to that. Never trust a singer." More throaty laughter.

Okay, Fran deserved that.

"We're nearly there." Ruby gave Fran a final tug, and they stopped at a clearing in the shrubbery. In four steps, Ruby made it to a wooden gate set back on the right. It was the width of two cars, the wooden slats reaching waist-height. She beckoned Fran over, then placed her own arms on top of the gate.

Fran did the same. She gazed out across the white field into the inky night.

"This," Ruby said, "is where I come when I need to think. To get peace and quiet. Just far enough off the beaten track, where nobody I know is going to ask me how I am or can I get some milk." She put a finger in the air. "Can you hear that?"

Fran cocked her head. "What?"

"The sound of silence. It's the same whenever I come here, day or night. You can't see its majesty fully at night, but this is the perfect spot to watch the sun rise and across the lane, the sun set." She pointed to the gate opposite. "I've solved many of my problems leaning on these two gates."

Fran glanced left at Ruby, who was staring straight ahead. "Is this where you bring women to impress them?" Fran winced. It wasn't what she'd wanted to say.

Ruby turned her head, her features blank. "I've never brought anyone else to this place," she whispered. "I've never brought anybody back to Mistletoe, full stop. It's too special. Too personal. But you live here now, so you're starting to understand."

Fran held Ruby's gaze, tasting fear on her tongue. "I'm honoured to be the first." There was something in Ruby's stare that was different to before, when they'd been on the road. Now they were hidden from view, Ruby had changed. Her guard was down. Now it was just Ruby, Fran, and a wide-open space.

A smile danced around the corners of Ruby's lips as she turned her gaze back to the field. "Who knows, you might need this place to escape to as well. Especially if you're staying a little longer now your dads aren't 100 per cent." She turned back. "You and me, we're different to everyone else around here."

"We don't live here full-time."

Ruby nodded. "We get both sides of the story. Country life and London life. But it's more than that. I never would have said it when I first met you, but you're not like anyone else

I've ever met. You surprise me every time I meet you." Ruby frowned, then turned away. "You know what, ignore me. I'm probably talking nonsense."

Something wet landed on Fran's face. She looked up to the sky, which was brighter than before, despite it being late. She knew why now. It was starting to snow. She glanced over at Ruby. "It's snowing."

Ruby stuck out her tongue. "I can see." She moved along the gate until she stood right next to Fran, their bodies almost touching. "We should huddle together. For warmth. Mistletoe rules."

"I don't want to go against those."

Ruby's body heat crackled next to Fran. Something kicked in her chest. This was dangerous. However, she didn't move. The Christmas card they were living in had just become animated. A little like her thoughts.

"How am I surprising you?" Fran couldn't let that comment slide. It had sounded delicious when it dropped from Ruby's lips.

"You're making an effort with everyone. You came back. You're *fitting in*. You're not who I thought you were." Ruby turned her head.

Fran squinted in the flakes. "Not such a city slicker?"

Ruby didn't flinch as she replied. "You're infinitely better."

Fran's heart rippled.

Ruby still stared, her cheeks flushed, her gaze intense.

The wind fluttered suddenly, sending snowflakes into their faces.

Both Ruby and Fran leaned away from the gate, shaking their heads. They straightened at the same time, turning to each other.

Fran gulped, and stared into Ruby's greener than green eyes. Right now, she felt like she could drown in them.

Ruby stepped into Fran's space.

Desire slid down Fran's body. They hadn't kissed, but it felt like they had. Fran was so *aware* of Ruby. Ruby was watching the rise and fall of Fran's chest, her every breath.

"I could never go out with someone who didn't get Mistletoe, or family."

Fran shook her head. "Me neither."

Ruby got closer still. "I want you to know also, this is not me at all." Her intense gaze was drilling into Fran's soul. "I don't usually act on my feelings. But you're making me act differently."

She was so close, Fran could feel her breath. "I am?"

"First the concert. And now…" Ruby left the sentence hanging as she grasped Fran's gloved hands and raised them to her mouth to kiss them. Her dark gaze kept Fran fixed to the spot.

When Ruby leaned in further, Fran forgot it was snowing.

Forgot it was freezing.

Forgot they were standing on a path, bathed in moonlight.

When Ruby's lips connected with hers, Fran forgot *everything*.

Ruby's lips were glorious. They tasted of hope, of freedom, of *her*. More than that, they fitted Fran's as if they'd been made to measure. No alterations required. As their kiss gained momentum, a glitter bomb of happiness steamrollered through her.

Then Ruby's fingers were on Fran's waist, staking their claim. Ruby pulled her close, their lips still pressed tight together. Ruby ran one hand up the side of Fran. She cupped her face. Ruby was strong and gentle, the perfect package. As the snow continued to fall, the tension spiked, dancing all over Fran's skin. Fran's kisses grew hungrier. Her lips danced across Ruby's. She couldn't get enough.

If someone had asked her this morning if she should get involved with another singer and kiss her in a snowstorm, she'd have told you it sounded like a Delilah song. Or perhaps one Ruby might sing in the future. If this was a mistake, Fran would happily live with the consequences.

Since Delilah left, Fran had been sad, then wary. Since she'd arrived in Mistletoe, excitement had returned to her life. Fran was tired of feeling like she was always running to catch up. In Mistletoe, she just was. Right now, that involved kissing Ruby like her life depended on it.

Fran moaned as Ruby slipped her tongue into her mouth.

The snow storm picked up, now matching the beat of her heart as it swirled and dived around them. Fran was in no hurry for anything to change anytime soon. Far from needing to get back to London, now the only thing in her mind was how to extend her stay. To be close to Ruby. To her mouth. To her divine kisses. Plus, whatever came after that.

After a few long moments, Ruby broke the kiss. There was a white heat in her stare that thrilled Fran.

Cold air buffeted them. Snow hit her face.

It didn't feel like it had a few minutes ago. Now, she was impervious to its chill. Plus, the heat of Ruby's breath warmed her cheeks, along with the languid smile painted on her face.

"You taste delicious." Ruby licked her lips.

Fran was just about to comment when Ruby kissed her again, this time with more force, more passion.

Ruby wrapped her arms around Fran and pulled her close.

It was all Fran could do not to fall backwards in her arms, in the manner of a Hollywood movie.

What the hell was Ruby doing to her? They should have done this sooner.

Had Fran been thinking about kissing Ruby when she saw her on stage the first time? No.

When they broke down? No.

When they fell in the snow? Maybe.

In The Bar? Perhaps.

Eventually, Ruby broke away. This time, her smile was so broad, Fran thought it might break her face.

"You look pleased with yourself." It wasn't Fran's best line.

Ruby grinned a little more. "I am. I wasn't sure we were going to kiss, but I'm glad we did."

Fran nodded. "Me, too. I could kiss you all night."

"I'll hold you to that one day." She glanced upwards. "But right now, as much as your kisses were perfect, you think we can get out of this snow?"

Fran looked into Ruby's gorgeous eyes and nodded. "Walk me home?"

Ruby leaned in and kissed her lips again. Her touch was feather-light, but its effect was anything but.

Fran shivered once more, as the reverberation landed in her core. "You're going to be trouble, aren't you?" She put a hand on Ruby's cheek as their gazes connected.

Ruby supplied a smouldering look. "I guarantee it."

Chapter 17

Fran woke the following morning before her alarm went off. Despite her thick, cream curtains, she could still sense the winter wonderland beyond, its power strong. When she got up and pulled back the curtains, she wasn't wrong. A fresh duvet of snow had fallen overnight, now at least 20-tog. If their old dog, Rhubarb, was still alive, she'd have run outside and disappeared. In Mistletoe, every December day was served chilled. However, red-hot nights could also be ordered, as Fran had experienced last night.

That kiss was still alive in her blood stream, in all her senses. Perhaps because it had been so unexpected.

The fourth quarter was for work, for the Christmas sales surge. Everyone knew that.

It wasn't for kissing folk singers on moonlit lanes.

At least, it hadn't been until Ruby O'Connell came along.

From the time they'd left the bar together, there had been something inevitable about the evening. Something film-worthy.

When Fran licked her lips, she could taste Ruby's lips all over again. Her body shook as she remembered its full force.

She'd kissed Ruby. It was going to be at the forefront of her mind for the rest of the day.

Fran turned to grab her phone. Today was Saturday. If she wanted to get back to London next week, she needed to book a train. Only, she didn't want to, did she? Maybe she could buy a day or two working from here. With a sick parent, she had the perfect excuse. Today was about them spending time as a family. Something she should have put to the top of her list a long time ago.

Fran scrolled through her phone to get the ball rolling with Damian: her absence affected him the most. If he could cover a couple of meetings and gigs, she could phone in to the rest. So long as Fast Forward stuck to their task and performed with no hiccups. But that would also depend on the outside world playing nicely, too.

Fran composed an email to Damian, then clicked send.

It bounced straight back. Mistletoe reception had struck again: hadn't Mary said it was better this year? Hollybush Cottage appeared to be a blind spot. Fran sucked air through her teeth. She'd have to try again later.

She pulled on some jeans and a sweatshirt with a reindeer on it — a present from her parents — then strolled downstairs. When she arrived, she found Pop sitting at the round wooden table in the country-style kitchen, reading a cookery magazine. His plastered leg rested on the tiled floor, his crutches within easy reach. Dad was at the hob making pancakes.

When he heard her, Dad turned. "Good to see your ability to sniff a pancake at 100 paces hasn't changed."

Fran grinned. "It's my superpower, you know that." She kissed both her parents good morning, then flicked on the kettle, and grabbed a mug and teabag from the cannister on the side. As the water heated, she glanced out the window, her breath still taken by the snowy scene beyond.

"Is this cheering you up?" She motioned out the window as she addressed Pop.

He nodded. "I know I wasn't in hospital for long, but the view was rubbish. This is much better."

"It's cracking," Fran replied. "I was just thinking about Rhubarb. How she'd have run outside in this snow and disappeared."

"Then reappeared, her ears like angel's wings," Dad added, laughing. "She loved the snow, didn't she?" He held up the mixture he'd made in his plastic jug, just as he had her entire life. "I take it you want pancakes?"

"Have I ever been known to turn down a pancake?"

"Not in living memory."

"Well, then," Fran replied. "Also, I'm thinking about staying on a bit longer this week. I want to make sure you're both okay. No more arguments with patches of ice or snow."

"I thought you had loads of work on?" Pop put down his magazine.

Fran nodded. "I do, but I can work from here for a bit."

Pop sat back, moving his leg. "Does that mean you're staying for Christmas? Because that would be really terrific."

The kettle boiled and Fran made her tea, skilfully avoiding the question. "Do either of you need a new one?"

Pop passed her his mug and she made it.

"We're still waiting for an answer, Francesca Jane."

Her full name. Now she was in trouble. "I'm not sure, so don't get your hopes up. I do have a lot of work on, and I was doubtful I'd be able to do it seeing as the Wi-Fi at the cottage is terrible. However, now I have The Bar to work in, it could make a difference. I need to check with my colleagues, too. I kinda volunteered to help Ruby do a gig at the farm next weekend, too." All dependent on Fast Forward, who were coming into sharper focus today. She needed to speak to Damian.

"You seem to be getting on well after a wobbly start? I'm glad. It seemed a waste that you knew each other, but were keeping your distance."

"It was a bit weird at first, but things have improved." Fran sat next to Pop and sipped her tea. Was she blushing? She certainly felt like she was.

"She's doing a gig next weekend? That's a lot to organise in such a short period of time. Plus, won't most people have bought their trees already, the week before Christmas?"

"Most will, some won't. But it's about getting people in to see what the farm has to offer. Also, they can pre-order next year's tree, too."

Dad put the pancakes on the table, and Fran grabbed the maple syrup from the cupboard, before tucking in. She smiled as she ate. Pancakes were Dad's speciality, the taste of her childhood.

"Whatever's keeping you here — my fall or Ruby's gig — it makes us happy," Pop said. "We want to see you more. I'm really glad you're getting on with the locals and pitching in. Especially when my involvement in anything this year might be curtailed because of my stupid leg."

Fran smiled at him. "I'll be your representative in the field. I'm asking my colleague if he can cover some of my meetings on Monday, and hopefully I can do some in The Bar. Plus, I've got one of our designers working on some social media stuff for the gig. He does this sort of stuff every day professionally, so it makes sense to ask him. What would take him half an hour might take a day to explain to someone else." She was justifying this too much, wasn't she?

Sure enough, Dad raised his eyebrow at Pop. In turn, Pop squirted maple syrup onto his pancakes, then gave Fran an interested stare.

"Wow, you really are on-board. I'm impressed. You said you had too much work on. Once your mind's made up, there's usually no shifting Francesca Bell. You're stubborn. You get that from your father." Pop inclined his head towards Dad.

"I am not stubborn!" Dad said.

Both Pop and Fran burst out laughing.

"You're stubborn, Dad, and so am I. Stop being so stubborn and just accept it." Fran had missed this. She glanced out the window, thinking back to last night. Her temperature rose. Was Mistletoe magic real? Maybe it was.

"Is this sudden change of heart and wanting to help out your local community anything to do with Ruby? Is there anything you're not telling us?" Pop couldn't crinkle his forehead any more if he tried.

Fran shook her head. "No."

But her body betrayed her, with a rush of blood to her cheeks.

Her dads had always been able to read her like a book. It was one of their very annoying traits. They were both studying her like she was a prize artwork in a gallery they both loved.

She knew it was out of character. She liked Ruby. She wanted to help her succeed. She was willing to change her work schedule to do so. To let Damian handle Fast Forward, even though she knew he was more than capable. That was new.

"Nothing at all? Because we are your parents. If you are lusting after another girl, we might be able to give you some wisdom."

"I'm not lusting after another girl. Sometimes you two being gay is *so* annoying. These are not the conversations children normally have with their parents." She sounded like she was 14 again and trying to deny it for real the first time around. She'd tried so hard to be straight and to fit in at school. At 17, she gave in and told her dads what they already knew.

"Yes, but those are people that usually have opposite-sex parents." Dad gave her a shrug. "Whereas you won the gay parent jackpot. So if you are after another girl — or even a man, we're not close minded — we're here for you."

Pop reached over and put his hand on her arm. "We are, even though I can't help you get up and run after Ruby. I'm here for you for all other needs, though."

Fran gave him a puzzled face. "I've told you before, I can run my own matters of the heart. But there is no matter of the heart here. I can't get involved with another singer after Delilah, you know that."

Her parents exchanged looks over their pancakes.

"Ruby's hardly Delilah, and I mean that in the nicest possible way. We never met Delilah as that would have made everything too real for her. But Ruby is a real person and she seems lovely. Plus, I prefer her music, too."

"You haven't heard it."

"I have," Pop said, pulling back his shoulders. "I know how

to work Spotify just like you do." He paused. "Plus, Ruby's from a lovely family, whereas Delilah's sounded like a nightmare. These things make a difference when choosing a partner. My parents never accepted us and it leaves a dent."

Fran knew that. But at least they had Dad's family who were lovely.

"I know Ruby's from a good family. But that doesn't mean I'm after her."

"Methinks the lady doth protest too much," Pop told her.

"Methinks you're talking nonsense." But Fran knew she *was* protesting too much. She clapped her hands together. "Anyway, let's eat these delicious pancakes, then I need to make one phone call. After that, I'm all yours. I'm making curry, and I thought we could watch a film this afternoon?"

Pop's face lit up. "A Christmas film?"

Fran nodded, happy to move the subject along. "I was thinking *Elf*, or whatever you fancy."

"*Elf* sounds perfect," Dad replied.

Fran glanced out the window again. "Have you thought about getting another dog now you're settled? It's been three years since Rhubarb, and Mistletoe is the perfect place for one."

Pop nodded. "We have. We were thinking of getting a couple of rescue dogs. Older ones that take it easy, and need a place to spend their final years."

"I love that. Two old dogs for two silver foxes."

Chapter 18

Ruby stood at the door of one of the barns, gazing out at the Christmas tree fields behind it. She took a deep breath in. The smell of fir trees was the smell of home.

The barn was one of the more insulated buildings they had. However, it was still freezing on this December Monday morning. It had been stacked high with Christmas trees, but was now two-thirds empty: proof that sales had picked up over the last couple of days. Maybe this year really would signal a change of fortunes for the farm. Hopefully, Ruby's concert would move the needle, too.

She jogged on the spot for a few moments, then did star jumps to get her blood flowing. She'd done her main vocal warm-up in the house, but decamped to the barn when Mum kept interrupting and commenting on her voice. To finish off her rehearsal, she needed a bit more warmth. She walked over to the barn office in the corner, shut the door, pulled the blinds and turned on the radiators.

Ruby liked to come here when she needed a little time away from the family to play, sing, or just be. The office housed two desks and a comfortable red sofa underneath a wall of Christmas tree photos. On the opposite side of the room was a hospitality station with a kettle, Nespresso machine, and a fridge below. This was where her dad and Scott brought their bigger corporate clients when they'd walked them around the fields and sprinkled them with Christmas magic. Ruby did a few more warm-up exercises, taking slugs of hot water and lemon from her steel-cased flask to ease her voice back into action.

She cleared her throat, pushing thoughts of Fran and how they'd kissed on Friday night from her mind. She could still feel how Fran had grasped her waist with her strong fingers. Still remember how she tasted. Ruby wanted to taste her again. That thought sent a scuttle of heat down her body. Ruby shivered. They'd exchanged a couple of messages since, but Fran had spent the weekend with her parents.

Ruby picked up her folder of song lyrics and got on with the job at hand. Being in the moment and singing. It was her speciality. She called up the backing tracks on her phone, and hit play. She'd just run through 'Winter Wonderland' and 'Rudolph The Red-Nosed Reindeer' when there was a knock on the office door, and Victoria walked in. It was just like their childhood: Victoria knocked, but then always walked straight in.

"All right, karaoke queen?"

"I hope I'm better than somebody having a go at karaoke." Ruby folded her arms and frowned. "Otherwise it's going to be a very short and grumbly concert."

"You're going to be just fine." Victoria gave her a hug. "Are you singing your own songs, too? Not just Christmas tunes?"

Ruby nodded. "I will be. But I have to sing the classics as well. You don't get Robbie Williams or Michael Bublé doing a gig at Christmas without some festive songs, do you?"

"They are Christmas cabaret, though."

"What am I?"

"You're the local superstar."

Ruby ignored her. She was terrible at taking compliments. "Anyway, I will be singing my stuff, but that doesn't need as much practice. I thought I'd run through the Christmas stuff, and leave my songs until I have some musical back-up. Is Eric going to be around to rehearse soon?"

Victoria nodded. "He is. He said to just let him know when. He's been practising with what you sent him."

Ruby put her lyrics folder down on a nearby chair. She shivered, even though the heat was on. She shouldn't stay out here for too long.

"How are you feeling about the concert? I know there was pressure in the bar, but I'm really excited to see my big-shot sister sing live. I've only seen you perform twice before." Victoria's smile was genuine, which only made Ruby more nervous. Was she going to cope with the pressure and make her family proud? There was a lot riding on this gig for her.

"I'm hardly a big-shot. I'm someone who gigs, and teaches on the side."

"Don't be so ridiculous. I'm a shopkeeper. You're a singer. If anyone ever asks me, that's what I tell them." Victoria pointed at her. "You need more belief in your ability. To be less fearful of it all. Maybe then you'd put yourself out there a bit more." Her sister tilted her head. "And yes, I know you're going to tell me you're happy where you are, you get by just fine, but I don't buy it. Neither does Fran, which I love." Victoria paused. "She's working in The Bar again today.

Hard worker, that one." Victoria waved a hand. "Anyway, we both think you should be doing more gigging and recording. You're a born singer. I'm looking forward to seeing you, and so are Mum and Dad. Even Scott."

Ruby snorted. Her brother was not a music fan. "Now I know you're lying. Scott would rather stick pins in his eyes than see me sing."

"He'll be there. If nothing else to admire the stage he and Eric built." Victoria paused. "Talking of Fran, anything to tell me about Friday night?"

Ruby perched on the edge of one of the office desks, and shook her head. She could do poker face, no problem. "No, nothing."

Victoria's look told Ruby she didn't buy it. "Nothing at all? I thought I picked up a little frisson between you two in the bar."

"You're seeing things that aren't there. Plus, how could you possibly have picked up anything while we were in the bar? There were people all around us fighting to be heard. Norman banging on about his pint. Audrey being Audrey. It's hardly the place where romance blooms, is it?"

"You can tell me that all you want, but I know subtle looks and smiles when I see them. Plus, you did lock up together. Nothing happened on the way home? No kissing under the snowy stars?"

A jolt of electricity hit Ruby as she recalled exactly what happened under the snowy stars. A snowy kiss that hadn't strayed far from her memory ever since it happened.

"No, no kissing at all." Ruby's stomach did cartwheels as she lied. "Besides, I can't get involved with a music exec.

I wouldn't hear the end of it from everyone I know. It's like sleeping with the enemy."

"She's not a music exec when she's here though, is she? She's your neighbour. An attractive, funny, available neighbour."

Ruby checked her watch. "She's coming over later to talk about the gig. Who knows, we might go for coffee afterwards. So stay by your phone for reports of us tearing each other's clothes off in the farm café."

Victoria's face lit up. "Some of us are older and married. We have to get our kicks somehow."

"I'm sure the other patrons might disagree."

"I don't know. Everybody needs a bosom for a pillow now and again, don't they?" Her sister was incorrigible.

"Haven't you got a shop to run, Mrs Shopkeeper?"

"You're no fun. You're also very prickly on the subject of your love life."

"I don't have a love life!" Ruby threw up her hands. "Now get lost so I can keep practising in peace."

Victoria held up her hands, palms facing out. "All right, I'm going. Happy singing and let me know if I can do anything. We've got all the stuff bubbling in the background for the food and drink for Saturday."

"Good. We put some stuff out on social media. We're already getting positive feedback. It looks like I'm really doing it now. Scott reckons we might pull in a few hundred." Ruby's stomach flipped at the thought, as it always did. But nerves were good. Just so long as there weren't too many of them.

"No backing out. The village is going to love it. Our own homegrown singing superstar for one night only."

"One night only is right, so tell your friends."

"I wouldn't miss it for the world."

When Victoria was gone, Ruby rehearsed a few more Christmas numbers, before she sat on the red sofa, going through her lyrics. She came across her new song, 'Pieces Of You'. The one she'd sung a few times in London. Every time she did, the crowd went wild. She'd written it about taking a chance on love. The irony wasn't lost on Ruby, because she hadn't done that in quite a while. She hadn't been in a relationship for two years. Hadn't had sex in 12 months. She also hadn't kissed anyone in that time, either.

Until she met Fran. Being around Fran was bringing to the fore a swirl of feelings she'd hidden away. Some that she'd wondered if she'd ever feel again.

Ruby scanned the words. She focused on the chorus. 'Even if the journey seems far, you need to follow who you are, sometimes all you need is a leap of faith." Was that what Ruby needed to edge closer to Fran? She'd already kissed her, and that had been the first leap. That kiss had made Ruby's blood steam. It had lifted her up. It had made Ruby want to feel *more*.

Of Fran, but also of herself.

Her phone vibrated in her pocket. Ruby fished it out. A text from Fran. A grin settled on Ruby's face as she opened it.

'I've got some social media designs to run by you. Can we meet for a coffee later to chat? Does 6pm at the farm work?'

Ruby stared off into the distance, her body humming with anticipation as thoughts skated around her brain. Every single one had her kissing Fran.

She texted straight back to say that would be fine. Her

parents would give her the time off for the concert. That it involved spending time with Fran was an added bonus.

Ruby shook her head. The gig began to pulse in her mind. She didn't have time to sit around and daydream. She checked her watch: 8:30am. Another half an hour before the farm opened to the public, which meant she had another 30 minutes to nail these songs.

She stood and cleared her throat. She could worry all she liked about the crowd's reaction, but she couldn't control that.

The one thing she could control was her performance.

She had to be perfect for Saturday.

Chapter 19

Fran strolled along Farm Lane at 6pm, having escaped The Bar before the locals turned up. She didn't want to get pinned down again. She'd learned her lesson on Friday. Norman drove by in his retro-green Morris Minor, tooting his horn. He lived down the road from the farm, and was probably heading to The Bar for a drink. He seemed to be a permanent fixture there.

Fran blinked as her eyes adjusted to being outside and not pointed at a screen. It wasn't snowing, but it was cold enough for what was there to stick.

Today had been an intense day, and she wasn't sure how it boded for the rest of the week. Fast Forward's single launch had gone well, but the group were still far too nervous about all the things that needed to be done. Damian and the rest of the team were doing a brilliant job, but in the end, the buck stopped with her, as Fran's boss had told her today.

Could she buy a couple more days in Mistletoe before she had to get back on Thursday? Fran hoped so. Her dads were loving having her, and then there was Ruby. Tall, gorgeous, unexpected Ruby.

Every time Fran thought about her, a shiver of anticipation ran up her spine.

That kiss had taken up brain space ever since it happened. How could it not?

Whatever occurred, Fran had to be back in Mistletoe for Saturday night and Ruby's gig. She couldn't miss that, not after suggesting it in the first place. Plus, she had a feeling Ruby was going to need all the support she could get. Fast Forward had a gig and TV appearances on Friday and Saturday, but Damian and the team could hopefully handle the finish if she was there for the start. She should have checked her schedule before she suggested the gig, but she hoped she could work it out. Every time she thought about it, her stomach sagged. She'd overcommitted, but she was going to have to live with it.

Now, it felt like Ruby was her artist, as well as Fast Forward. Fran knew whose music she preferred. Also, who she'd like to kiss again as soon as humanly possible.

As the farm sign came into view, Fran turned into the drive and spotted Ruby's silhouette walking towards her.

As she got closer, Ruby greeted Fran with an unsure smile.

In return, Fran gave her a small wave.

They were rubbish at this, weren't they? They'd shared one dynamite kiss in the snow, but what was the etiquette now? Did she hug her? Kiss her on the lips? Cheek? Shake hands? Did they do things differently in Mistletoe to London? Fran was in the same country, but life in Mistletoe might as well have been on the moon.

For one thing, she didn't generally run around London kissing women in the snow.

Mistletoe 1, London 0.

"It's good to see you." Fran went with no physical contact

and a lame opener. She should never give up her job to do improv. She'd be bankrupt within weeks. Particularly if it involved Ruby.

"You, too." Ruby's face was guarded in the flashing lights of their Christmas tree on the drive.

Fran shivered. "It's so much colder here. I thought I'd hate it, but I kinda love it."

"Especially now you have the right coat to deal with it. How was the curry? Did your dads love it?"

"It went surprisingly well." Ruby remembered. Fran beamed.

"And did you get a lot of work done today?"

"Loads. Also, sorted some stuff out with my colleague, so now I don't have to rush back tomorrow, fingers crossed. It's been a good day." Fran reached over and flicked some snow off a branch of the Christmas tree. It was force of habit now. "It's just a shame I didn't get to play in the snow today. Too much work. I need to make more time for play. I haven't built a snowman since I was 11."

Ruby tilted her head. "Not since you were 11? That's scandalous."

"I know."

"I would say we could play in the snow tomorrow, but we're both working." Ruby paused. "But there's nothing to stop us now."

"Now?" Fran flicked her head skywards. "But it's dark."

Ruby shrugged. "You can still build a snowman in the dark. We did it plenty of times when I was little. Scott and I used to sneak out of the house early and build them in the field around the back of the barn. If you turn the outside lights of the back barn on, it gives you just enough glow. How about you show me your designs, I'll agree with them, and then we can play?"

Fran knew Ruby was talking about building a snowman, but it didn't stop heat flooding her body. Playing with Ruby had just shot to the top of her to-do list. "Can we do the design part at mine so I can drop my laptop off?"

Ruby nodded. "Let me grab my snowman backpack and we'll go."

* * *

Fran let herself into Hollybush Cottage, wiping her feet on the doormat as she did. She pulled off her orange bobble hat, conscious of her hat hair. Was it doing that thing where it stuck up at the back? Probably. She finger-combed it in an attempt to repair the damage. In her heart, she knew it was futile. Fran put her hat and scarf on the coat rack, followed by her jacket. Then she hung Ruby's coat up, too.

Ruby eyed her approvingly. "Nice bright green top." A smile creased her face.

Fran wriggled under the spotlight. "Thank you." She pointed down the hall. "Better go and say hi to my dads." Self-consciousness dug its heels into her skin. She felt like she was 14 again, bringing home her first girlfriend. Not that she'd had a girlfriend at 14. Or been out. She wasn't that cool.

However, Fran's toes were curling at the thought of what her dads might say when they saw Ruby was here. They weren't embarrassing parents — far from it — but sometimes when she brought a woman home, they could be just a little too over the top. *Too* welcoming.

Which was why she hadn't brought a woman home very often. When had the last time been? Probably over ten years ago. Having gay parents was great, but they were still her parents. Even though she was 36 years old. Did Ruby even count as someone she was bringing home when she was their neighbour? Having told her dads there was nothing going on, this would send their imagination into overdrive.

When they entered the kitchen, Dad sprang up.

Pop reached for his crutches, too.

Fran shook her head, waving a hand at them. "Don't get up. Ruby's just come back so I can show her the designs I got today." That sounded like a line, didn't it?

Ruby gave them a smile. "Then we're going to make a snowman."

Fran shot her a panicked look.

Ruby looked like she wanted to curl up and die. Too late. It was out there now. Two grown women were going out into the twilight to build a snowman.

To their credit, her parents didn't laugh. Rather, they gave each other that look that parents did. The one that told Fran she was fooling nobody.

No matter. Fran was going to act as if she was a stealth agent. Cool, calm, collected.

"You wanna come upstairs?" The blood rushed to Fran's cheeks as soon as she uttered those words. She wasn't going to even look at Ruby, let alone her parents.

"Sure," Ruby replied.

Fran put her head down and walked out of the kitchen. Did Dad just let out a small guffaw?

She wasn't going to focus on that. She grabbed her bag

and headed up the carpeted staircase, Ruby's footsteps providing a reassuring beat behind her. Fran shut her bedroom door and let out a breath she'd been holding ever since she left the kitchen. Then she took another deep one as the enormity of the situation crept up on her.

Ruby was in her bedroom. She picked up a trophy Fran won playing pool when she was 15.

"A pool shark. I would never have guessed."

"We had a table at the youth club. I spent a lot of time there."

"Training to be a good lesbian."

Fran smirked. "I even got a trophy for my efforts."

Ruby smiled, then glanced over to the corner. The tell-tale guitar case was propped up against the wall. "You play guitar? You never told me."

"That's because you're a professional musician, and I can't do barre chords." Fran wriggled her fingers. "It hurts my hand too much."

"You get used to it."

"So everyone tells me."

Ruby held up her hand. "My fingertips have been years in the making. Hard as nails, but still soft when they need to be."

"Do you say that to all the girls?" Fran gave her a grin.

"Only the ones with guitars." Ruby sat on Fran's double bed, and bounced a little. "So are you really planning on showing me some designs, or is this just a ruse to show me your bed?" She bounced a little more. "Good movement. Not too noisy. Something we could work with."

Fran wanted to die on the spot, but she managed not to.

Good start.

"That was the idea. Parade you in front of my parents, then bring you up here to have my wicked way with you. It seemed a little obvious at first, but it worked. I don't know why I didn't think of this earlier in life. It would have saved so much time and angst wooing women."

Fran grabbed her laptop from her bag, then sat next to Ruby on the bed. The warmth of Ruby's body hit her immediately, and she gulped. They were sitting on her bed. This wasn't a situation she'd considered might happen so quickly this morning.

Ruby crossed her long legs one over the other. Then she turned her head.

Fran stared at Ruby's lips. She'd like to kiss them somewhere warm. Like here.

"You woo women? Is this something I need to know about? Do you have a harp hidden away too that you're about to spring on me?"

Fran gave her a slow smile, never taking her eyes from Ruby. "No harp, promise. My wooing skills are pretty average."

"Unlike your kissing skills, which I recall were way above that." Ruby's gaze dropped to Fran's lips.

Fran froze at the words, hardly believing them. "They were?"

They were so close.

Ruby closed the gap between them. "Uh-huh." Ruby's lips touched hers.

A spark of electricity streaked down Fran.

Ruby teased her tongue along Fran's bottom lip.

Fran mentally reclined, ready for bliss.

"Fran!" Dad's voice cut through the sexual tension in the room. Footsteps on the stairs, then a knock at her bedroom door.

They sprang apart, Fran's heart falling through her body.

The door opened.

Fran shot up. Her Mac dropped from her lap.

Her dad frowned as it fell to the ground with a thud.

Fran snatched it up, cradling it to her chest like her first-born. What the fuck was her dad doing?

"I wondered if you'd like some banana bread and tea before you head out into the cold?" He glanced at Ruby, then at Fran. Could he feel the crackle in the air? Or was he oblivious?

"Sure. Let me just show Ruby these designs, then we'll be down." She ushered him out of the room. Then she shut the door and let out a breath.

Fran caught Ruby's gaze. She gave her a wide grin.

Fran slid down the door, laughter taking hold of her. "We're far too old to be living with our parents, aren't we?"

Ruby laughed, then sat on the floor next to her. "In our defence, it's not what we normally do. This is a break from our normal lives. We're in Mistletoe. What happens in Mistletoe stays in Mistletoe."

Fran paused. Was Ruby talking about their situation, too? It was too early to ask. They'd shared two kisses. One way too short. She'd like a do-over.

Instead, Fran opened her laptop and showed Ruby the designs, which she approved immediately. To be honest, Fran could have shown Ruby anything. Neither of them was concentrating anymore.

"Tea's ready!" Dad shouted up the stairs.

Fran rolled her eyes. "It's definitely a break. Not normality, thank goodness." She stood, then held out a hand. "Shall we have tea and cake, then go make that snowman?"

Ruby got up and dropped another kiss on Fran's lips. "I thought you'd never ask."

Chapter 20

Ruby snapped on the light at the back of the barn. A bright yellow hue drenched the nearest part of the field. The Christmas trees stood in lines, spaced out liberally.

"If you want to build a snowman, the only way to do it is in a field full of Christmas trees. We can use this field, as this isn't open to the public this year. Your last snowman was built in your garden, right?"

"Most of us don't have a farm, so yes." Fran shivered, then smashed her gloved hands together, taking in the scene. "This is pretty epic, though. A Christmas tree forest. Even for this hard-hearted Christmas avoider, you can't get a better location. Or smell." Fran took a lungful of the pine air.

Ruby walked up to the nearest tree. "See the tag on the bottom? The trees are colour-coded so my family know how old they are, which to leave, and which to chop." She shook some branches and the tree danced side to side. "Most households want six-foot trees in the run-up to Christmas, but hotels, holiday parks and restaurants always need them taller and earlier. Plus, larger trees are needed for photoshoots from September onwards, too. Mistletoe Farm grows them to demand."

Fran gave a nod. "Makes sense. I never thought Christmas trees were needed until December."

"Most people don't. The first half of the year is spent planting, hand-pruning, shaping and fertilising. The second half is all about getting the trees to businesses, then getting the farm ready for the Christmas onslaught. It's a year-round business." Ruby patted the tree fondly.

"You never thought about going into it?"

Ruby shook her head. "I love being around it, especially at Christmas. People are always happy when they're buying a tree. It's impossible not to be. Plus, it's in my blood. But so is music. Dad, Mum and Scott have it covered, so Victoria and I can do our own thing."

"I love how important family is here. My parents have always been my rock. Perhaps I need to be around more for them, too."

"Mistletoe has a way of putting things in perspective." Ruby stared at Fran. Wrapped up in her new gear, she was still sexy. Ruby wanted to kiss her again. But the snowman came first.

"You're not wrong." Fran stared right back, then pointed at the quad bikes lined up outside the barn. "What do you use those for?"

"To zip around the fields, and to transport the trees after they're chopped down. And for looking cool to women, of course."

Fran grinned. "Wear a check shirt and I'm surprised you don't have lesbians queueing up. I'd love to have a go some time."

"It can be arranged." Ruby shivered. She could think of ways of heating up.

Fran blew out a frozen breath. "I know this is idyllic, but it's still a little cold. Can we start our snowman?"

Ruby crinkled her forehead. "I need a little more romance from you, city girl."

Fran laughed. "Real life is never quite as romantic as the vision in your head. Like having sex on a beach. Great in theory. In practice, sand in your foof."

Ruby shook her head, trying to get the image of a naked Fran on the beach out of her mind. "Foof? Really?"

"What do you call it?"

Ruby frowned. "Not foof. Is this what comes of having gay dads? No woman to tell you appropriate slang for your vagina?"

Fran walked up so close, Ruby could see the whites of her eyes.

"On the contrary, my dads probably did more research on how to be a mother than any mother alive. To say they were paranoid about it would be an understatement." Fran knitted her eyebrows together. "I have a feeling foof was my Auntie Christine's word. She was around a lot when I was little, playing the female role model."

Ruby licked her lips, never taking her eyes from Fran. "Have you had a lot of sex on the beach?"

"It's a one and done kinda thing, isn't it?"

Ruby leaned in. "I was talking about the drink." She gave Fran a loaded stare. "When you have sex on the beach, how do you like it? Strong and quick? Or slow and savoured?"

Fran looked her right in the eye. "Depends on my mood. But right now? Strong and quick."

A spark of desire ignited inside Ruby, and it was all she could do not to throw Fran down in the snow and kiss her into next week. However, a little like sex on the beach, sex in the snow wasn't advisable. At least the beach had heat. The snow had no saving grace.

"I'll remember that." Ruby tore her eyes from Fran and shook herself, then dropped the small backpack she'd been carrying to the ground. "Shall we make your childhood dreams come true and set about making Steve the Snowman?"

Fran laughed. "Steve? Really?" She stamped her feet. "I was thinking more Shantelle the non-binary Snowperson."

Ruby's laughter crackled in the air. "Shantelle it is."

They packed a large snowball each, then began to roll it, packing more snow around it as they went. Fifteen minutes later, they both had sizable snowballs. Ruby carried on with hers, instructing Fran to roll another. Then she stamped out a patch of snow in between two eight-foot Norwegian spruces, and rolled the largest ball onto it.

"Can you help me lift your first one?"

Fran walked over. Together they lifted the body onto the base, then the head onto that.

Fran breathed in again. "I could happily die in this forest, the smell is incredible."

"Please don't, your dads would not be pleased with me." Ruby patted the tree beside her. "The smell comes from the Norwegian spruce. This is the one to buy if you want the true Christmas feel." She paused. "Are you getting the Christmas feeling here?"

"If I wasn't, I might actually be dead." Fran frowned. "I just thought, though: we didn't bring anything for the face. It's a blank snowperson."

Ruby gave her a *hang-on-a-minute* look, then picked up her backpack. She took out a carrot and handed it to Fran. "Nose."

Ruby then produced two shiny buttons. "Eyes." She grinned. "You can draw the mouth."

Finally, Ruby took out a hat and scarf. "These are our special snowperson items. We've had them since we were kids."

Fran shook her head. "You really have thought of everything."

"I aim to please."

They dressed the snowperson. Fran drew its mouth, then they stood back.

"Not bad," Ruby said. "How do you feel? First snowman since your youth. Your first non-binary snowperson ever."

Fran gave her a beaming smile. "I feel a sense of accomplishment. Which is crazy, because I just rolled some snow. But it's so much better than if I finish a spreadsheet or meet a sales target. That's just something off my to-do list. Something else will replace it, as sure as night follows day." She patted their creation. "Whereas, Shantelle? She's a work of art. We created her from thin air. There's something to be said for that, isn't there?"

"It's what I do every day with music."

Fran held Ruby's gaze. "You make gorgeous music, have I told you that?"

Ruby flushed. If she'd heard those words dropping from Fran's lips a few months ago, she'd have dismissed them as music exec waffle. But now Ruby had got to know Fran, she felt the sincerity behind them. Plus, Ruby had just made a snowman with Fran. She'd kissed her. Right now, the pulsing thought in her brain was that she'd like to do it again soon. But preferably, somewhere warm. They'd already had a snowy kiss. She was ready for something different.

"Thank you," Ruby said. "I'm trying to get better at taking compliments, especially from you."

Fran curled her mouth into a smile. "That's the best you've done yet. Much better than your rebuff in the club months ago."

"I didn't know you then."

"You didn't give me a chance."

Ruby knew she was right. She held out a hand.

Fran took it.

"Let me make it up to you with some hot chocolate. If you ask nicely, I'll lace it with rum." Ruby paused. "I was thinking the barn office? It has heating, a hot chocolate machine and booze. Plus, it's away from all of our families."

Fran gulped. "I like the sound of all those." She dropped her gaze, staring at their joined hands.

Ruby squeezed it tight. "In that case, let's go." She turned her head. "See you tomorrow, Shantelle." Then she pulled Fran towards the barn.

* * *

Ruby ignored the heavy thud of her heart as she flicked on the office lights and shut the door. She switched on the radiators, quickly followed by the Nespresso machine. Then she grabbed a couple of hot chocolate pods from the stash in the drawer beneath, ignoring the slight shake in her hand.

Fran took in the space, before coming to a stop at the wall of Christmas tree photos. "These trees are so pretty." She reached out a hand to touch one. "Are these the photoshoot trees you were talking about?"

Ruby nodded. "Yep. Those are the nine-foot trees. We import them from Denmark or Newcastle when they're three years old, then we grow them for seven to ten years. We used to name them when we were younger, but we stopped after a while because we got upset when we had to say goodbye. It turns out, you can get attached to trees. I said goodbye to one I really loved earlier in the year. Nettie. She was 12."

"She had a great life here. Also, Nettie is a great name. You have good taste."

Ruby raised an eyebrow at Fran. "I'd say I've still got it now." Ruby gulped, then turned her attention back to the drinks. "I'm doing two hot chocolates, unless you prefer a coffee?" She caught Fran's gaze and every hair on Ruby's body stood to attention.

"Hot chocolate would be perfect," Fran replied.

Ruby tried not to focus on the lips that had uttered that.

Focus on the hot chocolate.

Not Fran's lips.

Hot chocolate.

Fran's lips.

Ruby took off her outer layers and made the drinks. Then she grabbed the rum from Dad's desk drawer. "My dad keeps this here so he can pretend he's in one of those old cop shows on TV, where they always kept booze in their desk drawers." Ruby paused, undoing the cap. "Can I tempt you?" She held up the bottle of Brugal.

"Tempt away." Fran took off her hat, gloves and coat, then sat on the sofa. She held out a hand to accept her hot drink as Ruby sat beside her.

Fran took a sip, and a sound escaped her mouth that did nothing for Ruby's heightened senses. "Just what the doctor ordered."

"I'm fully qualified in hot chocolate and rum therapy." Ruby's gaze collided with Fran's, and Ruby's confidence stuttered. She took a sip of her drink to keep her hands and mouth busy.

"Have you brought many women to this office?" Fran's stare was uncertain.

Ruby shook her head. "Just like Friday night, you're the first." She crossed her heart with her hand. "Not many good-looking, available lesbians travel through Mistletoe Farm, believe it or not."

Fran's shoulders relaxed as she laughed. "Okay, I do believe that part."

"As well as the field, this is where I come to escape the family. I love coming home in December, but living with your parents, as we know, can get a bit intense. Especially when you're used to your own space." She tapped the sofa beneath them. "This is even a sofa bed when needed." She pointed towards the door on the opposite wall. "Behind that wall is a shower room with a loo. Plus there's a duvet, sheets and pillows in the cupboard. You could live in this office."

Fran looked up at the massive windows that went from ceiling to waist-height, open to the barn. "It'd be a little like living in a goldfish bowl."

Ruby got up and dropped the blinds. When she turned to Fran, Ruby could tell she was thinking the same thing.

They had privacy now.

Exactly what they'd been craving since they met up this time.

Without a word, Ruby put her drink on the nearest desk, then took Fran's and did the same. When she turned around,

Fran was standing next to her, want flaring in her crystal-blue eyes. "I don't know about you, but I've been dying to kiss you ever since my parents interrupted us."

Ruby's bum hit the desk as Fran closed in on her. Now she was sitting, she and Fran were the same height, their lips level.

"Parental interruptus is a real thing. Let's make it a distant memory." Fran leaned in and pressed her lips to Ruby's. Slow, sensual.

Ruby's heart felt like it catapulted through her chest.

Then Fran gently pulled away.

Ruby caught her breath, and let her eyelids flutter open.

When she did, Fran's blue eyes were staring right at her.

"You asked me earlier if I favoured strong and quick, or slow and savoured." Fran dropped her hand to Ruby's belt buckle.

Ruby closed her eyes. *Holy shit.*

Fran cupped Ruby between her legs and pressed down. "What about you?"

When did Fran's tone get so low?

"When the mood takes you, do you like strong and quick, too?"

Ruby gushed *everywhere*. "Fuck, yes," she replied.

Fran gave her a sultry grin. "That's what I was hoping you'd say." Then she slid her hand around to Ruby's bum cheek, and kissed her like there was no tomorrow.

Ruby didn't care if it was true. At least they had today.

Fran slid her tongue into Ruby's mouth.

Ruby's senses exploded. Her fingers reached around Fran's waist and pulled her close. Ruby's breath tangled in her chest, her whole body shaking with anticipation.

This was no-nonsense Fran. The Fran that got business deals done. The one Ruby had issues with.

However, in this situation, Ruby was all for the take-charge-and-get-things-done Fran.

Especially when the thing getting done was her.

That thought sent Ruby's body into overdrive.

Fran's teeth pulled at Ruby's lips, sucking them into her mouth. Her hands slid up Ruby's front, grasping her breasts through her top. Her strokes were rough, and Ruby wanted to lie back on the desk and give herself fully. Strong and quick was *exactly* her type.

Ruby's breath began to sprint as Fran's fingers tackled her belt buckle, then made short work of the button on her jeans, then her zip. Fran held Ruby's stare as she eased down her jeans and underwear, and Ruby shuffled them that little bit further.

Then she trailed her fingers back up between Ruby's legs, inserting her thigh there, too, pushing Ruby's legs apart.

Fran parted their mouths, then bent her knees, licking her tongue all the way up Ruby's neck to her mouth.

Ruby trembled.

"I can't wait to feel you," Fran whispered in Ruby's ear, just as her fingers connected with Ruby's clit.

Ruby dropped her head backwards and took a huge intake of breath. What was Fran doing to her? The first touch and she was almost on the edge? Really? Ruby closed her eyes and focused. She was not going to come within seconds. She wanted fast, but also, something to remember.

Fran was certainly making sure the final part happened.

Fran brought Ruby's head back up and kissed her with hot

lips. Fran's fingertips worked in circular motions, until Ruby's vision went blurred. She was so wet. *So ready.* Fran's fingers on her were the *best*.

That is, until moments later, when Fran curled them into Ruby, grabbing Ruby's arse cheek to steady her.

The best just got upgraded.

Fran's touch ignited something inside Ruby, and she clutched the desk with her other hand.

As Fran moved into her, tantalisingly slow, she returned to Ruby's lips for a bruising, passionate kiss.

Ruby groaned into Fran's mouth, then spread her legs as far as her jeans would allow. The fire inside Ruby, contained until then, suddenly spiralled out of control. Her body shook some more. Her breath quickened. It was a personal wildfire and there was nothing Ruby could do.

Nothing she wanted to do.

Fran's tongue was all over her neck now as her fingers caused Ruby's heart to boom.

Ruby grasped Fran's shoulders and clenched her teeth. As Fran's rhythm increased, Ruby's brain buzzed, the fire inside burning bright. Ruby's breath came fast, shredding into the air as she struggled to keep up with the pleasure that was rampaging through her body.

But Fran didn't let up. Her kisses were perfection, her hands exquisite, her touch immaculate. It was almost more than Ruby could take.

Almost.

As Fran ramped up her passion, Ruby squeezed her eyes tight shut. When her muscles clenched, she knew she was close.

With one more exquisite stroke, Fran tipped Ruby over the

edge, and she came in a torrent of longing, clinging to Fran. Her body lit up with want as Fran ravished her some more.

A few moments later, Fran stilled, kissing Ruby's neck, her nose, her eyelids. Then those gorgeous, soft lips landed back at Ruby's mouth.

Ruby's eyes sprang open, her breathing still irregular. Not a surprise as Fran's fingers were still deep inside her. Ruby wanted to stay here forever. She took a deep breath and shook her head, staring into Fran's eyes. "I'd say strong and quick wins the day."

Fran gave her a smile, before withdrawing. Then she kissed Ruby's lips once more. "I'm in total agreement," she whispered.

Ruby turned up her smile. She was still coming down from her orgasmic high. Still floating on air. All because of Fran. "Wow. You didn't tell me you were such a top."

Fran's laughter lit the air as her gaze dipped and her cheeks pinked. "I'm not, but I have my moments." Now it was over, she was almost shy.

Ruby kissed her again. "Feel free to have those moments whenever they take you. To say you were hot is an understatement."

Fran responded with the most perfect smile in the world.

Pleasure tiptoed up Ruby's spine. Everything Fran did from now on was going to be the best thing ever. Ruby was hers, hook, line and sinker.

"What do you want to do now?" Fran eyed Ruby with a hooded stare.

Ruby gave her one right back. "Let's start by pulling out the sofa bed and getting you out of your clothes."

Chapter 21

A gigantic spider was chasing Fran. She went to scream, but nothing came out. She shuddered, then her eyelids sprang open. She blinked, heart racing. Her gaze landed on light grey blinds, then a desk. No spider, but where the hell was she?

Then she remembered. They were in the barn office, after a night of incredible sex. She rubbed her right eye with her hand, then tried to breathe without waking Ruby. Her mouth was open slightly, her head tilted on the pillow, her autumnal-coloured hair splayed down her skin.

Fran had broken her rules, hadn't she? She'd slept with a singer. She took a breath. She'd do it again, too. Perhaps multiple times. Could she be considering a relationship with a singer? She was a glutton for punishment, wasn't she?

However, Ruby was not on her books, as Delilah had been. Plus, she was way more sorted than Delilah. Keeping work and personal life separate was a lesson Fran had learned the hard way. Maybe it was fortunate that Ruby had turned her down all those months ago. She believed in fate. Everything happened for a reason.

A phone vibrated nearby. As slowly as she could, Fran leaned over the side of the sofa bed and reached down to her clothes. She had five messages from Damian: that was never good news. They were mostly about Fast Forward. The social media trolling had stepped up a gear. Tenny, in particular, was being targeted because she wasn't as skinny as the rest of the group.

Fuck this shit. When were people going to get over the fact that pop stars could be whatever they wanted to be, and not purely stick-thin?

But it was the modern world they lived in. Fran would happily go back to the pre-social media days. However, it wasn't going to happen this week, and Fast Forward needed more help than could be provided on the end of a phone.

Fran moved to get out of bed to give Damian a call. It was only 7.30am, but he was already up and working. However, her progress was stopped by a hand grabbing her waist.

Fran turned, then smiled at a sleepy Ruby. Damn, she was gorgeous. Fran dropped her phone back onto her clothes and gave Ruby her full attention. Damian could wait.

"Good morning to you." She settled next to Ruby, kissing her lips. Ruby even tasted good in the morning.

"Hey," Ruby replied, her voice sketchy. "I can't quite believe we're waking in my dad's office after our first date. Hardly glamorous, is it?"

"Yesterday was a date?"

Ruby grinned. "Kinda. Then you turned it into an ambush with your silky sex ways."

Fran threw her head back and laughed. "I think you gave as good as you got."

"I have my own skills."

"I'm well aware." Fran kissed Ruby's lips. The temptation

to fuck her again was strong, but Fran had business to attend to. Even though she hated that, and knew Ruby would, too.

"Where were you sneaking off to, by the way?"

Fran sighed, then sat up. "I've got good news and bad news. The bad news is I've had some urgent messages, and I need to head back to London today. Fast Forward and Damian need me." She glanced at Ruby. "But it's a wrench leaving you."

Ruby furrowed her brow. "Are you going to miss Saturday's gig?"

Fran shook her head briskly. "No, I'll get back for that." At least, she hoped she would if everything went well. But Ruby didn't need to hear that. Fran took Ruby's hand in hers. "I wouldn't miss you being heckled by Audrey for the world."

Ruby laughed. "Don't even joke." She pulled the duvet up her body as she shivered.

Fran jumped up and put her pants back on, followed by her T-shirt. Then she sat back on the bed. With her naked shoulders and tussled hair, Ruby looked every bit the sex goddess. "Don't you want to know the good news?"

"I'm still reeling from the fact you're going to fuck me and leave me."

Fran's eyes widened. Shit, was that really what Ruby thought?

But then the edges of Ruby's mouth softened. She got onto her hands and knees and crawled to Fran for a kiss. "That was a joke, by the way."

Fran gulped. "I can never be sure. I know you think I'm all business first."

Ruby shook her head. "Not true. I understand you've got

work to do. I just think you need to make more time for family and friends. And potential new love interests." She kissed her again.

A naked Ruby kneeling in front of Fran was somewhat distracting. "I totally agree with that." Fran kissed Ruby's breasts. "Don't you want to know the good news?"

"Apart from you kissing my breasts? Hit me."

Fran brought her head back level with Ruby. "Damian has got another band on-board to support you on Saturday. They're called Troubadour, and they're an up-and-coming folk/pop band who love Christmas and are happy to do it for the exposure. Also, they want to visit a Christmas tree farm." Fran held out her hands and gave Ruby a wide grin. "So only four of the five messages said 'get the fuck back to London'."

"That is good news." Ruby ran a hand through her hair. "Will you still be able to do all the designs for the gig?"

"Absolutely." Fran picked up Ruby's hand again. "But can I ask a favour? Can you call in on my parents, just check they're okay? I know they're big boys, but they both looked so frail at times this week."

Ruby squeezed her hand. "Of course. Mum's been doing it anyway since the accident, but I'll check on them, too. They're part of the village now. We look out for each other."

"I know. Thank you." Fran licked her lips, before holding up her phone. "I really need to call Damian. Do you mind if I do it here?"

Ruby shook her head. "Go ahead. I'll pack up the bed and get dressed." Ruby was true to her word, getting up right away, avoiding any more eye contact.

Yes, it was shit timing, but there was nothing Fran could

do about it. She hoped Ruby wasn't pissed off with her. She would do everything in her power to get back for Ruby's big gig, but she loved her job, too. No matter how much she'd taken to Mistletoe, London was where her life was. It was where Ruby's life was, too. How would they cope outside the Mistletoe bubble?

Only time would tell.

Chapter 22

Damian was already at the label's office when Fran arrived on Wednesday. The office was a hub of activity. The fourth quarter madness was in full swing and most of the 50 staff were at their desks. Phones rang, music blared and tinsel hung from most monitors. A Christmas tree, decorated with silver and red tinsel, with fake snow tinting its branches stood in a corner. Fran stared at it. Was it from Mistletoe Christmas Tree Farm? Probably not, but wherever it was from, somebody had cared for it. Planted it, pruned it, tended to it, perhaps even named it. She smiled as she thought about a teenage Ruby naming Nettie. Ruby put her all into whatever she was doing: singing or selling Christmas trees. Fran did the same with her work. They had far more in common than either of them first thought.

Fran waved at a couple of colleagues as she sat, dumping her bag on the empty chair beside her. It was already weird being back here, away from Mistletoe. Everything in London was so loud, especially in this office where DJ wars broke out every day. The air was thicker. The expectation heavy. In Mistletoe, only the moment counted. Of late, all of Fran's moments in Mistletoe had been glorious. One particular night stood out as five-star rated.

Damian got up from his desk opposite to give her a hug. "Thanks for coming back." He squeezed her tight. "Sorry to make you, but Tenny's not coping. To be honest, she needs more than me. Maybe more than *you*. Could we get another singer to have a chat with her? She'll really listen to them. When I talk, she tends to glaze over. The social media stuff isn't helping, but it's more she needs to speak to someone who's been there and done it."

Fran pursed her lips. Maybe that was what Ruby needed, too, to get over her big-stage fright. Fran was surrounded by singers who hated the big stage right now. "Let me think about it and have a word with Jules." Jules was Fran's boss and the label co-founder. She dealt with issues far better than her partner, Niall, who tended to flip out and create chaos. Plus, Jules would know who might be available this week.

"By the way, I love your outfit. Those colours really suit you." Damian pointed a finger at her. "You look alive."

Fran glanced down at her mustard top and teal-blue trousers. "Thanks." She bit down a smile. "How are the numbers looking, if we gloss over Tenny's possible breakdown?"

Damian nodded, walking back behind his desk. "Good. Fast Forward are holding their own with Skinny YouTube Star and Cupboard Boy – in sales and streams. Top three at least judging on the Monday figures, and that's better than we hoped."

Fran sat, drumming her fingers on her desk. "Good. They've just got to get through a barrage of press on Friday, a gig Friday night, and a TV appearance on Saturday." She looked up at Damian, keenly aware of her clashing schedules. "They're not being interviewed on Saturday as well, are they?"

Damian shook his head. "Nope. Just a single performance, nothing else."

"Okay." Fran paused. "When are they due in?"

"Midday for rehearsals and pep talks."

Fran blew out a raspberry in contemplation. It was always tricky with new artists. She remembered Delilah being a nervous wreck. However, Delilah always had steel inside her. Even when she was getting flack in the press and getting trolled on social media, she carried on regardless. The press had linked Delilah to a new man every week, which annoyed the heck out of her. It had annoyed Fran, too.

She clicked on her email and swatted a few away. Only 167 to go. Email was the curse of her life. Somebody a few desks away turned a song up and got moaned at for doing so. They turned it down right away.

Then a hush settled over the office.

Somebody clearing their throat made Fran look up.

The hairs on the back of Fran's neck prickled when she saw who it was. Delilah. With her long, blond hair and slender frame, she looked every inch the pop star. She'd been at least a stone heavier when she'd started, but the trolls and the cameras took their toll.

Fran didn't have to look around to know the whole office was gawping. It didn't matter how many times her workmates met pop stars, their fame always rolled out before them and tripped people up. Today was no exception.

Only Fran knew the look on Delilah's face was hesitant. Everybody else just saw the chart-topper.

Fran moved her bag and motioned for Delilah to sit.

Delilah glanced around the office, then did so.

"Everybody will get over you being here in a minute, just sit still like a normal person."

Delilah rolled her eyes. "I am a normal person."

Fran spluttered. "You were never normal."

Fran hadn't seen Delilah for ages, and she'd wondered how it would be when she did. So far, Fran's heart-rate was steady, her mind calm. It was an improvement on all the times Delilah had made every muscle in her body tense – not in a good way. Perhaps having no time to worry about seeing her was one reason. Plus, Fran had moved on. Having someone else meant Fran had let go of the past a little more. Now, seeing Delilah didn't cause her to panic. It was almost normal.

"What are you doing here? I thought you were on tour?"

"We built in a festive break, so I'm done for the year until we start the European leg on December 29th. I had a meeting with my producer here this morning, so I thought I'd stop by and say hi to you."

Damian walked over and gave Delilah a hug. They'd always got on when she and Fran were together. "Can I get you both a coffee?"

Fran could have kissed him. Damian always did have superb tact. "Yes, please," she replied. Then Fran ushered Delilah over to the sofa in the corner of the office.

Delilah sat beside her, kicking her legs out. Unlike Ruby, Delilah's legs were short. They'd sat next to each other like this a thousand times when they were together. However, now Delilah didn't need to police her every action around Fran, she seemed more relaxed. Which was more than a little sad.

"How's the tour going?"

"Really well. The crowds are so responsive, I'm blown away. It's everything I wanted, and it's all down to you."

Fran raised an eyebrow. "It might have something to do with you, too."

"You know what I mean. You signed me."

Fran snagged her ex's gaze. "Those start-up days were heady, weren't they? Playing those smaller clubs all around London. Look at you now, playing major venues."

Delilah nodded. "It's amazing. Also fucking exhausting. I'll be glad to just chill at my flat for a few days and do nothing." She paused. "Maybe you'd like to catch up over dinner one night?"

Fran's bum cheeks clenched. Dinner with Delilah was not a small thing. Paparazzi followed her everywhere. There would be photographs, and she knew how it would look to Ruby. They were still so new. Then again, it would be lovely to catch up. She'd just have to warn Ruby first.

"I'd love to," Fran said. "Gretchen not around?" Gretchen was the singer Delilah was dating, also still in the closet.

Delilah shook her head. "She's in Canada. Staying there for Christmas, catching up with her folks. She's coming back for New Year." Delilah sighed. "The most trying time of the year is on us again."

"No change with your parents?"

Delilah shook her head. "About as likely as a meteor strike. But you'll be impressed." She took a deep breath. "I've decided I'm going to do the deed this year and come out to them. My tour's wrapped until after Christmas, so my plan is to drive to their place and tell them."

"Over Christmas dinner?" Fran was horrified. "Maybe not the best time."

"Christmas Eve. Don't worry, I have a back-up plan. If they throw me out — highly likely — I'm going to my cousin's. But in the unlikely event they want me to stay, I will. I've done too much avoiding over the past few years, and it's causing me anxiety. My therapist and I decided to tackle it head-on."

"Therapist?" Fran was amazed. Delilah had resisted all help when they'd been together.

"Yep. I might not have acted on anything you said, but I *was* listening. Everything you said was right. It's time to be brave." Delilah fiddled with her hair. "How are your dads?"

"They're good. They've moved to a small village called Mistletoe. It's like living in a Christmas card."

Delilah spluttered. "How are you feeling about that? Ms 'Christmas is just an overblown roast dinner'?"

"I said that in the village bar. It didn't go down well."

"I can imagine." Delilah looked her up and down. "What about you? The label going well?"

Fran nodded. "It is. Fast Forward are breaking out in style. They could be bigger than you."

Delilah smiled. "I hope they are. Girl power and all that." She clenched her fist and pumped it up. "Talking of girls, how are things in that department. Are you seeing anyone?"

Fran bit her lip, trying to damp down her emotions. Was she? On their first unofficial date, they'd shagged in Ruby's parents' office. It was hardly what she'd call a relationship just yet. "Kind of. Sort of."

Delilah's clenched fist stayed that way as she nodded.

Fran threw up her hands. "I don't know. We slept together

on Monday, and then I had to rush back because Fast Forward are having a meltdown. I should have been here anyway, so that was my fault. But this woman is… She's…" Fran paused. What was she? So many things. Sexy. Smart. Gorgeous. Infuriating. But they probably weren't things Fran should be telling Delilah of all people. "I don't know what she is."

"It sounds like she's got you in a spin."

"Something like that." Fran held up her hands. "But now I'm back dealing with pop stars, like normal."

Delilah sat up. "Why are Fast Forward having a meltdown? I love their Christmas single."

Fran gave Delilah a tight smile. "They're new on the music scene. They're getting a whole lot of flack on social media because they're women. Remember what it was like being new to the business and having a vagina?"

Delilah raised both eyebrows. "I do, and I'm still dealing with it every day. They need to get off social media and ignore it, but it's tough at the start. I wish someone had told me in no uncertain terms."

"Maybe you could be that person." A light bulb flickered in Fran's brain. "In fact, they're coming in today and it's the lead singer, Tenny, who's having the biggest jitters. Would you stick around and talk to her? Damian's tried, but coming from you, it would mean so much more."

Delilah checked her phone. "Sure. I'm having lunch with Jules and Niall, but after that?"

"That would be brilliant. Thank you."

Delilah put a hand on Fran's leg. "Anything for you."

Right at that moment, Damian came back with the coffees. He put them on the table in front of them, then ran away.

Fran put a hand to her forehead. "Perfect. Now Damian thinks we're back on."

"Sorry." Delilah put her hands in the air like she was under arrest. "I'll keep my hands to myself from now on."

Fran shook her head. "It's fine." She grabbed the coffees and gave one to Delilah.

Delilah peeked under the lid. "Damn that boy. He remembered no milk."

"He's good. It's why I keep him on."

Delilah leaned back on the sofa and eyed Fran. "Who's this woman you might be having a thing with?" Something flickered across her face, but Fran couldn't quite place it. Regret? If it was, she was a little late.

Fran put her head back, before tilting it towards Delilah. "Ruby O'Connell. Her parents own a Christmas tree farm in Mistletoe, and my dads bought the cottage next door. And yes, I know that sounds like the plot of a Hallmark Christmas movie. She lives in London usually, but she's back there helping out her parents for Christmas." Fran paused. "She's also a shit-hot folk singer who I tried to sign, and she turned me down."

"Ouch," Delilah replied. "Before or after you slept with her?"

Fran laughed. "Way before. Seven months ago. Her living in Mistletoe was a head-fuck at first, but we're over our differences now." Fran got up and grabbed her phone from her desk, ignoring the interested looks from her colleagues.

"Have you heard of her?" Fran sat back down.

Delilah wrinkled her forehead. "I don't think so. I've been too busy touring to listen to any new music."

Fran called up Ruby's new song on her phone. "Her new single is incredible." She hit play.

Delilah listened, rapt.

When Fran clicked stop, Delilah nodded her head approvingly. "That song is dynamite." She paused, glancing at Fran. "You think this could go somewhere? Not the music, but with her?"

Fran swallowed down a breath. "I think it could. It's early days, but signs are promising."

"I'm pleased for you. You deserve love from someone better than me." She put up her hand. "And before you tell me I wasn't that bad—"

"I wasn't going to," Fran replied.

Delilah mimed a dagger to her heart. "Wow, you're harsh. But I know I put you through it, so I deserve it. I'm just pleased you've found someone who wants the same thing you do. We were wrong time, wrong place."

Fran nodded. "We were."

"But we can still be friends, right?"

Fran eyed her, then nodded. Perhaps enough time had passed and they really could be. Like proper grown-ups. "I guess we can."

"Fabulous." Delilah sat forward and sipped her coffee. "That single is amazing, by the way. It's still going around in my head." She got her phone from her bag, called up Ruby on Spotify and hit follow. "She's still not signed? Doing this on her own?"

"She is. Adamant. She's been burned by a label before. I'm leaving it for now, but I'd love to see her hit the big time."

Delilah shrugged. "You can't force her. People have got to

come to it in their own time. A bit like coming out and being yourself." She eyed Fran. "But I agree. She could be big."

It was good to hear confirmation of that from Delilah. It made a difference.

"Anyway, as my friend, how about dinner tonight?" Delilah asked.

Fran took a deep breath, then nodded. "You're on."

Chapter 23

Scott leaned a Christmas tree against Ruby's till point, then gave his sister a wink. At seven feet, the tree was 12 inches taller than him. Scott's dark hair was hidden under his black bobble hat, his cheeks red from the cold.

"The Varnish family tree. They should be around here somewhere?" Scott's gaze raked the barn. It stopped at an excited young boy running in their direction. "And there's the smallest. I gave him a ride on the quad bike earlier. I'm now his best friend forever."

As if backing up that claim, the young boy ran up to Scott and gave him a super-sized grin. "Hey, Scott!"

"Hey, Aaron." Scott stood back. "Here's your tree. Ready to take it home?"

Aaron's eyes were wide as he nodded, looking at the tree like it was the best thing he'd ever seen.

Ruby couldn't help but smile as his parents appeared, along with an older sister who was far too cool for Christmas. This family were like so many who came to Mistletoe Farm. Choosing their tree signalled the official start of their festive season. Mistletoe Farm was all about making memories, and Ruby was proud to be a part of it.

"I'll leave you in the very capable hands of my sister, Ruby, to wrap it for you." Scott walked away.

Mrs Varnish peered at Ruby. "Are you doing the gig on Saturday?"

Heat worked its way to Ruby's cheeks. "That's me."

The woman waggled a finger between herself and her husband. "We're coming, and we can't wait! We used to go to loads of gigs before we had kids. I've been listening to your stuff and you're amazing. I can't believe you're serving us a Christmas tree."

Ruby netted the tree with a smile, clambering over her embarrassment. "I hope you're happy with the tree and the concert."

"We can't wait. We love it here. Any excuse to come back."

It seemed like the gig was doing its job.

When the family left, Ruby glanced at her phone. No message from Fran yet today.

Fran had sent one when she got back to London yesterday, and it had left Ruby in no doubt that Fran had enjoyed Monday night just as much as she had. However, they were still separated by distance this week, and it was gnawing at Ruby. She had to remember she lived in London usually, and after Christmas, she and Fran would both be there together.

If they were an item by then. Ruby ran her fingers over the top of her woollen hat. She wanted her and Fran to work more than she'd care to admit. What's more, if Ruby had made a different decision, she could have been in London with Fran right now.

Somehow, Mistletoe had sucked her back in. But this year was different. She was happy to be helping out and spending time with her family. But something had shifted inside her. Was it time for a change? Could this be the last year she'd be netting Christmas trees? Her dad's words had got through. Fran's words had got through. Even the words from her last customer, who couldn't believe she was serving her. Ruby shouldn't be here. She should be in London with Fran. In London, working on her career.

That thought pulled her up short. Had Fran made that much of an impact on Ruby?

Ruby needed to get out of her comfort zone. But even as she thought that, doubts began to surface. Playing here was one thing. Playing to big crowds elsewhere was quite another. She made enough money doing what she did. It wasn't a lavish life, but she got by. Not every artist had to be a big star, did they?

Damn it, she confused herself. No wonder she'd been stalling, unable to move forward.

Fran's words rang in Ruby's ears. '*Putting your career on hold for a month every year is something most people wouldn't do.*' Was she self-sabotaging without realising it? Ruby ground her teeth together. Not only was Fran sexy. She was also shining a light on all the areas Ruby had been steadfastly trying to ignore.

Her phone ringing broke Ruby's train of thought. She glanced at the screen. It was Fran. She looked around the barn. Her mum was to her right, chatting with a customer. "Mum?"

Mary turned.

"Can you cover the till point for five minutes?" She held up her phone. "I just need to take this call."

Mary nodded. "No problem."

Ruby scooted over to the barn office, which did nothing to dispel memories of just how sexy Fran was. She still very vividly recalled two nights earlier, when Fran fucked her against the desk she was now leaning on. She could easily have sat on the sofa, or even in the office chair. But somehow, perching on this desk, legs spread, was her new favourite position.

"Hello to you," Ruby said. "Guess where I am?"

"The Bahamas, sipping a tropical cocktail?"

"Close. I'm leaning against a certain desk in the office barn."

Fran paused for a few seconds.

Ruby was pretty sure she heard her smile.

"Are your legs spread?"

"Don't." Ruby closed her eyes, feeling herself getting wet.

"It's my favourite desk in the whole world."

"That makes two of us." Ruby rolled her shoulders to stop herself dropping too deep into the memory. She was working, and this time, the blinds were wide open. She shook herself.

"Anyway, this is a lovely surprise. How's it going with your indie girl band?"

"A little better. They're here now, and Delilah is having a chat with them, which should hopefully go a long way to calming them down. If nothing else, they'll have to process being starstruck, so it'll take their attention away from their issues."

Ruby's jaw tightened. "Delilah's there? Did you know she was coming?" She tried really hard to stop those words coming out as possessive. She wasn't sure she succeeded.

"I didn't, but she's got a gap in her tour, so she came by the label. She's helping out with Fast Forward, and we've cleared the air." Fran paused, clicking her tongue on the roof of her mouth. "Just so you know, I'm having dinner with her later. Purely as friends. We've both moved on, and we've both met new people. That's you, by the way."

Ruby's muscles tightened, then relaxed a little. She wasn't sure which part of the previous sentence to focus on. The positive or the negative. "That's good to hear. Nobody wants to have incredible sex one night, and then hear that person is going out for dinner with their ex two nights later."

"I know," Fran replied. "But I promise, this is purely to catch up. Delilah and I are going to cross paths. We work for the same label. So just in case anything gets in the paper or appears online, remember that. I can't wait to come back to Mistletoe and see you again."

Ruby had no hold over Fran. They'd shagged once. They weren't going out. But Delilah was a megastar, and Ruby was not.

However, Fran's head wasn't turned by fame.

Ruby knew that.

She just had to keep reminding herself.

"The feeling's mutual." Ruby gripped the desk. The edge was now sticking into her leg. It wasn't quite as soft and sensual as it had been.

"How's the gig shaping up? I mailed Scott the designs, so hopefully he's getting the Facebook ads to work locally."

Ruby nodded. "He did, and he's having success. I walked him through the basics and he was awake half the night setting it up. He might become my social media manager after this."

"After your Mistletoe gig when everyone falls in love with you and your sales take off, you should definitely put him to work."

Ruby smiled. "There's only going to be a couple of hundred people. I'm not sure it's going to change my life."

"You never know who's going to be in the crowd. It could be someone big. It's what I tell all my artists. I've seen bands play to five people, but one of those worked for a major label and that was the gig that changed their lives."

"I know. But the preparation's going well. I practised some more today, and we've got posters, flyers, the lot." Ruby dug the nail of her middle finger into the pad of her thumb. "You are going to make it back for Saturday, aren't you? It would feel kinda hollow without you here."

Fran didn't answer right away. "Fast Forward have got a big day on Friday with press and a gig, then a TV appearance at the weekend. I shouldn't need to be here after Friday, and that's my plan. I'm going to do everything in my power to be at your gig."

It was as good as Ruby could hope for. She desperately wanted Fran to be there. Her world might screech to a halt if she wasn't. "Make sure your power is super-charged." Ruby pushed herself off the desk, trying to stay upbeat. "What about Troubadour? When are they getting here?"

Fran slipped back into professional mode. "They're driving down on Friday with all their gear. They're staying at my parents' house, which is all sorts of weird. I'm normally very strict with my boundaries between work and home, but I'm bending them like crazy of late. I'm calling it the Mistletoe effect. Or maybe the Ruby O'Connell effect. I can't quite decide."

That perked Ruby up. She couldn't help but grin as she swapped the phone from one ear to the other. "My support band are staying with your parents? That's brilliant. Also, really fantastic of them. I'll tell them thanks when I see them. I called in on them this lunchtime, by the way. Your Dad was baking again and the house smelt delicious. Your Pop was watching a Christmas movie and weeping, although he denied it, telling me he just had something in his eye. I don't think you need to worry."

"I'm looking forward to baked goods at the weekend," Fran replied. "I just want you to know, Saturday is a priority, okay? It's just, the label have been so helpful with your gig, I want to help them out with Fast Forward."

Ruby winced: it would sting more than she could let on if Fran didn't make it. "I understand. Anyway, I better get back. I left Mum on my till."

"I gotta run, too. Delilah's just come back in the office after speaking to the band. Give my love to everyone and I can't wait to see you at the weekend."

Ruby pocketed her phone, then stared into space, before dropping onto the sofa. She'd known what she was getting into with Fran. She had a big job that she cared about, and it had always been in London. That hadn't changed. Plus, someone who cared about their job was a good quality in a person. However, if Fran didn't make it back, Ruby couldn't deny she'd be gutted. What's more, since this had been Fran's idea in the first place, Ruby would also be a little hurt and disappointed. She wanted to sing for the farm, but she also wanted to do it for Fran. For them. It mattered.

Why would Fran say she could make it, help Ruby to organise it, and then not turn up? It wouldn't make any sense. If that happened, it would tell Ruby that Fran was still entrenched in the corporate world, putting her job first: above friends and family.

Ruby blew out a breath. She was catastrophising. Whatever happened, this gig was going ahead. With luck, Fran would be there. She'd promised to do everything she could to do so.

Fran hadn't bailed on her yet.

Ruby should give her a chance.

Even if she was meeting up with her ex for dinner.

Chapter 24

Fran stood in front of a poster of Fast Forward. In it, their posture was loose and their confidence shone. What's more, every performance they'd done, they'd smashed it. Getting them to believe they were doing a great job was the trick. Fran tapped her phone to get the latest charts. They were still number three. They were never going to beat Skinny YouTube Boy and his novelty song about wheelbarrows, but Cupboard Boy was there for the taking.

Fran wanted to do it for young women everywhere. To show them they could compete with the boys and achieve their dreams. From being somewhat dismissive of the group at first, Fran was now willing them to succeed. Plus, she'd never had a hand in a Christmas hit. That would be a novel achievement.

A loud cheer from the other team across the office caught her attention. They were unwrapping their Secret Santa gifts. A bottle of wine was held aloft, followed by some pink, fur-covered handcuffs, and a tin of biscuits. Quite the combo. Fran pondered the order of use. Post-handcuff biscuits or post-handcuff wine? She'd plump for both.

The biscuits took Fran right back to Ruby. To their ill-fated car journey, the start of the thaw in their relationship. It was only just over two weeks ago, but it seemed like a lifetime. That contraband biscuit had tasted delicious, one of the few things Fran ate that day. But it wasn't as delicious as what had happened since. Getting to know Ruby and then sleeping with her on Monday. Today was Thursday. Fran could just picture Ruby selling trees in the barn, a blur of people and activity.

Did she have any more messages from Ruby? Nothing since last night, when Ruby had messaged saying Eric wasn't well and they'd had to postpone their rehearsal until today. Ruby was fretting that she wasn't going to be as prepared for Saturday as she should be.

Fran wasn't worried: she'd seen Ruby perform. Ruby had the pedigree, the experience, and Mistletoe was the perfect stepping stone. Fran was sure once Ruby took the leap, she wouldn't stop there. Ruby was stronger than she gave herself credit for. Fran hoped the same could be said for Fast Forward in the months and years to come.

She sat and dialled home. It was a daily practice since leaving Mistletoe, one that thrilled and bemused her parents. "We're only in our 60s, not heading towards death anytime soon," Dad had told her.

"Hello, daughter dear." Pop breathed out and groaned, which told Fran he'd hobbled to a chair for her call.

"How's your leg?"

"Still attached," he replied.

"I hope you're sitting down when you're in your studio." When he was fit, Pop loved to stride about while creating.

"For the most part. Don't worry, your Dad makes sure of that. How are things going with your girl group?"

"Pretty good, I hope. They might even make number one."

"That would be incredible," Pop replied. "Ruby was here this morning, checking on us. She's dropping in her chicken and pasta bake later. She said to ask you for the secret ingredients that make it delicious. Do you know them?"

A warmth washed through Fran at how thoughtful Ruby was. "Parmesan and cream. Gird your loins and don't take your cholesterol level the next day."

"My mouth's watering already." Pop paused. "By the way, is everything okay with you two?"

Fran sat up. "I think so. I hope so. Why?" The hairs on her arm stood to attention.

"Because I saw some photos of you and Delilah online today and Ruby looked a little glum when she came around at lunchtime. I didn't say anything, but if I were her, I'd be put out."

Fran winced. She hadn't seen the photos. Even though they'd gone to a small, back-street bistro, it was always a risk they ran. "Shit. I did warn her I was going out with Delilah, but I'll drop her a message. We just went out for dinner to catch up. But I promise I was home by ten."

"It's not me you need to tell. A little reassurance never hurt anyone." Pop said something off the phone to Dad, then came back. "Are you still going to make it on Saturday? That would put a smile on Ruby's face, and onto ours. We're used to having you around. It feels wrong you're not here."

That made Fran smile, too. "Unless something goes drastically wrong, I'll be there. But I don't want to commit totally and make promises I can't keep."

Dad was quiet for a few moments before he replied. "She was quizzing us earlier on whether we thought you'd make it, and obviously we were non-committal. We know your work always comes first."

Ouch. That one stung, even though Fran deserved it. She'd not turned up for her parents too many times. She should change that pattern and commit. Starting now.

"I know this is important and I'll be there."

"It is. Not just for Ruby. For the village. But don't make promises you can't keep."

Fran didn't even live in Mistletoe, but she was already connected. "I'm not. By hook or by crook, I'll be there. Don't overdo it and I'll see you at the weekend."

Fran clicked off the call, then put Delilah's name into Google. Sure enough, when she clicked on the images tab, the first ones to pop up were from last night, with Delilah walking beside Fran. Delilah was turning her head and laughing. Fran was referred to as a 'friend'. She winced. Why couldn't Delilah have been frowning? Looking like she wasn't having a good time? At least there was no physical contact. Mainly because there hadn't been. But Fran saw how it might look from Ruby's side.

She opened up Ruby's message again. She needed to reply. Should she bring up the photos and Delilah? Ruby was busy, she might not have seen the photos. Fran hadn't. She decided to ignore it and focus on what was more important.

'I'm sure you're going to kill it on Saturday. Fast Forward could use a little of your stage magic. I can't wait to see you then. Xxx'

Fran stared at the message for a good few minutes before hitting send. She hoped Ruby knew the effect she was having on her. Ruby wasn't just another girl, or just another singer.

Ruby could be huge professionally. But also, *they* could have something huge, too. Fran was going to make it back for the gig, whatever. Her and Ruby's future depended on it.

Even though she'd have to get the train and it wouldn't stop bloody snowing.

Chapter 25

"Let's go again. From the top?" Ruby clutched the mic and sighed deeply. This evening wasn't going to plan so far, and it was doing nothing for her nerves for Saturday. She glanced around the empty bar. It was Thursday, but they were opening an hour late so they had time to rehearse. Ruby had no doubt Norman was outside in his Morris Minor, frowning.

"Do you want to take five?" Eric rested his right elbow on the top of his electric-acoustic guitar, currently hanging from the well-worn brown leather strap around his neck. Eric was a seasoned performer and had been in many bands. This gig wasn't fazing him one bit.

Ruby shook her head. "No, I have to get this right. I can't believe I keep fucking up the words to 'Fairytale Of New York'. It's a Christmas standard, for fuck's sake."

Eric furrowed his brow. "You're very sweary today and you're making me a little nervous."

Perhaps the tendrils of doubt from yesterday's call with Fran were beginning to seep through. It hadn't helped seeing photos of Delilah and Fran together today. Ruby's mum had helpfully pointed them out to Ruby over lunch. Mum had no idea of Fran and Delilah's history. Or what their present might be. Ruby, however, was fully aware. Fran had sent a vague text earlier telling her she'd be great on Saturday, but was she even coming? What if Delilah wanted to go to dinner again, and Fran chose her?

Ruby blew out a long breath. She'd tried to conjure up the feelings from Monday night, but they seemed far away. The more Ruby thought about her current situation, the glummer she got. It certainly wasn't helping the rehearsal.

"I'm sorry, I don't mean to be snappy." She gave Eric a half-smile. Ruby couldn't quite form a full one. "Ready?"

Eric gave her a less-than-certain nod, and began playing the intro to the song.

Ruby gathered up her strength and began to sing. She got through the first verse, then the chorus, then stumbled over the second verse again. Just like she had done the last three times they'd tried it. Her nerves were shredded. How could she not remember the words? And if she couldn't remember the words to this song, what about all the others? What if it wasn't just the Christmas songs, but also her own? She'd seen singers hit the stage with lyric sheets on music stands before, and suddenly, she understood.

Or perhaps it was early onset dementia.

Either way, she was screwed.

She let out a yelp of frustration, then stamped her foot. "Sorry, maybe I do need a break." Ruby put her mic down on one of the bar tables and walked over to the corner table normally occupied by Norman. She slumped back, splaying her long legs in front of her.

The door between the shop and the bar swung open. Both Ruby and Eric looked up.

Victoria swept in, giving them both a wide smile. When she saw their faces, she stopped mid-grin and put a hand up.

"What's going on? I swear I just heard the opening bars to 'Fairytale Of New York' a few minutes ago. I was expecting high fives and smiling faces. Instead, I walk in to Ruby slumped in a corner, and my husband fiddling with his capo. Not a euphemism."

Ruby threw up her hands, then rubbed her palms up and down her face. She needed to put thoughts of Fran aside. She and Eric needed this time to rehearse. If the past hour had taught her anything, it was that.

"Everything's fine." Ruby sat upright. "I keep forgetting the words to all the Christmas standards. The gig is in two days. The whole fucking town is coming to see me and I can't sing a song without buggering it up. It's just peachy."

Victoria walked over to Ruby, sat beside her and rubbed her thigh. "You've forgotten words before. You'll be fine on the night. If you're worried, take lyric sheets on with you and tape them to the floor. It's always good to have back-up."

Ruby sighed. "That's not a bad idea."

"No need to sound so surprised." She stared at Ruby. "Plus, you can't forget the words to 'Fairytale Of New York'. It's like forgetting the words to 'Last Christmas'. You are doing 'Last Christmas', aren't you?"

"Of course."

"Good." Victoria squeezed Ruby's knee. "Are you okay otherwise? Everything good in Ruby Town?"

Ruby ducked her head. "Fine." When she looked up, Victoria was studying her intently.

"What?"

"This is about a girl, isn't it? Mum said you crawled in early on Tuesday after spending the night out. I can only assume it was with Fran?"

Ruby's cheeks flared.

"What happened?"

Ruby slumped again. "It's fine. I mean, it's not, but it is."

"You're not making much sense." Victoria paused. "Did you sleep with her?"

Ruby hesitated, but knew Victoria would see through the lie.

She nodded.

"I knew it!" She glanced at Eric. "What did I tell you?"

Eric rolled his eyes.

"And what was it like?"

Ruby gave her sister a stern look. "I'm not telling you that!" Ruby glanced at Eric.

Victoria slapped Ruby's leg. "Eric and I have no secrets. I'll only fill him in later, so he might as well hear it now."

Ruby snorted, then relented. "It was great. But now she's back in London and she might not be able to make it on Saturday because of her work."

Ruby wasn't going to mention Delilah.

Victoria made a sad face.

"Plus, she was out for dinner last night with her ex, which isn't ideal."

Victoria frowned. "I thought she was out last night with Delilah. At least, that's what I saw in the papers today."

Ruby watched as realisation dawned.

"Her ex is *Delilah*?" Victoria blinked rapidly.

Ruby had vowed not to say anything, but it just slipped

out and then Victoria filled in the blanks. Ruby jumped up, waving her arms in a 'cut!' motion. "Forget I said that last bit. Forget I said *anything*. Delilah isn't out, and this *can't* get out. I promised Fran." Horror thoughts ran through Ruby's mind. Of all the people to tell, she'd told *Victoria*?

"Promise me you won't say anything to anyone? None of your friends or our family? Swear on Eric's life." Ruby gave Victoria her sternest face.

"Of course, I can keep a secret!"

Eric snorted. "She can't, but I'll make sure she keeps this one." He gave Ruby a nod. "Don't worry."

It was as good as Ruby could hope for.

"Delilah is gay? Well, shit the bed." Her sister paused. "Fran has a thing for singers, huh?"

"Hopefully just a thing for me, but the photos of her and Delilah gadding about town have done nothing for my ego."

"I saw those photos, but just assumed they worked together. She seemed pretty into you, didn't she?"

Ruby nodded. "She did. And she does still work with Delilah, I know that. Plus, I hardly have any claim over her. We slept together once." But ever since, every day had dragged like it was a year. Ruby wanted to know what Fran was doing, what she was thinking. The distance, albeit temporary, was killing her.

Victoria shook her head. "You and I both know that counts for something."

Ruby pouted. "We only started being civil to each other two weeks ago. It's too soon to tell." Ruby's words were rational, but her feelings were anything but.

"No wonder you're forgetting words." Victoria took Ruby

by the shoulders. "Fran had to go back to London, but she will be back and you will work this out — whether she gets back for the concert or not. Even if she doesn't, you've got tons of people who are looking forward to it, so you have to push your fears aside and do it. You're going to smash this, little sister. You know why?"

Ruby shook her head. "I have no clue."

"Because you're a superstar! I knew that when Mum and Dad gave you your first microphone, aged three. I still know it today. I'm sure Fran will try her best to be here, seeing as it was her idea in the first place. She's invested. But even if she doesn't, there are still a million reasons to be excited about it. Mistletoe. The farm. The community. The exposure. This is your night to shine and make a difference. Don't lose sight of the reasons you're doing it in the first place." Victoria paused. "It's all going to work out with the gig and with Fran. I guarantee it."

Ruby gave her a smile. She loved her sister for trying. "How can you be sure?"

Victoria gave her a wink. "Because you don't fall off a ladder for just anyone. You *want* this to work. So, it will."

Chapter 26

Damian slid into the chair beside Fran. He spun around once, twice, then let out a long sigh before he stopped, facing her.

"Why the long face?"

"Why the long sigh?"

Damian gave her a slow shrug. "I spoke to marketing to see if we could get Fast Forward's next single moved up to jump on the success of this one. But the dates don't work, which sucks." He paused. "Your turn."

"I was just looking at the trains back to Snowy Bottom on Saturday and wondering if they were going to be running. There's currently a tree on the line and more snow forecast." She glanced out the window, where a light flurry was still falling. Fran blew out a breath and Googled car hire. The prices made her wince.

Damian put both his palms up and sat forward in his chair. "Can we just take a moment to stop and marvel at the fact you're getting a train in the snow to Snowy Bottom, and then heading to Mistletoe? If I didn't know this was true, I would never believe you."

Fran laughed. Damian was always good at light relief. "You can't help but say the names and feel happier, can you?

Everyone is happy in Mistletoe." She thought of Audrey, Mary, Norman and the gang. "Eccentric, but happy. I just hope I can make it for tomorrow."

Fran also hoped Ruby had remembered her words. She'd texted last night to say she was having issues.

Damian studied her, went to say something, then sat back.

"What?" Fran asked.

Damian shook his head. "Nothing. It's just… This is about Ruby, right? You really want to get back for the gig. I get it. But you've never been like this before with anyone else. Certainly not with you-know-who."

"I wasn't allowed to be anything with her." Fran remembered everything about being in a relationship with Delilah. Most of it was bad. She was glad they could be friends now.

Fran just hoped Ruby felt the same.

"But you're distracted. You're different." He paused, tilting his head. "I think you've found someone you really care about."

Damian was only 29. The same age as Ruby. However, he was wise beyond his years. He'd also been in a committed relationship for three years with a lovely woman named Isla. If anyone was the relationship expert of the two of them, it was him. Damian managed to juggle work and love, a trick Fran had never mastered. Instead, she'd just put love on hold and thrown herself into work. The only reason she and Delilah had met was because it had happened at work.

But Damian had a point. Fran was distracted. She wasn't focused purely on her job.

Ruby had her attention.

"I like this new side of you, by the way. It makes you seem more human. More vulnerable."

Fran knew vulnerable was all the rage. However, it wasn't normally her thing. She glanced at her pink trousers. Just as colour hadn't been, until she met Ruby. "Vulnerable wasn't what I was going for, but I'll take your word for it." She paused. "But yes, I would like things to work out with Ruby. But it means I *have* to get home on Saturday."

Damian raised an eyebrow. "Home?"

Fran sat up, rolling her shoulders. "Back to my parents' place. You know what I mean."

Damian said nothing, just shot her an amused smile.

"Stop staring at me like that." Fran checked her phone. No new messages from Ruby since her good morning message today.

What was she doing?

Fran had work to do, and she was fretting over a woman and allowing Damian to see it all.

"You're mooning," he told her.

"I'm going crazy not being able to talk to her. Also, I'm worried that she's seen photos of me and Delilah online."

"So long as Delilah wasn't pawing you like she was when I came in the other day." More eyebrow raising.

"It was a momentary thing and it was hardly pawing." But Damian was right. "Why is real-life dating so hard?" Fran lowered her voice so nobody else overheard the next bit. "Dating Delilah was easy because I just had to pretend she didn't exist."

"It's ironic you're worrying about being seen with her now you can be, isn't it?"

The irony was not lost on Fran.

"If you're going a little crazy, that says to me you're falling for this woman."

Fran's flush began in her toes and hit the very edges of her eyelashes. "It's a bit early for that. We've slept together once." But she already knew there was some truth in Damian's words. She couldn't stop thinking about Ruby. Their sex had been off the chart. She desperately wanted to do it again. It was another reason she wanted to get back to Mistletoe as soon as she could. London, which had always held such glamour, paled beside Ruby.

Damian shrugged. "I knew the first time I kissed Isla that I wanted to kiss her for a very long time."

"But tell me truthfully: can it ever work with a singer? You're with a teacher. A far more sensible profession."

"Ruby O'Connell is not Delilah." Damian's words hit home. He lowered his voice. "She's as far away from Delilah as she could possibly be. She's sorted and sane. Plus, she has a better voice, but don't tell Delilah I said that."

Fran snorted. "Your secret's safe with me." She closed her eyes and spun in her chair, still thinking. "But I've tried going out with a singer and it was a car crash. I can't escape that."

"Thanks very much," Delilah said.

Fran's eyelids sprang open, and she jumped up, clutching her chest. "Where did you come from? Shit. I didn't mean for you to hear that." *Bugger.* She threw Damian a *why-didn't-you-warn-me?* look. Had Delilah heard Damian's comments, too? They'd just got back onto solid ground with their friendship. She didn't want Delilah to think badly of her.

Delilah shook her head, glancing around the office. There

was nobody close by. "I was a car crash, no need to sugar-coat it." She threw Fran an apologetic look, then glanced at her screen. "Why are you hiring a car?"

"She needs to get back to Mistletoe for Ruby's concert tomorrow," Damian replied.

Delilah glanced at Fran, then shook her head. "Don't hire a car. Take my Porsche. You're still on the insurance, and I'm not using it."

Fran's mouth gaped. "Are you sure?" Delilah was proving more useful this week than she ever had when they were together.

"Positive. I'll get someone to drop it around to yours in the morning and give you the keys. Just let me know a time."

"That would be perfect, thank you."

Delilah shrugged. "Happy to help. I just stopped by to check about Fast Forward's gig tonight. I can get there for 8pm. Is that okay?"

Damian nodded. "I'll tell security to expect you."

Delilah squeezed Fran's shoulder. "Great. Gotta dash, I'm meeting my new producer. See you later."

Fran stared as she left the office. She turned to Damian. "Did that just happen? My ex, who used to cause me no end of problems, is now the expert problem-solver?" Fran's mind was still whirling.

"Maybe singers aren't the tyrants you make them out to be," Damian replied.

Fran shook her head. "Maybe not."

"Now you can go back to Mistletoe with no worries. I'll take care of things this end."

Emotion rose up through Fran. Damian wasn't just a

work colleague. He was a friend, too. She got up and hugged him.

He hugged her right back. "One condition, though," Damian said. "I want a present from mystical Mistletoe. Plus, I want to come to the Tree Contest next year. It sounded awesome."

Fran smiled. "You're on. My parents can put you and Isla up." She put a hand to her chin. "A present from Mistletoe." She twisted her mouth. "How about some shit on a twig?"

Damian let out a howl of laughter. "That would be perfect."

Chapter 27

Ruby jumped off her quad bike and grabbed the chainsaw from the back. The Nolan family — two mums and twin girls around seven — stared at her with wide eyes. That it was a queer family made this extra-special. What did the girls call their parents? Mum and Mummy? Mum and Mamma?

Ruby recalled the chat she'd had with Fran about what she called her two dads. It seemed an awfully long time ago. Especially because she hadn't heard from her since yesterday morning, and today was Saturday, the day of the concert. Ruby was still forgetting words. Still googling those photos. Still thinking the worst.

"Okay, I need you to stand back behind that tree with the yellow flag on it." Ruby wasn't going to focus on Fran. Instead, she was going to chop this tree and start this family's Christmas.

The family moved, then Ruby grabbed the chainsaw and ripped the cord. Power rippled through her. She pulled her visor over her eyes, then got to work felling the tree. When it collapsed to the ground with a thud, one of the girls grabbed her mum's leg, the other whooped. Ruby had been a whooper as a child, following her dad around the farm like he was some kind of Christmas magician. Now, she held the magic.

She collected the farm's walkie-talkie from them, and made sure they knew how to get back to the barn. "See you there in half an hour to collect your tree!"

Ruby had one more tree to cut before she made her way back. That was going to be her final one for the day, before she headed back to the house and started getting ready for tonight. A gig it looked like Fran wouldn't make it back for. The trains weren't working, and Fran was clearly too busy. Chopping down trees had helped Ruby to rationalise it a little.

But this was showbiz. The show must go on.

The buzz of another quad bike approaching made Ruby look up. She waved at her dad, but at that distance, she couldn't make out the person he was giving a lift to. However, she recognised the yellow coat. Her dad cut his engine, and the passenger hopped off.

It was only when the woman removed her helmet that Ruby was sure. Fran. She'd made it back.

Ruby's skin tingled all over.

"You got any more to do before you go back?" her dad asked.

"One more," Ruby replied, keeping one eye on Fran.

"Okay. Do that, then give Fran a lift back to the barn. Scott can take over from there. You need to get ready!"

Her dad hauled the Nolan's tree onto his bike. "See you later." He put his helmet back on and rode off.

Ruby gazed at her dad's departing bike, before turning her attention to Fran.

She clutched her helmet in her hand, but looked anything but comfortable.

"Of all the forests in all the world," Ruby began. She

walked nearer to Fran. "Why didn't you let me know you were coming back? I thought Fast Forward and Delilah had won."

"It was never a contest. I'm sorry I didn't let you know." Fran winced. "Yesterday was manic with the gig, then I was going to tell you on the drive here, but my phone ran out of charge. So I thought I'd make it a surprise."

"It's certainly that," Ruby said.

They stood awkwardly looking at each other. Ruby couldn't quite work out what the next move was.

Fran took a lungful of air. "Have I mentioned the smell in this forest is still insane?"

Ruby eyed Fran. "Once or twice."

"The courtyard looked busy. How's business?"

Ruby went with it, although business wasn't at the forefront of her mind. "We've had a good week. We're expecting a big crowd for tonight, too."

"It's why I'm here. I told you I'd try my hardest."

"I'd resigned myself to you *not* coming after I heard about the trains. You said you drove?"

Fran looked down and dug her hands into her pockets, before catching Ruby's gaze.

The way the sunlight caught Fran's face and hair through the trees was stunning. Fran was so beautiful. Why hadn't Ruby told her yet? Why hadn't they touched? Because they were still sussing each other out.

"Delilah lent me her car and I drove over." Fran sucked on her top lip.

Delilah. There was that name again. Ruby's defences rose. She pulled her shoulders back. "I need to cut down one more tree. You want to jump on the bike and do it with me?"

Ruby didn't want to dwell on Fran's words. Actions would make them go away.

Fran nodded. "Love to."

Ruby put on her helmet and jumped on the bike, waiting for Fran to do the same.

When Fran's body cosied up to Ruby and her arms wound around Ruby's waist, Ruby could hardly breathe. It had only been five days since they saw each other, but it felt like longer. So much had gone on since then. Fran had lived a whole other life with a pop superstar. Ruby couldn't match up to that. Ruby had no idea if *she* was who Fran still wanted.

However, having Fran's arms around her felt *exactly* right. Like this is where Fran should have been the whole time.

Delilah wasn't going anywhere. Come January, London would be where they all lived. There had to be room for all three of them in such a vast city.

Ruby fired up the bike and turned to Fran. "Hold on tight!" she shouted over the engine noise.

Fran nodded, then clutched her tighter.

Ruby concentrated on driving, but it wasn't easy.

They rode down the line of trees, colour-coded with orange tags that meant they weren't going to be chopped for another two years. Ruby had a dream to have a house big enough to fit a ten-foot tree one day. She wanted to put it in her hallway so everyone could comment on her tree from Mistletoe Farm.

Ruby pulled up at the next tree to chop, and waited for Fran to jump off. Ruby grabbed the chainsaw from the back and flipped her visor.

Fran took off her helmet and shook her blond hair.

Ruby wanted to reach out and touch it. "You want to chop down a tree?"

Fran wrinkled her brow and shook her head. "I'll leave that to the experts." She paused. "But I have to say, a chainsaw suits you. You wield it well."

If that's what Fran thought, Ruby was going to put on a show. One that told Fran she was a better bet than Delilah — even though she couldn't give her a car, or any other riches. Ruby fired up the chainsaw and approached the bottom of the tree. She cut at an angle, and within minutes, there was a dull thud as the tree hit the ground. Ruby put the chainsaw back on the bike, then took off her helmet. "Was it as good as you'd hoped?"

Fran smiled. "It was better."

Ruby wanted to say something cool and effortless in reply, but nothing came to mind. There was an awkwardness to their speech and movements, as if they'd never met before. They were laboured. Ruby was desperate for something to ease the gears and for them to click again, but it wasn't coming easy.

"How did the gig go last night?" Ruby decided to stick to safe ground with Fran. Work.

Fran nodded. "The girls overcame their nerves and did a great job. Delilah helped out, too." Fran winced. "Sorry, I seem to be mentioning her name a lot, but she's been around a fair bit this week. She's been really helpful with the band, and lending me her car."

Ruby ground her teeth together. It was still a little hard to swallow. "You worked out your differences with her? I saw the photos of you."

Fran gave her a steady stare. "As I told you, it was just

220

dinner with a friend. She's going to come out to her parents over Christmas, so it's a big deal. I think the thought of losing her current relationship spurred her into action. She knows she fucked up with me." Fran's gaze never wavered. "But we're in the past. I'm looking to the future now and I hope you're in it."

Ruby breathed out and banged her gloved hands together. "I hope so, too." Her heart was pounding. That was good news, right? "Can you give me a hand getting this onto the bike?"

Fran nodded and together, they heaved the tree into position.

Fran stood one side, Ruby stood the other. Six feet and thousands of pines separated them.

"Before we head back to the barn, can we clear the air? Things don't feel settled between us and I really want them to be." Fran fiddled with her gloves.

Ruby held back. She was still annoyed at this week. Mostly at herself for how jealousy had crept up on her. Fran had been honest with her. She shouldn't be holding a grudge. "No better place to clear the air than here."

Fran took in her surroundings. "You're right," she said. "I want you to know that I hated being away this week. Especially after Monday." She paused. "I've been replaying that night in my head a lot. It's helped me get through this week."

Ruby broke. "I have, too." She gave Fran a smile.

Fran's shoulders sighed in relief. "I've hated the distance and not being able to chat properly."

"Me, too." A gust of wind sailed through the forest. Ruby glanced at Fran. "It wasn't easy seeing photos of you with Delilah. I've got no hold over you, you're not my girlfriend.

We never spoke about anything beyond Monday. We slept together once. Yet, it *felt* like more. Which scared me a little."

Fran walked to her, then put a hand on Ruby's arm. "I missed you, too. And it *was* more." Fran put a hand over her heart. "I felt it right here."

Ruby's breath caught in her throat. "I'm glad it wasn't just me." She glanced up at the sky, the bluest of blues. "But you scared me." She brought her eyes back level with Fran. "When you said you might not make it back. I thought you didn't care as much about us. About the gig. About Mistletoe."

Fran shook her head. "I was covering my bases. But I shouldn't have. I should have committed. To you, to my parents. I know that now. I'm sorry I've come off a bit flaky this week. But the thought of seeing you again today has been keeping me going."

"Even though I'm not a superstar or vying for the Christmas number one?"

Fran shook her head. "I'm not after that, I never have been. You're a star in your own right. I hope you know that."

Fran really thought so? Ruby's pulse thundered. "I don't quite believe it yet, but I'm going to fake it until I make it." At least having this heart-to-heart with Fran was taking Ruby's mind off the gig. Hundreds of people staring at her.

"You're going to be great. And you know what the best thing is? They're here to see *you*. This isn't a rock club and nobody's going to heckle or boo you off stage. Just remember that when the lights come on tonight."

Ruby blew out a breath, nodding. "I'm glad you came back."

Fran took Ruby's gloved hand in hers. "I'm glad, too. I'm

looking forward to what we might have in the future. We can be neighbours. Friends. Lovers."

Ruby shuddered. "I hate the term lovers. It sounds like all we do is shag."

Fran gave her an amused look. "And that's a problem because?"

Ruby gave her a proper, cheesy grin. "You know what I mean." She pulled Fran closer. Now, from not quite knowing what to say or do, Ruby knew *exactly* what to do.

"What term would you prefer?"

Ruby hesitated, then decided to be brave. "Girlfriends?"

Fran's smile grew wider. "I was hoping you'd say that. I'm sorry if I made you doubt me this week."

"Are you coming back for Christmas, too?"

Fran nodded. "I can't miss my first Christmas in Mistletoe, can I? It would be nearly as bad as missing my girlfriend's big homecoming gig." Fran pulled Ruby closer and pressed her lips to hers.

Red-hot desire throbbed through Ruby. She kissed Fran back, emotion swirling inside. When they eventually pulled back, her breath was shaky.

"I better get this tree back to base, otherwise we're going to have a riot on our hands. Jump on the bike?"

Fran nodded. She put her helmet on, then wrapped her arms around Ruby once more. Only this time, it was perfect. This time, their bodies slotted together like they were meant to be. Ruby turned the ignition under her hand and revved the bike. When they went over rougher terrain, Fran grabbed her tighter, which made Ruby want to do it more. They pulled up outside the barn minutes later.

Scott ran over and grabbed the tree, giving them both a grin before he walked away.

Ruby took off her helmet and shook her hair. Her skin prickled. She threw her helmet onto the back of the bike and did the same with Fran's. Then they stood looking at each other.

A shy smile graced Fran's face. "That was pretty cool. This morning I left London a little uncertain and praying I made it back. Now I've got a girlfriend who can wield a chainsaw and ride a quad bike. I feel like all my lesbian Christmases have come at once." Fran ruffled her hair and moved closer to Ruby. "Thanks for believing in me."

Ruby's smile loosened. "I had my doubts this week, but you're here and that's the main thing. But I need to get ready. Walk me back to the farmhouse?"

Fran threaded an arm through Ruby's.

They walked through the tree barn, busy with Saturday buyers, then out into the equally buzzing courtyard. Ruby's feet crunched on the grit her parents had put down this morning, just in case.

"Have you remembered the words to the Christmas hits yet?"

Ruby shook her head, eyeing the stage as they passed. "Don't." She walked up to it, nodding at the stage floor. "Victoria came up with a wicked back-up plan." Laminated lyric sheets were already stapled to the floor. "Just in case stage fright renders me numb." They carried on walking towards the house. "Tonight's sold out," Ruby added. "The weather's good, so it's going to be in the courtyard. 500 tickets all gone. There aren't many gigs around here, so people are really coming out."

Fran squeezed Ruby's arm. "They're also coming to see *you*. Because you're amazing."

Ruby took the compliment on the chin. It was a perfect winter's day, that would hopefully lead into the perfect winter's night. Crisp, clear, a success.

They pulled up outside the front door.

Fran dropped Ruby's arm.

Ruby already missed her. "Stop by the barn to say hi beforehand if you like." She tried to sound casual, but she wasn't sure it worked.

"I don't want to ruin your preparations."

Ruby leaned forward and kissed Fran's lips. "I promise: you being there won't ruin a thing."

Chapter 28

Fran walked back down the farm drive a few hours later with her parents: it hummed with activity. She could taste the anticipation in the air.

From being sure about Ruby, now Fran had nerves on Ruby's behalf. However, nerves were good. Fran had worked with enough acts to know that. But tonight was different.

This was Ruby getting over her personal demons, as well as performing to all the people she loved the most.

The crowd ahead was already thick, and Fran had to shout to clear a path for her pop. He hobbled towards the stage on crutches, Dad guiding his every step. They were so sweet together, and they'd been the perfect role models for Fran. She wanted that in her relationship, too. She hoped she might have found it with Ruby.

They located the elevated seats Mary and Paul had reserved for them, and Fran got her parents settled.

"We're in the VIP section by the look of it," Pop said.

Dad gave Pop a smug smile. "It pays to be in with the farm owners."

"Beer? Mulled wine?" Fran asked.

Dad shook his head. "Mulled cider. Paul introduced me to it this week and it's delicious."

Pop scoffed. "I'm surprised you're going back in after the way you felt the morning after."

Dad gave him a shy grin. "I'm not planning on drinking quite as much tonight. I just got a bit excited on Wednesday." He paused. "Can you get us a couple of buttered pretzels, too?" He rubbed his hands together. "I love living near a Christmas tree farm. Christmas treats on tap!"

The queues at the bar were minimal, and Fran got a hug from Victoria when she got there.

"I'm so pleased you made it, I know it means the world to Ruby. Especially after this week and everything that went on with…" Victoria's eyes widened. She dropped Fran's gaze and cleared her throat.

"Everything that went on with what?" What had Ruby said?

Victoria shook her head. "Just the gig, her forgetting her lines. It's been a stressful week." Victoria's cheeks coloured purple. "Have you seen Ruby yet?"

Fran let it go. What Victoria knew or didn't know wasn't important tonight. "Not tonight. I saw her earlier. I'm going to try to poke my head around if there's time."

A strum of an electric guitar made them both turn their heads. The support band were tuning up. The gig kicked off in ten minutes.

"I know she'd appreciate it." Victoria ladled three mulled ciders from her massive steel urn, putting lids on the cardboard cups to keep the heat in.

Fran took them, breathing in the scent of orange, cinnamon and spices. The smell of Christmas. She made her way back through the chattering crowds, the buzz in the air heightening.

To her right, a fire pit crackled in the corner, and Paul was holding court around it. She delivered the drinks back to her parents, then headed out again to the pretzel truck which was doing a roaring trade. She got three, then brought them back to eat with her parents just as the support band began. Fran had seen them play before, so her focus was more on the crowd. How attentive they were, because that would affect Ruby, too. The answer was, very. Even her parents, who were average music fans, were rapt by song three.

Fran took the opportunity to slip away, rounding the bottom of the stage and slipping past the pick-and-mix truck, and one selling posh socks. She shivered as she approached the barn, then walked through the yard to the office she was very familiar with. Ruby was inside, blinds drawn. Fran could hear her doing her scales.

She hesitated once, then knocked lightly on the door.

Ruby opened the door in seconds. When she saw Fran, she tried a half-smile. It almost worked.

Fran's heart lurched. She wanted to wrap Ruby up and protect her, but that wasn't what she needed.

"Hey." She went to step inside, but Ruby shook her head.

"I was just coming out anyway. I need to hear a bit of the band, feel the crowd." She took a deep breath and shut the door.

"How are you feeling?"

Ruby blew out a breath. "Nervous as hell, but that's expected."

She walked on her tip-toes, faster than normal.

"You're going to be great."

"Ruby!" Mary waved from the other side of the barn. She raced over and gave Ruby a bear hug. "You're going to be brilliant." She kissed her cheek. "I gotta run, people are still buying Christmas trees. But this is the last sale, then I'm taking my place." Mary checked her watch. "Twenty minutes!" Mary pressed something into Fran's hand, then ran back to her station.

Fran opened her palm. Mary had given her a sprig of Mistletoe. She raised an eyebrow at Ruby. "I've no idea what your mum's suggesting."

Ruby took it from Fran's hand and held it above their heads. "Maybe this?"

Fran didn't need a second invitation. She reached up on tiptoes and pressed her lips to Ruby's. Lust rippled through her. She snaked an arm around Ruby's neck and pulled her lips closer. Now they'd reconnected, Fran never wanted to let Ruby go.

When they parted, Fran stared up at her. Ruby didn't know how gorgeous or talented she was. That was part of her charm.

"Can you believe it took us this long to kiss under the mistletoe in Mistletoe?"

Ruby laughed. "My *mother* had to step in."

"Let's keep that between you and me." Fran smiled. "It was worth the wait."

"It was."

Outside, Troubadour finished a song and the crowd whooped and clapped. "We've got two more for you until you get the woman you're all here for. The incredible Ruby O'Connell!"

This time, the cheering and applause were so much louder.

Ruby's face dropped a little.

Fran took hold of both her hands. "Listen to me: you're

going to be great tonight. I'm not your label or your manager. But I am your girlfriend." She touched Ruby's cheek with her fingertips. "If you'd let me, I could be your biggest cheerleader. This is your moment. I can't wait to hear you sing 'Pieces Of You'. I can't wait for your home town to realise how great you are." She kissed her lips a final time. "And who knows? Bigger things might come from this."

When Fran pulled back, Ruby's green gaze was on her. "Let's deal with this gig for now. One step at a time. Maybe in six months I might feel differently about going bigger, who knows? For now, I'm happy being a small fish in a small pond." Ruby kissed Fran again.

Fran's head spun.

A wolf whistle split the air.

Fran glanced up to see Victoria and Eric walking towards them, Eric with his guitar aloft.

"Get a room, you two!" Victoria shouted.

Ruby narrowed her eyes. "I apologise for my family."

"Never apologise." Fran winked, then stepped back. "You look every inch the superstar, too, by the way. Now go out there and break a leg." She tilted her head. "Not literally, of course. One of those in the family is quite enough for one year."

* * *

Ruby strummed her guitar twice, then stepped up to the mic. "One, two, Mistletoe!"

The crowd roared back their approval, and a shiver of pride rattled through Fran. Her girlfriend was on stage. From the look on Ruby's face, she was loving it.

Fran breathed out a sigh of relief.

And relax.

"One, two, Mistletoe!" Ruby said again.

This time, someone in the crowd shouted it right back. Fran scanned the front couple of rows for the instigator, even though she recognised the voice.

Audrey. Sure enough, in seconds Audrey was on her feet, hands in the air. "Everybody!" she shouted. "One, two, Mistletoe!"

Ruby repeated it, then tuned her guitar.

Meanwhile, the crowd, led by the unstoppable Audrey, slowly began to chant. "One, two Mistletoe! One, two, Mistletoe!"

Beside them, Paul and Mary's faces were a picture. "That's what I always say!" Paul shouted at Fran's parents. But he also chanted it right back at his daughter.

"Thank you so much, Mistletoe! This is my first time playing for all the people I love most in the world." Ruby's gaze landed on the elevated seated section to her left. She blew them a kiss. "I hope you enjoy my Christmas set."

She launched into her first song, and the crowd began to sway along, voices loose. Right there in that first song, Ruby came alive. As if she'd been given permission to flourish, to showcase herself, to have fun. She was going to do just that.

Fran could do nothing but grin, just like the rest of Ruby's family and friends. The looks on their faces were priceless. They knew what Ruby could do, but they almost never saw her perform. Tonight was the culmination of all those gigs Ruby had done, all the hours of practise she'd put in. Even the gig that had gone so wrong. It hadn't diminished her. Ruby was born for the bigger stage. Bigger than the one she was on.

Five songs in and the crowd were going wild, Audrey now silenced, everyone hanging on Ruby's every word. Ruby's fingers dazzled on her guitar, and Fran's mind jumped forward to what they might do to her later. Heat stole over her at the thought.

"Thank you so much!" Ruby shook her head as she scanned the courtyard. She looked like she couldn't believe where she was. She also looked the most content Fran had ever seen her.

"I cannot believe I'm playing the courtyard where I grew up. I've built snowmen on this ground. I've scraped my knee, drunk too much mulled wine. I think I may have even thrown up in that corner over there. Don't worry, Mum made me clean it up." Ruby waited for the laughter to die down. "I want to say thank you to everyone for being here, and for supporting Mistletoe Christmas Tree Farm. Please order your trees for next year. But mostly, thank you to the people who made this all possible. My parents, my brother and sister, my wonderful brother-in-law, Eric, on the guitar." She waited for the clapping to die down. "And also, to Fran Bell for dreaming it up in the first place."

Fran stilled. She hadn't expected a shout-out. She glanced at her parents who were giving her wide puppy eyes. Happiness danced through her. Ruby was so far from Delilah, just as Damian had said. With her, Fran could be out, be herself. She wasn't a dirty secret with Ruby. It made all the difference.

"Now, I'd like to play you my new song which is very special to me. Very personal. And I want to dedicate it to a remarkable person in the crowd. She knows who she is."

Fran's stomach rolled. She gritted her teeth and held it together. Ruby had dedicated her new song to her. Emotion bubbled up inside her. Fran wasn't a crier, but if she had been, this would have been the time. Instead, she grabbed her phone from her pocket, turned it onto Ruby and hit record.

When Ruby began to sing, the crowd hushed. By the middle eight, she had them in the palm of her hand. When Ruby hit the high notes, Fran swooned. Everyone was glued to Ruby's every breath. Fran made sure her hand was steady, as she got every note of the song, plus the crowd's reaction when it ended.

Fran knew stardom when she saw it. Ruby had it, the elusive 'thing' that all labels looked for. She could be a folk/pop crossover like so many before her. But she had to want it.

Fran glanced down at the video, then shared it on her Instagram feed.

If nothing else, her followers could hear it and marvel, too.

* * *

The crowd were still basking in the afterglow of the gig, and her public weren't keen to let Ruby go. She'd threaded her hour-and-20-minute set with her own songs, a smattering of Christmas favourites plus some folk classics, and it had gone down a storm. Ruby had hugged Audrey and Norman, chatted to farm staff and locals alike, and now she was with her family.

Ruby's parents hugged her, then Victoria, before Ruby greeted Fran, Dad and Pop.

Her parents couldn't wait for their hug.

"Ruby, you were incredible. Fran told us how good you were, but that was such a performance. Fran was right, you should be a megastar!"

Ruby cast her gaze to the floor, then shook her head. "My

hometown made it easy." She glanced at Fran. "But without your daughter, it wouldn't have happened."

Fran shook her head. Ruby was too quick to attribute her success to others. It was time she owned it. "This wasn't me. This was all you."

Ruby glanced at her parents. "Do you need me to do anything else here?"

Paul shook his head. "I want you to do nothing here. The café staff are going to take down the stage. We've got the food and drink stands covered, and our Christmas tree pre-orders are through the roof. One thing, though. Everyone has demanded another concert next year, so can we make this an annual event?" He paused. "I should let you know, I've already said yes." He walked over and put an arm around Ruby, kissing her cheek.

"I would love to," Ruby said. "From being scared stiff, it's turned into the best night of my life. I could feel the love from the crowd. If you have that, you can't fail."

Fran shook her head. "You can't."

"By the way," Paul added. "That 'one, two, Mistletoe' chant got me a little jealous. Nobody's ever chanted it back at me before."

Ruby laughed. "I'll credit you next time, Dad."

Paul smiled. "It's my gift to you." He kissed her cheek again. "Why don't you and Fran have a drink and we'll join you later when we've cleared the farm. Don't argue. We've got enough staff here to help, so just go and relax."

Ruby glanced over at Fran. "Can I interest you in a mulled wine and a mince pie by an open fire?"

Fran nodded. "It sounds perfect."

* * *

"You really were incredible."

Ruby squeezed Fran's hand as they walked through the farmhouse front door. Chipper greeted them, jumping up at Ruby and pawing Fran.

"Hey boy, good dog!" Ruby ruffled his fur, before ushering him through to the lounge. Then she shut the door.

"Aren't we going in there?" Fran inclined her head.

Ruby shook hers. "I've been thinking about you all week, wanting to kiss you without an audience. Just me, an audience of one." She wrapped her arms around Fran and pulled her close so their bodies were touching. Then Ruby pressed her lips to Fran's.

Fran's toes danced in her boots.

"I haven't shown you my room, yet. Plus, there's nobody in the house right now. How about a mulled wine afterwards?"

"Fuck the mulled wine."

Ruby shook with gentle laughter. "You're my kind of woman."

Ruby tugged Fran's hand and they walked through the kitchen and up the stone stairs with frayed carpet. Fran focused on the rich thud of her heart, stirring her insides with style.

Ruby opened a door on the right: her bedroom. It housed a double bed with a white duvet and pillows. The walls were white, the two chests of drawers the same colour.

"You like white." *Shut up, Fran.*

The room could have been painted neon pink for all she cared. It didn't matter.

What mattered was the electricity in the room, so raw, so wired, about to ignite.

Ruby reached for her, but stopped when she touched Fran. She brought Fran's hand to her mouth and kissed it gently. That didn't help Fran's mini-tremors.

"You're shaking," Ruby whispered.

Dark eyes tracked Fran's every move. Her breath quickened. "It's what you do to me." She raised her head and caught Ruby's glittering stare. "It's what you did to all those people out there tonight. You dazzled them. You're dazzling me now."

Ruby shook her head, her gaze steady. "You dazzle *me*. I haven't stopped thinking about you all week."

Fran shuddered. "What were you thinking about specifically?" Because she knew for sure that she'd been thinking about *this* moment all week long. This gorgeous, languid moment, heightened with anticipation. When it was just the two of them, with no interruptions.

Ruby shook her head as a sultry smile appeared on her face. "Your body. Your skin. You." She put a finger under Fran's chin, her strong thumb stroking the soft skin of Fran's cheek.

That slight action made Fran's breathing hitch.

Then Ruby tilted Fran's head upwards until there were only millimetres between them. There was no hesitation as she pressed forward and their lips met again.

A firework exploded in Fran's soul.

Hot damn.

Ruby slid her tongue into Fran's mouth with the surety of a lover who'd done this many times. It already felt like that. Like Ruby knew Fran. But also, like this was the first time.

It had only been a few days since they'd been together, but there was a ferocity in Ruby's kisses from the start. Fran was all for it. In response, Fran sucked Ruby's top lip between her own, and Ruby groaned. It was more than enough to send spikes of pleasure through Fran.

The heat in the room ramped up. Ruby pulled back, eyeing Fran. Her breathing was ragged, and they both had too many clothes on. She hoped her gaze told Ruby that. Apparently, it did.

Buttons popped as Ruby's fingers worked deftly to rid Fran of her top. When it slid from her shoulders, Ruby tossed it onto a nearby chair. Fran did the same for Ruby, kissing her skin beneath the buttons as she went. They both shed their bras, never taking their gazes from the other.

The air around them rippled with hunger. Fran brought Ruby's hand to her lips, kissing the tips of Ruby's fingers one by one. The desire inside her was so overwhelming, she could hardly breathe. "I can't believe I'm getting to touch the hot star of the moment."

Making short work of her jeans and underwear, Ruby guided Fran to her bed. She shook her head. "I can't believe I get to be here with you. You're the star in my eyes." Ruby paused. "And I hope you don't mind, but I *really* need to feel you."

Fran shook her head. "That's the craziest question. The pleasure's all mine."

"It will be," Ruby replied, and Fran's stomach flipped. Ruby kicked off the rest of her clothes, then lowered herself on top of Fran, their groans connecting at the same time as their lips.

When Ruby slid her tongue into Fran's mouth again, desire drenched her. It was too much. She'd watched Ruby all night long. Now she wanted more.

"I want you inside me." Fran's voice came out fractured. Her feelings were anything but. They were connected and she knew exactly what she wanted. She wanted Ruby inside her, on top of her, all over her. She wanted to be consumed by her.

Ruby bathed Fran with her emerald-green stare, darkening by the second. Then she raised two fingers to Fran's mouth, and moved her lips to Fran's ear. "I know you're probably wet enough," she whispered. "But just in case."

If Fran wasn't soaked before, she definitely was now. She opened her lips as silently instructed, and sucked Ruby's fingers inside. Was it possible to die of desire? Fran never wanted to let Ruby go.

Above her, Ruby closed her eyes and groaned again, which only stoked Fran's fire. Then Ruby slid her wet fingertips down Fran's body and in one swift move, slipped into her with liquid ease.

If Fran had been anticipating this moment all week long, the reality was ten times better. She'd wanted Ruby to fill her, to swamp her, and she'd got her wish. Fran's mind went blank as Ruby did just what she asked, and more. Her hips bucked and she closed her eyes.

"You feel so good," Ruby told her. "Exquisite. Like silk."

Hot breath pleasured Fran's earlobe. Her pink nipples went rock hard as Ruby sucked them into her mouth. She tried to catch her breath, to remember anything. It was impossible. She gave in, and fell under Ruby's spell. She spread across the bed, her body an invitation, with Ruby the honoured guest. She arched up, letting her fingertips dance across Ruby's back.

Meanwhile, Ruby's fingers performed a dance all of their own inside her.

Ruby licked Fran's neck, and thrust into her with perfect precision. "There?" Hesitation flecked Ruby's voice.

A shiver rippled through Fran at Ruby's low tone. "Yes."

"Just there?"

"I promise you, yes."

Satisfied, Ruby relaxed into her rhythm, before connecting with Fran's clit.

Fran pressed the back of her head into the pillow as pure heat spread through her. It wasn't just today or this week she'd wanted Ruby, *ached* for Ruby. Having Ruby inside her felt like something she'd been waiting for her whole life. Like they were two parts of the same puzzle. As if Ruby had been missing from her life all this time.

Ruby's lips came back to Fran's, pulling her mouth into a searing kiss that scrambled Fran's brain. Passion drizzled down Fran's body. She clung to Ruby's shoulders as they moved as one. Her insides throbbed with longing as she tried to hold on. She wanted this to last forever, but then again, she wanted her sweet release.

The passion roaring within took hold. All the colours behind Fran's eyes turned to red, as she clutched Ruby that bit tighter still. Every heated moment they'd shared flashed through Fran's mind, and every fibre in her body tightened to breaking point. Then desire crashed through her and her thoughts fell to dust. Fran came undone in a blur of movement and sensation she'd never experienced before.

Ruby's fingers were buried deep inside her, and Ruby's whispered words urged Fran on. The light flashed once, twice, three times before Fran stilled Ruby's fingers, whispering to her "enough, enough." Fran didn't want to, but she had to. For now.

The sheet was soft under her skin as she pulled Ruby close. Fran was on the podium, the race won, champagne popped. She wallowed in the glory, soaked up the applause. It wasn't hard. Ruby made it easy.

Fran floated back to reality, the sugar rush of sex still fizzing through her. She kissed Ruby's lips, then cracked open an eye.

Ruby stared at her, a lazy smile on her face that told Fran she was feeling pretty pleased with herself. She had every right to be so.

"You're delicious, you know that?" Ruby shook her head. "Scarily so."

"I could say the same for you." Ruby had no idea of the cartwheels Fran still had going on inside. Of the utter delight screaming from her every bone. Ruby was missing the fact she was a sex goddess.

"You think everyone's still out?" Fran pressed her face into Ruby. "If your parents heard me come, I'm never leaving this room."

Ruby hitched an eyebrow. "There's an invitation."

Fran's laugh was deep and guttural. "This is all your fault." She kissed Ruby's lips. "You strut around on stage outside, holding the village in the palm of your hand. Then you bring me in here, pull me into the bedroom and seduce me. How could I resist? It's my duty to womenkind."

Ruby snorted. "Your duty? Wow. Women have described sleeping with me as many things, but never as 'their duty'." She quirked an eyebrow. "Their pleasure, maybe."

Fran grinned, then put a hand on Ruby's face, stilling the chat. A rush of desire raced through her. She reached around and squeezed Ruby's bum cheek. "You're a little smug, you know that?"

Ruby tilted her head. "Which bit of what just happened was most smug?"

"All of it." Fran smiled. "You're annoyingly talented in all departments."

"You're not so bad yourself."

Fran wriggled her hips. "I'm glad you remember." She reached down and trailed her fingers through Ruby's core.

Ruby's eyes closed and she shook at Fran's touch.

"You're so fucking wet." Fran rolled Ruby off her and reversed their positions. She pressed her naked body into Ruby, before trailing her fingers up and down the inside of Ruby's thighs. Fran locked eyes with Ruby, then slid right inside her.

Fran let out a long, low moan of pleasure. "Fuck, you're so sexy." Her voice was a growl. "Now, show me how quick you can come."

But Ruby shook her head, her breathing laboured, and reached out to Fran, too. "Show me how quick we can *both* come."

Ruby's words made Fran quiver as another orgasm thrummed inside her. She slid onto her knees and opened her legs wide, making it easy for Ruby.

Fran curled her fingers into Ruby, hitting her high and making her cry out. Fran's other hand found Ruby's clit.

Ruby squirmed beneath her, her eyelids closing.

Fran's movements became frantic, as did Ruby's. If Fran thought Ruby was all over her earlier, this was another level altogether, one she welcomed with open arms.

Their rhythms merged as they both became more vocal, until Fran could hold off no more. Her hips bucked, her heart roared, and then Fran soared. In seconds, she began to shake, just as Ruby's insides clutched Fran's fingers, and they cried out as one. They both kept their rhythm, coming together in one earth-shattering moment.

When they could take no more, Fran slumped on top of Ruby, and their racing heartbeats seemed to merge. Fran placed open-mouthed kisses on Ruby's shoulder and her neck, loving how Ruby twitched under her lips. She tasted delicious. Then Fran put her head in the nook of Ruby's neck, the only sound their breathing returning to normal. She gripped Ruby's waist tight, warm and sated. She hoped Ruby felt the same. If she didn't, there was plenty of time to correct course.

Eventually, Ruby looked at her, grinning. "As girlfriends go, I think we're going to be a good fit."

Fran burrowed her cheek into Ruby's neck and laughed. She had the biggest smile on her face.

Chapter 29

Ruby crept out of bed the following morning, threw on her jeans and a T-shirt and slunk downstairs to get coffee and toast. She needed sustenance this morning, having been up all night with Fran.

She boiled the kettle, then cut thick slices of tiger bread and put them in the toaster. Ruby buried her head in the fridge for milk and butter. When she popped out, her mum was behind the fridge, her hair sticking up, her dressing gown pulled tight.

Ruby jumped out of her skin. "Don't do that!"

Her mum hugged her, Ruby having to bend down as she was so much taller. She didn't mind. She breathed in her mum's smell, still the smell of home.

When they pulled back, her mum got another mug and added a teabag to it.

"Sorry I bailed on helping out last night."

Her mum raised an eyebrow, then indicated Ruby's two mugs. "You had other things to attend to." She paused. "Is Fran still asleep?"

Ruby nodded, embarrassment seeping up her body. Having a woman in her Mistletoe bedroom was a first for both of them. Ruby buttered the toast while Mum cleared some plates from the side into the dishwasher. She hadn't tidied up last night. She must have been tired.

Ruby put their breakfasts on a tray and picked it up. "I'll see you in a bit."

Her mum laid a hand on her arm.

Ruby stopped.

"Just so you know, you did so well last night. You were incredible. We're very proud of you."

Ruby flushed. It was always nice to hear. "Thanks, Mum."

Back in the bedroom, Fran was awake, checking her phone. When Ruby walked in, she looked up and gave her a wide grin, before pulling the duvet up to cover her breasts.

"Don't do that on my account." She gave Fran coffee and toast.

Fran made a famished sound. "You've no idea how hungry I am."

Ruby sat on the bed. "I do, because I'm the same."

"You okay with crumbs in the bed?"

"So long as you're served with them, I'm good." Ruby ate her first piece, savouring the flavour. "By the way, I forgot to ask. Did Fast Forward make number one?"

Fran shook her head. "Beaten by Skinny YouTube Boy. But we made number two, and there's still one more chart before Christmas, so who knows. I checked my messages, too, and yesterday went well for them." She ate some more toast. "It's interesting working with Fast Forward. They could be really big. Girls and boys like them, so the sky's the limit. Plus, the lead singer's getting over her fears. A little like someone else I could mention."

"It was only a first step, let's not get ahead of ourselves,"

Ruby said. "Remember, I'm still me. I don't do massive shifts in momentum. I'm a tortoise, not a hare. Slow and steady wins the race." She paused. "Although, I better make sure I service my music mogul before she hits the big time and leaves me for the lead singer of Fast Forward, hadn't I?"

Fran chuckled. "Have you seen her? Tenny's 19. I'm 36. I could be her mother."

"Stop it," Ruby replied.

"Have you seen your streaming numbers this morning? I bet they've gone up overnight. I posted a video of you singing 'Pieces Of You' and it's got a couple of hundred likes already."

Ruby turned her head. "You did? I must watch it back."

"You should. You're incredible *and* sexy. Buy one get one free. You're my favourite BOGOF." Fran smirked at her own joke, then kissed Ruby's lips. "Good morning, by the way."

Ruby kissed Fran's shoulder. "It certainly is with you in my bed."

Fran gave Ruby her phone and clicked play on the video.

Ruby watched a minute of it, then clicked off. "It feels weird watching it now. Like masturbating in front of you."

Fran gave her a sultry smile. "I find both of those hot, so feel free to act anytime you want," she replied. "Do you believe me now when I say you're more than just a normal singer? That you could be a household name?"

Ruby sighed, but happiness spiked her body. "Of course not." She put down her coffee and sat up on the bed, taking Fran's hand in hers. "What I know is that you spur me on. Like you said last night, you're a great cheerleader. I appreciate that. I'm going to write a song for you one day."

Fran put a hand to her chest. "Nobody's ever done that for me before."

"I better get there before Fast Forward lady does then, hadn't I?"

"Talking of Fast Forward, I still really need to go back to London this week. It's our Christmas party tomorrow night, and I still have the final week to wrap up. Which I could do without, but I need to go. Plus, I need to deliver Delilah's car back to her."

"I was hoping for a spin in the Porsche."

"We can still do that. I don't have to leave until later." She put her coffee down and crawled on her hands and knees to Ruby.

Desire slid down Ruby. She reached down and cupped one of Fran's breasts, before kissing her hard on the mouth. "I wish you didn't have to go. I wish we could have the most perfect Christmas week."

"We will," Fran replied. She knelt in front of Ruby, wrapped her arms around Ruby's neck and kissed her. "I'll be back for Christmas. You can trust me on that." Fran cocked her head. "Do you trust me now? Have I done enough to let you know I may be in the industry, but I also have a heart and a soul?"

Ruby nodded. "You have. I trust you."

"Good, because I'll be seeing Delilah again this week, but you need to remember I'm your girlfriend, okay?"

"I'm the only one you're getting naked with?"

Fran cocked her head. "If we discount Fast Forward lady."

"Touché."

"If you miss me, just remember this moment. Me naked in your arms. And if this isn't proof of what Mistletoe has done to me, I don't know what is. When did I turn into such a cheesy romantic?"

"It was always buried within. I just coaxed it out," Ruby replied.

Chapter 30

"Wow, you look hot." Damian put a hand to his mouth, frowning at his own words. "And I can't quite believe that just came out of my mouth. I apologise. I will file that under 'things never to say again to your boss'."

Fran looked down at her outfit. She'd decided to wear the blue suit she bought for her cousin's wedding two years ago that had sat in her wardrobe ever since. She'd teamed it with some navy heels and a crisp white shirt. "Thanks, I think. Although is now the time to tell you I'm gay?"

Damian opened his mouth wide. "Stop, you're killing me." He waved a hand. "But seriously, you look… I don't know. I'm not going to say hot again." He stared at her, then clicked his fingers. "You look like someone who got laid at the weekend. Am I right? Is that what I'm picking up?"

Fran willed her cheeks not to colour, but she was pretty sure they had. If not, her silence was deafening.

Damian grinned at her. "I'm right, I know it. Good decision for you to go home, then?"

"Great decision. The gig was a hit and I have a new girlfriend."

Damian put his hands in the air like he'd just scored a goal. "OMG! That's fantastic. Is she signing with us, too?"

"That was not in the criteria of her being my girlfriend." Fran hadn't even thought about that the whole time. She must be smitten.

"You're slipping," Damian said, laughing. "But looking like that, you're going to draw attention at tonight's Christmas party, mark my words."

Fran grimaced. "I hope not. I plan to have a couple of drinks, grease a few palms and be home before I lose my shoe and need to be rescued."

"That's everyone's plans until the shots take hold." Damian paused and straightened his party shirt. "Anyway, everyone smashed it at the weekend. Fast Forward killed the performance, in a good way. I watched that video you posted, too." He shook his head. "That song needs to be heard. Ruby was amazing."

"Wasn't she?"

Damian nodded, then checked his watch. "We better get to the marketing meeting and then to the party." He slicked back his hair. "How do I look? My make-up on-point?"

"To die for," Fran replied.

* * *

The label party was in an old warehouse in East London that used to be a huge wasteland of space, and was now a huge wasteland of space that had been swept twice and had a bar installed. It was freezing, but the amount of booze on offer was the way to stay warm. Fran stalked the room, waved at Jules and Niall, and headed in the direction of Fast Forward's lead singer, Tenny. As usual, Dronk Records had invited everyone on their roster — from interns to superstars. Even

Delilah was coming. Everybody was under strict instructions to take no photos or videos of the guests.

Fran recalled Delilah getting drunk at her very first Dronk Christmas party, when nobody knew who she was. In fact, it had been the Christmas party where they'd first kissed. Fran didn't want any walks down memory lane fuelled by a heady mix of tequila and nostalgia, hence she was sipping sparkling water. She was a taken woman now.

She passed a chocolate fountain, with sugary doughnuts and marshmallows to dip. She got out her phone, snapped a photo and tapped out a message to Ruby.

'I'd like to cover something else in chocolate and lick it off. I'll leave your imagination to figure out what. Miss you x'

Fran hit send, pocketed her phone, and carried on walking until she landed next to Tenny. "Hey you," she said, nudging Tenny with her hip.

Tenny gave her a hug, before taking a swig of her beer. Something about her stance had always tweaked Fran's gaydar, and tonight was no different. Can someone hold a beer bottle in a gay way? If it was possible, Tenny was doing it.

"Great to see you. Great party, too."

Fran nodded. "It is." She paused. "Are you performing later?"

"We are." She gave Fran a tight smile.

"Are you feeling more relaxed about it?"

Tenny shrugged. "I wouldn't say relaxed, but at least this performance won't be judged by the public or by the music press. This is just playing for our label, so the pressure's off."

A little like Ruby's performance at the weekend.

She put an arm around Tenny's shoulder and squeezed. "Damian said the weekend was fantastic. You're doing brilliantly. Just keep going, and that's the very best way to answer the haters. They're doing nothing with their lives. You're doing *it all*."

Tenny gave her a tense smile. "Thanks. I wasn't sure I was ready for the exposure, but the team have shown me I can do it. I just needed to believe in myself a little more, and cut out the noise — from my past and my present."

Which sounded all too familiar. It's what Ruby needed to do in order to get over her fear of success. Because that's what it was. All these women had trained themselves to think they were one thing, because society told them they were. In actual fact, they could be anything they wanted to be. They just needed to believe it. Fran was pretty sure that Ruby's weekend gig, plus her growing streaming numbers were the first step to her rebirth. Fran wanted to be there for all of it.

Tenny slipped away some minutes later to get ready to play.

Fran stood at the back waiting for them to appear when Delilah rocked up next to her. She chatted at speed in Fran's ear about some producer she hated that Niall was trying to get her to work with.

"Can you have a word with them?" Delilah swayed as she spoke. "You're the only person in the world who gets me, Fran. Nobody else does. Nobody else ever has."

Fran's defences went up as she glanced at Delilah. "Have you been drinking?" She already knew the answer.

Delilah shrugged, then held up her right hand, indicating 'a little' with her thumb and index finger. "I needed something to take my mind off the fact Gretchen hasn't been answering my calls this week. Probably another relationship I've fucked up. First you, then her. I'm doomed to singledom."

Fran grabbed her arm and moved Delilah to the side of the room. "What do you mean? Have you broken up?" She spoke slowly and at high volume, to make sure Delilah understood her over the music.

Delilah shook her head. "No, we haven't. But why is she ignoring me?"

"She's probably busy with her family. The whole world doesn't revolve around you, Delilah."

"Easy for you to say, with your new, talented girlfriend." Delilah pouted. "Did she like that you posted that video? Is she getting more views?"

Fran didn't like Delilah's tone. "She is, but she's still nervous about it."

Delilah got out her phone and called up the video. "What if I post it on my socials and tell everyone to go and listen? That would get her noticed."

Fran shook her head. No, she didn't want Delilah to do that, but she had to handle it delicately. "That would be great, but I'd have to get Ruby's okay, first. She's nervous about exposure and what it would mean for her career. She likes to be in control. She's been burned before."

Delilah waved her phone in the air. Her eyes were glazed. She might be more drunk than Fran had first thought.

"But it might be what she needs. When everyone sees this, hears her vocals, they'll lose their shit."

It was Ruby losing her shit Fran was more worried about. Especially if Ruby's big break involved Delilah.

"No posting." Fran's tone was stern. "Let me ask her first. I don't want to rock the boat. Delilah, look at me."

Delilah squinted.

"This is really important, okay?"

Delilah gave her a slow nod. "No boat-rocking. I promise."

A tap on Fran's shoulder made her turn. It was Damian.

"Our girls are on in five. You want to come and stand at the front with me?"

Fran nodded, glancing at Delilah. "Sure thing. Let me just get this one settled on a sofa first and I'll be with you." Fran guided Delilah to a sofa on the far wall, then knelt beside her. "No posting any videos, got it?"

Delilah tried to focus by placing a hand on Fran's cheek. "None at all. Or Fran will be very angry with me. Must not make Fran angry."

Chapter 31

Ruby always said December was the month she got in shape. Who needed the gym when you had a Christmas tree forest? Add Fran into the mix, and she was getting all the exercise she needed.

She grinned as she walked across the barn and delivered the tree to her mum and the excited family. Ruby went to leave when something pulled her back. When she turned, a small hand had attached itself to the sleeve of her thick coat.

"Were you the singer from Saturday?" The young girl of the Christmas tree family stared up at Ruby.

Ruby squatted down, nodding. "I was," she replied. "Were you there?"

The young girl nodded. "You were my favourite." She reached into her small pink rucksack and pulled out a notebook and pen. "Can I have your autograph?"

Ruby glanced up at the child's mum, then back to the young girl. "Of course." This wasn't the first time she'd been asked for her autograph, but it was the first time outside a gig venue. This was significant. "Who should I sign it to?"

"Me," said the girl, pointing at her chest.

Ruby grinned. "What's your name?"

"Sophia."

Ruby did just that.

Sophia gave her a shy smile. "When I grow up, I want to be a singer, too."

"I'll keep an eye out for you in a few years' time, then."

Ruby said her goodbyes, then slid into the barn office and fired up the computer. She logged into Spotify. Her streams were off the scale. Her sales were up, too. How many did it take to get in the charts? Ruby had no idea. All she did know was this time last week, her numbers were average. Now, they were like nothing she'd ever seen before, and they'd *really* soared overnight.

She leaned back in the office chair. She had no idea what had gone on, but she had a strange feeling in her stomach. Could it be things were finally happening, all from one gig? She found it hard to believe. What's more, she had a ton of messages to reply to, including a few from labels and venues she recognised.

They weren't for today, though. Ruby had work to do. Plus, she'd responded to labels too quickly before. She had to remember she was the artist, the one with the gold. If they wanted a piece of her, they'd have to wait.

The office door opened and her dad walked in, whistling. This was a new thing, too, and Ruby loved it. Over the past couple of years, her dad's worry lines had got more pronounced. But this year, with pre-orders up and the crowds swarming in, he had a new spring in his step.

"Rubytubes! What you up to? I hear you've been asked for an autograph in the barn!"

Ruby looked up. "Bit crazy, isn't it? I just looked at my

streams, too. They've been going mad since Saturday, and even more overnight. It seems bonkers one gig could do that."

Her dad parked his bum on the sofa, letting out an "ooof!" as he did. "No surprise. You were magnificent." He paused, tilting his head. "Although, the gig made me realise this has to be your last year working at the farm. Your mum and I appreciate everything you've done for us over the past few years. Coming home, putting your career on hold year after year. You are a very special daughter."

Ruby swallowed down emotion, covering it up with a shrug. "It's what we do, isn't it? Christmas is not Christmas without selling trees."

"But it should be for you." Her dad looked her in the eye. "The farm is finding its feet again. The pumpkin patch, the contest, your gig. You need to put you first. You were incredible. You should be incredible everywhere."

Ruby glanced back to the monitor. The streaming numbers were still there. Belief surged through her. Could next year really be her year, finally?

"Have you been talking to Fran about this?"

Her dad frowned. "No. Should we have been?"

Ruby shook her head. Everyone in her life agreed. But Ruby still wasn't sure she was ready to take the next step.

Coming back to Mistletoe year after year, she was able to hide, to pull back. If she put her music first and really committed, what happened when it all went wrong? Or, more to the point, what happened when it all went right? Was Fran right? Was Ruby scared of success?

"What I'm saying is, we're all paid to be here. This is

going to be Scott's business if he wants it. Your Mum and I, it's what we do. It's not what you do. You're destined for bigger things."

Ruby stared at him. If she didn't have to come back to Mistletoe for six weeks and effectively take two months off her year, she could put so many more things into motion. She could make that video she'd been promising. Finally record a few more solo songs and some with Tom. She could open all the emails and messages she'd been avoiding forever. She could really plan ahead.

Was she ready for it? Ruby knew what Fran would say: yes.

"If you give me one thing for Christmas this year, I'd like it to be you putting your whole self into your career. Will you do that for me?"

Ruby was just about to answer when Victoria burst into the office, out of breath. She'd clearly been running. Victoria hated running.

"Great, you're here. I've been trying to call you, but you're not answering."

Ruby shook her head. "My phone's over there charging." She pointed towards the drinks station where the coffee machine was unplugged to juice Ruby's phone. "Where's the fire?"

"On Instagram. On Delilah's Instagram, to be precise."

Cold fear slid down Ruby as if someone had just dumped a bucket of ice on her. Had Fran and Delilah been photographed again? She jumped up and grabbed her phone, then called up Instagram. She'd been tagged. By Delilah.

A part of Ruby said this was good news. A chart-topping pop star had tagged her.

But the other half told Ruby this was bad. That Delilah was trying to ingratiate herself with Fran.

Fran was Ruby's girlfriend. The sooner Ruby got back to London to press that home to Delilah, the better.

Ruby clicked on the tag and blew out a breath.

"What is it? What's going on? And who's Delilah?" Dad asked.

Victoria threw her hands in the air. "She's a major-league pop star, Dad! She's had a few number ones. She's a big deal, and she's posted a video of Ruby singing on Saturday night on her feed!"

"That's brilliant news!" Dad looked from Ruby to Victoria, taking in their stern faces. "Isn't it?"

Victoria looked at Ruby. "I'm not sure, ask her."

Ruby should be thrilled, but her emotions towards Delilah were all mixed up with her emotions towards Fran. Did Fran know about this? Had the two of them discussed Ruby? Why wasn't Delilah back on tour? Because she still harboured feelings for Fran?

Ruby scrolled down Delilah's Instagram feed. The next photo was a shot of Delilah, Fran, and Damian. Ruby's insides churned.

She walked back to the monitor. Her streams were still going up. The comments were rolling in. Her inbox was busy. This explained it all. It wasn't about Saturday night. It was about Fran posting her video. Then Delilah taking that video and running with it. Ruby could already feel the control of her career slipping through her fingers.

Ruby's stomach fell. Had Fran planned this with Delilah? Had she been scheming to force Ruby's hand, then play the hero by signing her? Had it been about business all along? Ruby had told Fran she wanted to take it at her own pace, but Fran had ignored that.

Ruby felt like someone had just put on size ten boots and stamped out her insides, leaving her hollow. Had Fran betrayed her, after everything?

"Isn't Dad right, though? Isn't this good news?" Victoria put a hand on her hip. "Your music's finally getting out there."

Ruby gritted her teeth. "But I wanted to do it on my own terms. To get into the spotlight through working, through my songs, through gigs, word of mouth."

"You've built that already," her dad said. "This is a helping hand."

"From my girlfriend's ex."

"Does it matter who it's from?" Victoria asked.

Ruby glanced up and held her gaze. "It does to me." Disappointment rippled through her, along with red-hot anger. Could she trust Fran? Was she going to run to Delilah with every part of Ruby's career?

She stood and grabbed her phone. "I need some air."

Ruby ran out of the office and through the barn, out into the Christmas tree fields. She wanted to run into the rows of Nordmann firs, lie down and hide from the noise. But she couldn't. She had to speak to Fran. Who might at this moment be all over Delilah, thanking her for this generous act. The thought made bile climb up Ruby's throat.

She took some deep breaths, thinking back to where it had all started with Fran. The snowperson they'd rolled among the trees. The snowball fight. The incredible sex. But if she couldn't trust her, did it all count for nothing? It was the music exec thing rearing its ugly head again, wasn't it? Creativity versus commerce. The old struggle. Would they forever be butting heads? Could Ruby and Fran navigate their way through, even if they cleared the ex-girlfriend hurdle?

Ruby turned and jogged towards the house. She ignored her mum's wave. She didn't want to be near people right now. She wanted calm. Silence. She had a feeling she wasn't going to get it.

She was steps from the farmhouse when her phone rang. She looked at the screen. It was Fran.

Ruby's heart froze. She slowed to a halt. Did she want to talk to Fran? It would certainly clear up a few things. She decided to be brave.

"Thank goodness I caught you. Listen, have you seen your Instagram feed yet?"

"I have." Ruby's tone was steely.

"Shit." Fran paused. "I need you to know, I asked Delilah not to post anything until I okayed it with you. She promised, but then she had a bit too much to drink last night at the office party and she did it anyway. I had no idea until I woke up this morning. By that time, it'd been viewed by thousands of people, so there wasn't much I could do. But I want you to know, I didn't ask her to do this. I know it would freak you out."

"You're right about that." Ruby let herself into the house.

Chipper barked and jumped up. She walked into the lounge and he followed her in. She loved this room, but she hadn't spent nearly enough time in here this year. There had been too much to do, with working, preparing for the gig and spending time with Fran. This year had been the best Christmas run-up she'd had in ages. She should remember that. Fran wasn't the enemy. Or was she? Ruby had no idea what to think.

"Can Delilah take it down?" Ruby closed her eyes and massaged her temples with her fingertips.

Fran was silent for a moment. "Do you really want her to? Yes, it's not ideal that she did it without asking, but it's publicity that most artists would kill for."

"I'm not most artists."

"I know that."

"You're not in my brain, Fran. I always told you I wanted to do this my way. At my pace. But you had to get involved, didn't you?"

"I asked her not to post it. This isn't my doing."

"But you showed her the clip in the first place."

"Because you're amazing. Because I'm proud of you. Because I'm your girlfriend." She let out an exasperated sigh. "You know, I already did this with Delilah. With her, I wasn't allowed to be me, to even exist. Now, you're asking me to play you down, to not show everyone how brilliant you are? I can't do it. I have to tell people how great you are. I didn't tell Delilah because I wanted to cash in on your fame. I did it because Delilah and I are friends. She posted it because she was drunk. I'll confront her, but she's not answering her phone right now. She's probably too hungover to talk."

Ruby's stomach churned some more. What Fran was saying made sense. But then again, Ruby's past label experience was like an open wound that had never quite healed. Could she trust Fran? Ruby couldn't stop the gnawing feeling Fran had been planning this all along. "It's not just a ploy to get me to sign with you? Has our whole relationship been about that? It's what you wanted from the start, after all."

Silence on the other end.

More bile travelled up Ruby's throat. A neon red sign flashed in her mind.

Oh, fuck.

As soon as the words were out of her mouth, Ruby knew they were the wrong ones. Scrap that, they weren't just the wrong words, the meaning behind them was wrong, full stop. However, the insinuation was out there, parading around, waving its arms. Ruby had just accused Fran of using her to further her career. Told her she didn't trust her. How could she have said that? Accused Fran so blatantly? Ruby knew in her soul it was untrue.

They'd got to know each other over the past few weeks and nothing Fran had done pointed to anything like that. Their connection was true. Their sex had been orgasmic. Fran wasn't the person Ruby had first thought. Fran wasn't out for herself. She was gorgeous and fearless. Everything Ruby wasn't.

If Ruby could take back that sentence, she would. But her insecurities had taken over and run riot. She'd never quite dealt with her past, and now it was trampling on her future, and she was powerless to stop it.

"Fran—" Ruby began again. Even if it was too late, she had to try. Her brain was on fire as she spoke. She clutched her phone tight, desperation ripping through her.

"You know what, fuck you." Fran wasn't about to mince her words.

Ruby didn't blame her.

"How *dare* you say that to me. How fucking dare you!

I seriously don't have time for this. I've got artists getting shit thrown at them online for no reason other than they're young and new. But at least Fast Forward are putting themselves out there, taking a chance. Unlike you. Have you ever taken a chance in your life? You did it once with a label, you got burned, and then you've run scared ever since. But you know what? Life is about taking chances, it's about getting up when you've been knocked down and trying again. You're not the first person to experience a setback, Ruby.

"You need to get over yourself. Get out of your own way. Realise the talent you've got. Stop running back to Mistletoe and hiding. Because if you don't, maybe you're always going to be looking for someone else to blame as an excuse for you to do nothing."

Fran was right. Ruby knew it. Her hand shook as she tried to think of something to respond with. But she was scared of opening her mouth. Scared of saying the wrong thing again. The hole she'd started was deep enough, and she didn't want to dig any further. Would Fran take her silence as not caring? *Fuck*. Ruby had to conjure a sentence. A word. A letter. Anything to stop this train wreck of a conversation from getting worse. She searched her brain, but drew a blank.

Fran filled in the gap. "If you really don't trust me – because that's what this is – if you *really* think there's some grand plan, maybe we'll never work out. And you know what? That would be a crime because we're good together. *Damn good*." Fran sighed deeply. "I'm not out to get you, Ruby, and I honestly can't fucking believe you would think that. We've shared so many moments. We had amazing sex and you *still* think that?"

Fran raised her voice higher. "That's the thing that really

sticks in my throat. Did you really think I was fucking you and instead of enjoying the mind-blowing sex, I was wondering how to get you to sign with me? You're *unbelievable*. I thought I knew you, but maybe I don't. Maybe we're not on the same page, just like you thought all along. Maybe you were right from the start."

Ruby hated every second of this call. Acid panic burned her throat. "I'm sorry Fran. I said the wrong thing—"

"You're damn right you said the wrong thing! Or maybe you said the right thing so that I can really see who you are before I jump into a relationship with you. All that stuff you said about me being what you needed, about us fitting together. Was that ever real?"

"Yes, it was. You have to believe me!" Ruby's stomach dropped and her mouth went dry. It was only days ago they'd laid in each other's arms. In the stretched-out days since, Ruby had been longing to see Fran again. Now, she could see their whole relationship unravelling before it even started, and it was all down to her. Ruby and her big mouth, along with her past that she'd boxed up and backed away from.

Fran had forced Ruby to confront her fears, and she'd been right to do so. Ruby had been hiding away for too long. But now, faced with taking it further, Ruby had lashed out and said *completely* the wrong thing. She knew it in her bones. She knew it in her heart. But she was pretty sure it would take a colossal effort to convince Fran of that.

"Plus, you know what the real kicker of this is?" Fran was far from done, but Ruby had to take it. "You're so hell-bent on doing everything yourself that you don't realise a label could help you, take the weight off. The *right* label this time.

People who get you. You can't do it on your own. And even if you don't want to sign with anyone, you could get some help anyway so that you're freed up to take some chances. If you don't, you're never going to realise your full potential."

Every word was true. Ruby's gut told her so. She wanted to rewind. She'd do *anything* to rewind. To take them back to the gig, and what happened afterwards. She didn't want to be jealous of Delilah. She didn't want to make Fran upset and disappointed with her. She wanted to be the perfect girlfriend, and the perfect singer. But she was neither. She was failing miserably on all counts. Her breath rasped as fear lodged in her throat. This was it. She'd blown it. She clutched her phone in desperation. "Fran, you have to believe me. I don't think you're scheming against me—"

"You just said you did! You accused me of getting you publicity for my own gain. Which is just ridiculous. And insulting. Like you think I'm a sort of prostitute, which every woman always wants to hear. You really fucking need to work on your charm skills, Ruby. But fine. Go ahead. Blame me for getting eyeballs on you. Blame me for wanting more for you than you even dare to dream of. If you think this is all one elaborate ruse to get you to sign with me, then *fuck you*, Ruby. Maybe we should call it quits."

The line went dead. Fran had hung up.

Ruby stared at her phone. If she thought she'd been hollowed out before, she certainly was now. Her skin sagged. Her bones buckled. Her heart slumped on the floor. Was that really it? Was that how this ended? Her brain refused to believe it.

Ruby had just pressed the self-destruct button on the truest connection she'd ever felt in her life, with one of the funniest and smartest women she'd ever met. Smart move. Way to go, Ruby. What a fucking gargantuan moron she was.

Ruby took a breath and dropped her head. She pressed her feet firmly to the ground to stop her from falling.

Fran had just broken up with her. Ruby's whole body was numb. She couldn't feel a thing. Christmas was next week. She'd entertained such fantasies about their lives when they got back to London. Museums they'd visit. Restaurants they'd eat at. Lazy weekend mornings when they'd make love. All gone. Just like that. All thanks to Ruby. *Bravo*.

What the hell had she just done?

Chapter 32

Fran massaged her temples and leaned back in her chair. What a week. First the Christmas party. Then the Delilah storm. Then her break-up with Ruby. And now, more social media trouble for Fast Forward, who were getting trolled from all sides, especially by the rabid fans of Cupboard Boy and Skinny YouTube Boy. It never rained, but it poured.

"Did you sort it out?" Damian poked his head around his monitor.

Thank goodness for Damian, otherwise Fran might well want to jump off a cliff at this point. She nodded. "Yes, got the accounts blocked, reported them, had a word with the team about how it got through in the first place. These girls are dealing with enough sudden fame; they don't need this shit as well."

"Couldn't agree more." Damian carried on staring at her. "Any Ruby news?"

Fran let her eyes flicker shut, then reopened them. She had Christmas presents at her feet. New bakeware and gardening stuff for Dad. New candles and some painting supplies for Pop. Also, presents for Ruby she'd bought before their phone call last week. She was still angry, but now she was more sad.

Today was Christmas Eve, a week since they'd spoken.

Fran had decided to put Ruby on pause, to try to work out her own feelings and make sense of what had happened. Every brain cell in her head told her Ruby wasn't ready for a relationship, never mind a rocket up her career. However, Fran's heart was singing a different tune. It still recalled the way Ruby had made her feel. It still wanted to believe they had a future together.

"I dunno what to think. She sent me a few messages and a couple of voicemails saying she's sorry, but they petered out when she realised I wasn't going to call back. I should hate her. But I can't believe she meant it. But why say it in the first place?"

Damian tilted his head. "We've all said things we didn't mean in the heat of the moment. Plus, you look pretty sad for someone who's thinking of giving her up."

"Is there a future if she doesn't trust me? If she always thinks I'm out for myself? She has a paranoid hatred of the music business."

"She's been burned before. You happen to be the one in the firing line. It was the same when my older brother met his wife. He thought she was going to do the dirty on him because that was his experience with women. When she turned out to be a lovely person, he wasn't quite sure whether to believe it or not. It took her threatening to leave and my mum telling him to stop being such a twit for him to wake up. But he nearly lost her. They've got three kids together now and everything's fine."

"I don't want three kids."

"Just have two and a dog, then." Damian grinned at her. "The key thing is, Ruby is reacting because of past experience and fear. You're in a position to help her. Don't give up on her. I don't think you want to, either." He paused. "Plus, you're going home to Mistletoe today. Isn't it against the law to be unhappy there at Christmas?"

Damian had a point.

"Would you like another random Mistletoe fact?"

Fran smiled. "I would love one."

Damian held up his hand. All of his fingers had far too much hair on them. "Mistletoe has been associated with kissing since the 1500s. If that's not a sign that you need to kiss someone when you get back there, I don't know what is. Also, the berries on it are toxic to humans, so don't eat them."

"Do some snogging, don't eat the berries. Got it. Are you going to your parents?" Fran had been so preoccupied with her own disaster week, she hadn't asked Damian yet.

He nodded. "We're driving over for lunch on Christmas Day, then we're going to Isla's parents for the evening. By Boxing Day, I will be the size of a cow."

"A lovely, wise cow." Fran sighed. "I thought my parents moving to Mistletoe would mean an idyllic Christmas with lashings of snow and no drama."

"You've got the snow." Damian pointed out the window where snowflakes were falling. "And you might still get a drama-free Christmas. Although, drama-free Christmases are over-rated if you ask me." He paused. "Have you checked the trains, by the way? The snow's affecting them."

Fran clicked her jaw left, then right. She hadn't. When she did, there were a raft of cancellations on her line. *Of course there were.* She had to get home or her parents would be crushed.

"How you feeling, Delilah?" shouted someone in the office.

Fran sat up, her gaze scanning the space until it fell on her ex walking towards her.

"Better than Tuesday!" Delilah shouted back, and the whole office laughed. Delilah was getting good at laughing at herself. Wonders would never cease.

"Hey, Damian," Delilah said, giving him a wave.

Damian waved back.

When she got to Fran, Delilah held out some keys. "I come bearing gifts. A grovelling gift to say sorry again for Tuesday's fuck-up. I've been given another car, and I know you need one over Christmas. So here are the keys to the Porsche." She held up a finger. "No arguments, I know the trains are shit." She paused. "Think of it as an indefinite loan." She leaned in and whispered in Fran's ear. "Let's just say it's yours if you want it. But if it causes issues with your new girlfriend, you don't have to keep it." She pulled back. "Will it at least help you out today?"

Fran looked down at the bags of presents at her feet, and her suitcase. "Like you wouldn't believe."

"Good." Delilah pursed her lips. "Can I have a 'you're forgiven' hug? Even if it's half-hearted?"

Fran smiled. Ruby's reaction wasn't Delilah's fault. She hadn't committed the crime of the century. If Ruby couldn't see that, then fuck her. Although, Christmas was going to be all sorts of awkward.

Fran got up and gave Delilah a hug. She held on longer than necessary, squeezing Delilah tight. It was good to have her as a friend again.

When they broke apart, Delilah eyed her. "Everything okay?"

Fran nodded. "All good." She hadn't said anything to Delilah about Ruby. Fran was too embarrassed at love failing again.

Delilah quirked an eyebrow, but let it go. "Also, and I know you probably won't take me up. But if Ruby needs someone to talk to — someone who's been there and knows what it's like to overcome stage fear — call me."

Fran snorted. "You're right, she probably won't, but thanks." She paused. "Are you leaving for home soon?"

Delilah nodded. "Into the lion's den. Wish me luck heading to my worst Christmas yet."

"It might not be so bad."

Delilah cocked her head. "Stop it with your glass half full, you're freaking me out." She kissed Fran's cheek. "Have a great Christmas."

* * *

Fran got back to Mistletoe around 7pm, after the Porsche purred its way along the M11 and got her home in record time.

Her parents wouldn't stop hugging her.

"You don't need your car back when you've got this, do you?" Dad ran his hand along the Porsche 911's sleek exterior.

"Talking of that, any update from the garage?" Fran asked.

Dad shook his head. "I spoke to the bloke yesterday. The part still hasn't arrived. It's looking like January." He gave her a small pout, then grabbed her bags and they walked inside.

"You look laden with presents this year." Pop closed the front door with one of his crutches.

"Got to spoil my favourite men," Fran replied.

"But first, let us spoil you. We haven't eaten yet, we've been waiting for you. Dad made your favourite: salmon en croute!" Pop's face lit up.

Dad stood next to him, his festive apron covered in flour. Fran hugged them again. Her love life might be up the spout, but she could rely on her parents to put a smile on her face. Also, the dinner smelt incredible. She already knew there was an obscene amount of butter in Dad's pastry.

"It smells delicious and sounds heavenly. Let me put my stuff upstairs, freshen up and then I'll come down for a glass of wine and some food."

Fran hung up her coat, scarf and hat, then followed her dad upstairs, after he insisted on carrying her case. Left alone, she changed, then gave herself a pep talk in the mirror about putting on a brave face and not spoiling her parents' Christmas Eve. She was ready to do just that when she walked down the stairs, smoothing down her light-grey jumper. Her Christmas face was on, even though being in such close proximity to Ruby made her heart quake. She'd deal with tomorrow when it happened.

Fran reached the bottom stair when there was a knock at the front door.

She opened it with a smile that was soon wiped from her face when she saw who it was.

Ruby.

Fran gulped. She wasn't prepared to see her yet. She had a speech written in her head for tomorrow, a list of how their relationship could and couldn't work.

But now Ruby was in front of her, all that was out the window. Looking into Ruby's green gaze, Fran's body lit up.

She recalled how dark her eyes got when she was aroused. How sparkly they got when she spoke about Christmas. How just being this close to her made Fran's pulse race. These were the factors she couldn't account for on paper.

"Hi." Ruby shivered, then folded her arms across her chest. Her eyes darted to Fran's face, then pulled away. Ruby's gaze skittered around until it eventually landed back on its initial target.

"I know you only just got home. I was in the front garden when I saw your Porsche drive by." She held up a hand. "I'm not stalking you, I promise. I just thought I'd act now, before I lost my nerve. I got the message you didn't want to talk with me last week when you didn't answer my texts and calls. I know I was in the wrong. I know I still am. I just wanted to come over and smooth things out before tomorrow. To make sure we can be civil to each other for Christmas, at least." Behind Ruby, the snow had stopped, but the night was still freezing.

"Who is it, Fran?" Dad called, before appearing in the hallway.

When he saw it was Ruby, he raised both eyebrows. "I'll leave you to it." He disappeared at speed.

Fran had given him skeleton details on the phone earlier in the week. She stared at Ruby, battling with herself, then relented. She wanted to talk to her, so she might as well do it now. "Come in." Fran shut the door when Ruby was inside.

"I've never seen a parent disappear so quickly."

"Sometimes, they're well trained. Most of the time, they're not." Fran stared. "You want to come up?"

Ruby nodded. "Sure." She took off her boots and coat, then followed Fran upstairs.

This was the second time Fran had invited Ruby to her bedroom, but this time, annoyance pulsed inside her. Fran had no idea how this was going to go. Ruby had broken their relationship, and Fran had no idea if it could be fixed. The doctors had mended her pop's leg with a cast, and time. Fran was sure if their relationship could heal, it would also take time. The first move would determine their future, and it was Ruby's to make.

Fran cleared the bags of gifts from the floor by her bed and invited Ruby to sit. Her parents had left her fresh towels, along with a sprig of mistletoe. Fran frowned. She wasn't sure that was going to be needed. She moved them to the opposite side of the bed.

Ruby smoothed down her jeans as she sat next to her.

Fran stared at Ruby's gorgeous face, her shiny lips. The same ones that had accused Fran of using her.

Fran wasn't going to be won over so easily.

"I just want you to know that I'm sorry. *Really sorry*. I reacted badly, and I accused you of something that was a bit ridiculous."

"A lot ridiculous."

Ruby hung her head. "Okay, a lot. But I want you to know that this is my issue and it's all about trust. I know I need to deal with it. I also know that you have always had my best interests at heart, even when I really didn't deserve that. Again, I'm truly sorry. For everything."

Fran heard what Ruby said, but she wasn't budging just yet. Ruby spoke a good game, but words were cheap.

"I saw Delilah lent you her car again."

If Ruby was about to have a go about that, it would be

the final straw. Every muscle in Fran's body stiffened. "She did. She gave it to me, actually. As a thank you, and a sorry."

"She gave you a Porsche?"

Fran nodded. "She also told me I didn't have to accept it if it was going to cause issues with you. But if you can't take me being in contact with exes who are still my friends, then we're not going to work." She hadn't planned to say that, but it was true. Delilah was in Fran's life, like it or not.

Ruby stared at Fran for a few moments. "Look, I know you're pissed off with me and you have every right to be. You're not trying to manipulate me. I get that. Delilah did what she did, and in the cold light of day, I'm grateful. I'm getting so much interest, it's blowing my mind. My song is in the charts. I'm making money. That's amazing."

Fran kept her game face on. "It is." Ruby acknowledging that was a good thing.

"I've only glanced at the emails quickly. I've been too busy here. I'm not making any decisions yet because it's Christmas, so they can wait." Ruby looked Fran in the eye. "I know I messed up, but I really want to try again. I missed you so much this week. I missed *us*." She paused. "If you're willing, I'd love for you to look at these offers of festivals and collaborators with me. To give me some advice. You know the business better than anyone and I'd love some help to make the right decisions." Ruby's lip wobbled, and she took Fran's hand.

Confusion rippled through Fran. Ruby might be the biggest bundle of insecurities she'd seen in such an accomplished artist, but it came with the territory. All artists were a curious mix of confidence and self-doubt. Ruby just needed to work on the former. She was tough enough. She just needed belief. Fran could help her.

What's more, holding Ruby's hand was *everything*. Whatever they had was still there, beating loudly inside her. It hadn't gone away in a week. Perhaps their relationship did just need a plaster cast, and some time.

"I'm not sorry about that video going viral."

Ruby shook her head. "Neither am I."

"Good. Also, just to be clear, I don't want to sign you anymore, either. You'd be a nightmare. I already have enough of them on my books."

The corners of Ruby's mouth twitched at that. "We're on the same page, then. Plus, I'm still not signing with anyone."

"I charge a £500 a day consultancy fee for my help, too," Fran added.

Ruby's eyes widened. "Oh. I…"

"I'm kidding." Fran finally allowed herself a half-smile. "Damn, you're easy to wind up."

Ruby's gaze was uncertain. "And you're very forgiving."

"You're not forgiven quite yet. I want to know that any advice or nudging I give you, you're not going to throw the 'pushy music exec' line at me. I am who I am. I want to help make you a success."

Ruby nodded. "I know that. I promise, no music exec jibes. They're banned." She squeezed Fran's hand. "Just know, this week has been hell. I've hated what I said to you and I've been battling myself. I'm my own worst enemy, I know that. But time away from everything has given me perspective. I've talked to the trees and they think I should get out of my own way. Even my dad told me he doesn't want me back here next year helping out. He wants me to forge my path. Pursue my goals." Ruby gave Fran a grin. "Feel the fear and do it anyway, as someone wise once told me."

Fran held Ruby's gaze, hope blooming in her soul. "They sound very wise."

Ruby nodded. "Terrifyingly beautiful, too." Her gaze sank to Fran's lips.

Fran snapped her fingers. "Stop looking at my lips. We're not done."

Ruby sat upright.

"I need you to mean what you're telling me. To stop hiding behind limiting excuses. You could do many things, but the one you're best at is being a singer-songwriter. Lean into that one."

"I'm starting to believe that."

Fran put a hand to Ruby's face. Then she went to take it away. Was it too soon? Should she make Ruby wait longer?

But Ruby didn't think so. She caught Fran's hand as she moved it and pressed it to her cheek. "I want to pick up where we left off. I want to give us a go back in London." She paused, fixing Fran with her stare. "I'm sorry for this week, more than you can imagine. When I said I want to start making the right decisions, this is my first one. Also, my most important." Ruby took a deep breath. "What do you say? Clean slate from now on?"

Fran moved towards Ruby before she could stop herself. In seconds, her lips were inches from Ruby's. "I'm still fucking mad at you."

"I know." Ruby's breath was hot on Fran's lips.

"But you're asking for help. Finally." Fran shook her head. "Let's try a clean slate. Don't make me regret doing this. Although, I don't want to wipe out certain memories we've made together." Fran flicked her gaze to meet Ruby's own.

"Those memories are burned into my mind forever." Ruby moved forward. "Can I kiss you now?"

Fran stared into Ruby's vibrant eyes. Then she leaned forward and their lips met. Ruby's mouth finally on hers after so much upset this week felt like salvation. Fran moved her hand into Ruby's hair, and Ruby released a sharp breath against her lips that made Fran's stomach dip. The bubble of resentment and worry that had built this week inside her burst on contact.

She didn't want to be angry at Ruby. She wanted to be her girlfriend, and for them both to be happy. One of the ways that could happen was by Ruby kissing her exactly as she was at that moment.

A kiss that spoke of their future together. One filled with passion, romance and love. Ruby's hand pulled Fran closer, and Fran didn't resist. She didn't want to. Now she'd given in to her heart, she was ready to embrace the next stage. Ready to embrace Ruby.

When they pulled apart, Ruby's eyes were misty. "I wondered all week if I'd get to do that again."

"Me, too." Fran kissed Ruby once more. "But I have a first test of your commitment to us. I promised my dads I'd have dinner with them."

Ruby stood. "I'll leave you in peace."

But Fran shook her head. "That's not what I'm saying."

She took Ruby's hand. "Would you like to join us for a spot of salmon en croute? My dad makes the best one ever."

Ruby's smile was so wide, it almost took up the whole room. "I would absolutely love to."

Chapter 33

The next morning, Ruby jerked awake as pain shot through her foot. She sat bolt upright as her foot contorted. She tried to straighten it, but knew she was fighting a losing battle. When she glanced right, Fran was already awake, sitting up in bed, phone in hand. Her face wore a frown.

"Are you okay?"

"Cramp!" Ruby reached down and grabbed her foot, forcing it into a stretch. She let out a cry of angst. This was not the alluring wake up she'd been hoping to showcase on Christmas Day.

"You want me to massage it?" Fran dropped her phone and knelt up, giving Ruby an alarmed look.

Ruby gritted her teeth and shook her head. Eventually, she got her breath back and sat up the bed again, her back against the padded grey headboard.

Fran twisted her head and ran a hand up Ruby's arm. "Better?"

Ruby's body thrilled to her touch. She leaned down and kissed Fran's arm. "Yes. Although I've just realised it's Christmas Day and I don't have any presents for you. They're back at the house, so you'll have to wait until later."

"You mean Santa didn't come?" Fran pouted.

"He came to the farmhouse," Ruby replied. "It's your first year here. He'll know for next time."

Fran jumped out of the bed and rustled in one of her bags. "In the meantime, I have something for you." She sat back on the bed with a gift in her hand, neatly wrapped in gold paper with a matching bow.

However, Ruby's attention was snagged by the mistletoe on Fran's chest of drawers. She reached across to get it, then sat next to Fran, holding the sprig over their heads. "Here's my first present to you." Ruby pressed her lips to Fran's, and Christmas Day got that little bit brighter. "Happy first Christmas, new girlfriend." Ruby gazed into Fran's eyes. "I'll never get tired of kissing you."

"You might, you've only been doing it a few weeks." Fran gave her a wicked grin, then took the sprig from her hand. "Open your gift, please!"

Ruby laughed, and kissed Fran's naked skin. She tore open the wrapping paper to reveal a red box. When she opened that, she pulled out an intricately made shiny golden star.

"I saw it and thought of you, because that's what you are: a shining star." Fran paused. "But now you're holding it, I'm worried you're going to think I'm being pushy again—"

Ruby silenced Fran by kissing her again. Ruby's fingers clutched the star as her lips slid over Fran's, and Ruby's heart swelled in her chest. When she pulled back, she smiled at Fran. "I don't think you're being pushy. I get it. I know you want me to embrace whatever happens, and I'm going to try. To be brave. With you beside me, it's going to be a whole lot easier." She held up her present. "I love my star. Thank you."

"You're welcome." Fran blushed bright red.

She was adorable.

"Thanks for last night, too. It was fab having dinner with your parents. They're so cute together."

Fran smiled. "They are, aren't they? I've neglected them over the past few years, but I'm not going to do that anymore. Especially now we're together. I was thinking this week — before you threw a huff at me — that if you do have to go away for festivals or to tour, I could take some of my holiday and come with you. I never take time off, but that's going to change."

"You're getting a bit ahead of yourself. My bookings at the moment are both in small pubs in London. No time off needed."

"I'm thinking long term. Your song's in the charts now, right?"

Ruby nodded. "Amazingly, it is. I'm being interviewed on national and international radio this week. My inbox is overloaded. All thanks to you and Delilah."

Fran shook her head. "I think it's down to you." She kissed Ruby again. "But back to my point. You're stuck with me now. We've sung 'Last Christmas' in the world's smallest bar. Built a snowperson. Had sex in a barn. There's simply no way you can escape now."

Ruby laughed. "There's no way I would want to, either. Not after the barn sex. Although having sex in a bed is way more comfortable.

"Where's your sense of adventure? Honestly, pop stars these days…"

"I'm not a pop star yet!"

"You will be. If Taylor Swift can do a country-pop crossover, why can't you do the same with folk-pop?"

"Because she's Taylor Swift?"

"And you're Ruby O'Connell."

Ruby pulled up the charts on her phone. Her song, 'Pieces Of You', was at number 15. She still couldn't quite believe her eyes. She scrolled down to the number one slot, occupied by the Skinny YouTube Boy. Fast Forward were at number two.

"Sorry you didn't get your Christmas number one." Ruby flashed her phone screen at Fran.

Fran shook her head. "Fast Forward have done amazingly well. We can build on it. Plus, I got the number 15 star naked in my bed. I'm pretty pleased with my work."

She took Ruby's phone from her hand and pushed her back on the bed, climbing on top of her.

Ruby groaned as their skin connected. She could happily stay like this all day, but her parents might not be so happy.

"By the way, did your dads make you a cool Christmas card like you told me all those months ago?"

"I climb on top of you and you start talking about my dads?" Fran gave her a crazed look, then a kiss. "The short answer is no. The broken leg derailed their plans. They just watched a lot of Christmas movies, baked, and had fun." Fran grinned. "When we get back to London, I want to have fun and go on an official date with you. Take you out to a restaurant. Wine and dine you, instead of just falling into each other's beds. What do you think?"

"I never realised you were so conventional. It's not what pop stars do." Fran's lips were so close, Ruby could feel her breath.

"No? What do pop stars do?"

"This." Ruby kissed Fran's lips. She didn't see a time she'd ever tire of it.

Fran slid down Ruby's body, kissing a path from her neck to her belly button.

Anticipation danced on Ruby's skin. "Can one of our dates be you cooking me dinner, too? Because I've wanted to taste your Malaysian curry ever since you told me about it when we broke down."

Fran parted Ruby's legs and slid her shoulders between them. "You're thinking about eating right now?"

Ruby grinned down at her, licking her lips. "In a way."

Fran licked her lips, too, her hot breath hitting Ruby's centre. "Happy Christmas, my shining star."

* * *

"Something's burning! What's burning?" Mum had her fingers in her hair. "Not the turkey again. Paul!"

Victoria rolled her eyes at Ruby as their dad ran to the oven and grabbed the handle.

"Argh!" he cried when he forgot the handle would be hot. He grabbed a tea towel from the counter, and opened the oven door at the second time of asking. Grey smoke billowed from the oven. Her dad's glasses steamed up so he couldn't see a thing.

Ruby tried not to laugh. Eric wasn't as successful. It was the same every year. Dad burned the turkey. Mum shouted at him. Everyone ate the turkey and made reassuring noises that it wasn't dry. It always was, but that was where her mum's gravy saved the day.

"What do you normally do at Christmas when you haven't just moved to the madness that is Mistletoe, Michael and Dale?" Victoria handed them both a glass of Merlot as requested.

"We normally see Michael's parents or his sister and her family, but they've taken themselves to the Caribbean this year. I think they'd always wanted to and us having other plans was the excuse they needed," Dale replied.

"Particularly good now our families are joined together in a new way." Victoria bumped Ruby's hip with her own. "I called it when I first met Fran, but Ruby was very insistent that just because they were both lesbians did not mean they were going to get together."

"To be fair, when we met here, I did vomit sausage roll onto her slipper, so it wasn't the best start," Fran said.

"Isn't that how all the best love stories start? With some sort of mishap? Then they morph into something beautiful." Michael's face went all dreamy.

"Ignore him," Dale said. "He's been overdosing on far too many Hallmark Christmas movies."

They made way for Audrey, who bustled in waving her Christmas cracker. "I want my hat. It's not Christmas without a silly hat. Who wants to pull me?"

"There's an offer you don't get every day," Victoria said.

Audrey ignored her. Her gaze landed on Fran. "You can pull with me, seeing as you look like a Christmas cracker in your green top and red trousers. Ready?"

Fran grabbed the end of Audrey's cracker and pulled.

It snapped, and Audrey came away with the winning end. She fished out the silver paper hat and put it on, then waved around her prize: a mini pot of Mary's home-made gooseberry jam. "Delicious! Ready for the joke? What kind of motorbike does Santa drive?"

Nobody offered an answer.

"A Holly Davidson." Audrey shook her head. "That joke was terrible, Paul. It's got you written all over it."

Mary clapping her hands got their attention. "Can everyone please sit and pull your crackers. I'm not responsible for the jokes. To save arguments, I've put name tags on everyone's places, so play nice and sit where I put you. That includes you, Audrey."

Audrey clucked like she'd never dream of doing anything else. She stalked the table until she found her place. She sat next to Norman, rolling her eyes. "I can't believe you put me next to him."

Norman, used to Audrey's lip, roared with laughter. He put an arm around Audrey and kissed her cheek. "Merry Christmas to you, too, Audrey Parrot."

Mary caught Dale's eye. "Dale, I've put you on the corner to give you room for your cast."

Ruby sat in her place — Victoria on her left, Fran on her right. She glanced around the table: she had so much to be grateful for. A loving family, food and drink to celebrate, and Fran. The Christmas gift she hadn't ordered, but the one it turned out she wanted the most. So much so, she was willing to turn her life upside down for her.

It was about time.

Ruby put a hand on Fran's thigh under the table.

Fran turned and gave Ruby a wink, before accepting the tray of roast potatoes from Scott.

Ruby had never had Christmas with someone special at

her family table before. She'd never even imagined it. But now it was happening, it felt exactly right.

Fran and her parents were the perfect addition to the O'Connell family Christmas. The previous owner had lived in Hollybush Cottage for eight years and never come to dinner once. The Bells had lived there for three months but it might as well have been forever.

A warmth burrowed its way into Ruby's thighs. She looked down to see Chipper's pleading eyes staring up at her. It was the same every dinner, every day. Anyone would think the dog never got fed.

"Chipper, in your bed."

Chipper didn't move.

Ruby got her firm tone out and repeated the instruction.

Chipper slunk away.

"Glad to see you've got turkey and ham on the table, Mary and Paul," Audrey said. "Not bending to the London types who want tofurkey."

Ruby laughed. "I'm still not vegan, Audrey."

"Ridiculous," Audrey muttered, piling turkey onto her plate. "Shall I do yours, Norman?"

"Careful," Norman replied. "People will think we're a couple."

In response, Audrey shoved the plate into his hands. "Second thoughts, do it yourself."

A tapping of metal on glass stilled the chatter and din of plates being filled. The whole table looked up.

Dad stood at the end of the table, glass raised.

"Before we all eat this delicious turkey that I lovingly cooked, I just wanted to say how grateful both Mary and

I are. To our family, to our friends old and new, and to the community of Mistletoe. We came together like we always do this year, and the farm has had a great festive period that will hopefully set us up for years to come. Mistletoe Farm is a destination, a place to make Christmas dreams come true, a place to make Christmas memories." He glanced at Ruby. "Our wonderful daughter gave us a lasting Christmas memory this year, and we're so proud she's finally getting the recognition she deserves."

The whole table broke into spontaneous applause.

Ruby blushed the colour of Santa's suit.

"But today is all about being together with the people who matter most, and I'm glad to say we've achieved that. So raise your glass with me to the true spirit of Christmas, before we all eat far too much food than is good for us." Dad raised his drink. "To Christmas in Mistletoe!"

Ruby brimmed with happiness as she raised her glass. "To Christmas in Mistletoe!" she chorused with everyone else. Then she looked at Fran. "And to my first Christmas with you," she whispered in Fran's ear.

"The first of many," Fran replied, kissing Ruby's lips.

Epilogue

Two years later.

"Rubytubes! You made it back! How was Rome?" Dad and Chipper greeted her at the farmhouse door. Chipper, now ten, wasn't quite as jumpy as he used to be.

"Italian." Ruby bent and rubbed Chipper behind his ears, then gave her dad a hug. "How's the Treasure Hunt going? Fran and I were admiring the trees on the way in."

Her dad pushed his glasses up his nose. "Going great! We've got nearly 50 trees this year. Nearly running out of places to put them."

Ruby walked through to the kitchen and stopped in her tracks. She hadn't been home since the summer, and things had changed massively.

"Am I in the right house?" Ruby glanced at her mum, who was standing by the sink with a massive grin on her face. "This new kitchen looks incredible. You've gone from country crumble to country slickers." Ruby leaned against the new quartz counter-top her mum had raved about to her on the phone. "An island, too. Your dreams have come true, Mum."

Mary walked over and hugged her tight. "To have you both home for Christmas is my dream coming true." She paused. "Where's Fran?"

Ruby indicated with her head. "Michael and Dale were out in the garden, so she was hijacked by them. She'll be over in a bit. We met their new rescue dogs, Cagney and Lacey. They're adorable."

Mary nodded. "Cagney is blind in one eye, but they're so sweet. They've found a wonderful home for their final years."

"Looks like it," Ruby replied. "I'm going for a shower as we've been travelling for what seems like forever. I swear, the dirt is ingrained."

"Take all the time you need. The Christmas gig's not for another," her dad checked his watch, "eight hours. Plenty of time."

"Paul! The girl's just walked through the door, let her relax." Mum put a hand on Ruby's arm. "This kitchen is all because of you. The number of fans coming to the farm to see where Ruby O'Connell is from grows every time you release a song. They're all buying coffee, scones, wreaths, the works." She shook her head. "Good job you're not out there selling trees; you'd be knee-deep in autograph hunters."

Ruby was just about to brush her mum's comments off, but then she remembered what Fran always said to her: take the compliment and be gracious. Ruby had learned so much from Fran since she'd given up her job to become Ruby's full-time manager. The pair of them were now travelling the globe touring. It was tough work, but it was so rewarding.

One downside was that the new flat they'd bought together

in London was hardly lived in, yet. But now, Ruby got to play to crowds there just for her. It was everything she'd never dared to dream of, and it felt just right. A little like coming back to Mistletoe for Christmas. Even if it did mean staying with her parents again.

"I'll go out there in a bit, sell a tree for old time's sake. Test your theory." Ruby picked up her suitcase.

"You will not!" Mum replied. "Go get cleaned up. I've made sausage rolls, turkey-and-stuffing bites, cranberry-and-brie parcels. Plus, mince pies, of course. All the Christmas favourites. Fill you up before you go on stage."

Ruby smiled. It was good to be home.

* * *

"There she is, my sister, the superstar!" Victoria and Eric hugged Ruby and Fran, before handing over their daughter, Eleanor.

Fran and Ruby had met the baby once before their tour schedule had whisked them away.

"She is so adorable." Fran held Eleanor up in the air.

Eleanor gurgled and grinned as if on cue.

"Couldn't you just eat her up?" Victoria grinned. "She's very excited about seeing her Auntie Ruby sing tonight."

Eric nodded. "Wouldn't stop going on about it earlier." He turned to Victoria. "Or maybe that was you."

Victoria drew herself up to her full five feet three inches. "I'm unashamedly proud of my sister, so sue me."

"You should be," Fran told her. "She's been killing it on tour."

"We've been killing it on tour," Ruby corrected Fran.

Fran let out an exasperated growl. "Please take a compliment! She's a bloody nightmare."

"We'll leave you two to fight about who's the best. See you out there." Victoria squeezed Ruby's arm. "Break a leg." She took her daughter from Fran and kissed Eleanor's chubby cheek. "Come on, my little munchkin. Let's go and let the whole village coo over you. Try not to cry when Audrey holds you as you do every single time."

The new family left the barn office, and then it was just Fran and Ruby.

Fran walked up to Ruby and pushed her back against the desk, a smirk on her face. "Remember this move?"

Ruby coughed. "How could I ever forget? The first time you fucked me was in my dad's office. That's a country song if ever I heard one."

Fran laughed. "Begging to be written." She kissed Ruby's lips. They were still her favourite place in the entire world.

"Did I tell you my parents gave me my Christmas bauble this year, and it's a photo of the two of us, not just me?"

Fran sucked in a breath, then clasped her hands over her heart. Coming home to Mistletoe was always special, because all the people she loved most were here. Even Damian and Isla were in the crowd tonight. They had VIP seats right next to her parents, who they were staying with again.

"I love that more than I can say. I think that means your parents approve of me, right?"

Ruby kissed her. "How could they not?"

Fran hugged Ruby tight, squeezing until Ruby coughed.

She pulled back, laughing. "Talking of parents, my dads are livid, by the way. They entered a tree in the contest again this year. Second year running they didn't win. As someone who has a hotline to the O'Connell family, they wondered if you could put in a good word."

"They should speak to Victoria. She hasn't won either after years of trying." Ruby's lips quirked into a smile. "She never will, either. It's a Mistletoe scandal."

But Fran's attention had moved on. She held Ruby's stare, then slipped a hand between her thighs. "Back to me, you and the desk. How about it? For old time's sake?"

Ruby was just about to reply when there was a knock on the door. "Ruby! Fran! Can I come in?"

Fran grinned, then stepped back. "Parental interruptus strikes again."

Ruby laughed, then smoothed down her favourite tweed suit, normally too hot for indoor venues. For tonight, though, it was perfect.

Fran opened the door to find Paul standing there. "I brought some special guests." He stepped back to reveal Delilah and Gretchen. "I'll leave you to it."

Delilah and Gretchen gave Fran a hug, closely followed by one for Ruby.

The farmhouse kitchen wasn't the only thing to alter drastically in two years. Delilah, Gretchen, Ruby, and Fran were now good friends.

"You've got some beefy blokes doing security out there," Delilah said. "Bet it wasn't like that when you played two years ago."

Fran shook her head. "Back then, we wondered if anyone would turn up. Now, we're squeezing 1,500 in and we could have sold the place out a few times over." She pointed at

Delilah. "Imagine if you were on the bill, too." A plan began to form in Fran's mind.

Delilah glanced at her ex. "I can see pound signs in Fran's eyes. Can you see it, Ruby?"

Ruby nodded. "Tell-tale signs. She's gone quiet and her face is a little pale."

Fran pursed her lips. "Mock all you like, but who's the best manager?"

Delilah, Ruby and Gretchen all pointed at Fran.

"We could put on a festival with an all-female line-up." Fran pointed her finger at the performers one by one. "You, Delilah, Gretchen, and also Fast Forward. Do your parents fancy starting the next Glastonbury?"

Ruby made a face. "I think they're more interested in retiring. But we could ask Scott. We've got the extra land." She held up a hand. "But can I get tonight ticked off first, please?"

Fran nodded. "Of course you can." She glanced at Delilah. "Any shift this year from your parents? Are they still saying you're going to hell?"

"Last time I checked." Delilah put an arm around Gretchen. "But *they* can go to hell for all I care. Gretchen and I are getting married, my fans and career are intact, and my life is actually better without them. I don't have to look over my shoulder anymore. I should have come out years ago." She smiled at Fran. "But you knew that."

"I'm thrilled for you," Fran replied.

"We just came to say hi and we'll stick around after for a drink." Delilah fist-bumped Ruby. "Looking forward to your set."

Fran waited for them to leave, then resumed her position.

She took Ruby's hand in hers and kissed her knuckles one by one. When Fran raised her eyes, Ruby's gaze was on her.

"You're beautiful; have I told you that lately?"

Ruby smiled. "Once or twice." She kissed Fran again. "Have I told you lately that I love you?"

Fran shook her head and frowned. "Not for a good two hours. You're slacking, O'Connell." She winked, then slapped Ruby's bum.

"By the way, I've got a surprise for you tonight."

Fran gulped. "What kind of surprise."

"Don't worry, I'm not going to propose at a gig."

"I would absolutely kill you."

"I know." Ruby laughed. "But I do have a new song in the second half of the set. One I wrote just for you."

Fran melted. "Oh, fuck. Are you going to make me cry?"

"Happy tears, I hope."

Fran stared at Ruby, then shook her head. "You really are something, you know that? I'm so proud of you." She checked her watch, then snapped into professional mode. "Ten minutes to the anniversary of the gig that changed your life."

Ruby shook her head. "You changed it," Ruby replied. "You change it every day. I love you, Fran Bell."

Fran pressed her lips back to Ruby's. Her heart swooned. "One, two, Mistletoe," she said, kissing Ruby once more. "I love you right back, Ruby O'Connell." Fran took Ruby's hand in hers and pulled her towards the office door. "Now, let's go and wow your hometown all over again, shall we?"

Ruby took a deep breath. "Let's do it."

THE END

Did You Enjoy This Book?

If the answer's yes, I wonder if you'd consider leaving me a review wherever you bought it. Just a line or two is fine, and could really make the difference for someone else when they're wondering whether or not to take a chance on me and my writing. If you enjoyed the book and tell them why, it's possible your words will make them click the buy button, too! Just hop on over to wherever you bought this book — Amazon, Apple Books, Kobo, Bella Books, Barnes & Noble or any of the other digital outlets — and say what's in your heart. I always appreciate honest reviews.

Thank you, you're the best.

Love,
Clare x

Also by Clare Lydon

Other Novels
A Taste Of Love
Before You Say I Do
Nothing To Lose: A Lesbian Romance
Once Upon A Princess
One Golden Summer
The Long Weekend
Twice In A Lifetime
You're My Kind

London Romance Series
London Calling (Book One)
This London Love (Book Two)
A Girl Called London (Book Three)
The London Of Us (Book Four)
London, Actually (Book Five)
Made In London (Book Six)
Hot London Nights (Book Seven)

All I Want Series
All I Want For Christmas (Book One)
All I Want For Valentine's (Book Two)
All I Want For Spring (Book Three)
All I Want For Summer (Book Four)
All I Want For Autumn (Book Five)
All I Want Forever (Book Six)

Printed in Great Britain
by Amazon